The Knot

Joan Broughton

TWIN CATS PRESS

The Knot
by Joan Broughton

Published by Twin Cats Press.

Cover and interior design by Edie Freedman.

Printed in the United States of America
First Printing, 2019

ISBN: 978-0-578-50386-8

CONTENTS

for John

<u>2012</u>

CHAPTER ONE

Genie wouldn't kid herself; today was going to be miserable. At least she could go outside for a while before she had to leave. She slipped on a fleece jacket and took her mug out onto the deck. Low-lying wisps of fog hung over grapevines that stretched toward the Sonoma County foothills. Beyond, Mount Saint Helena wore a cap of snow, a testament to the wet weather of the last few days. Today would be clear, though, and warmer. Genie took a sip of coffee and sat on the iron bench Charlie had found at an estate sale years before. He'd scraped away the rust and painted it dark green. Proud of his first DIY project, he'd had vowed to do more. He never did, though. Work had kept him busy, and the months and years had slipped by.

Tramp, their well-padded black and white cat, sauntered through the cat door and hopped up on Genie's lap. Genie leaned down and put the side of her face on the top of his head. "What's your plan for today, old man?" She reached under his chin and rubbed gently along his jawline as he purred and flexed his toes in contentment. When she and Charlie had met Tramp in the shelter, he was alone in his cage, the last of his litter to be adopted. As they'd driven home he'd cowered in the cardboard box and had refused to come out of it for hours. Fifteen years later, he was still healthy and ran the household.

From the south, a rainbow-patterned hot air balloon drifted over the vineyards. Genie looked up wondering who was aloft, shivering in the early morning air. Was it newlyweds, toasting each other with champagne before breakfast? Or maybe a couple from the Midwest were making plans about where they'd go wine tasting later in the day. Tramp, sensing Genie's attention had drifted away, jumped off her lap and landed with a thump. He went back through the cat door in search of breakfast. Genie had washed his bowl earlier and filled it with his favorite kibble. He'd polish it off before she went back inside.

She sighed and took a last sip of coffee. More than anything, she'd like to sit outside all day, with a book or her journal. In time, she'd feel the sun on the top of her head and take off her jacket, happy to sit in her T-shirt and jeans and let the warming breezes slip over her bare arms. Charlie would join her, earbuds in place, and listen to an audio book. He'd lean back in the Adirondack chair and soon he'd be snoring, waking up with a curse at having missed a chapter. They might drive out to the ocean and hike around Bodega Head; maybe they'd even see the last of the gray whale migration from the cliffs.

A car pulled into the driveway, and for just a second Genie thought it was Charlie. Then she remembered that Debra was coming by to help her pack for her trip to Boston. Genie's brothers would soon arrive for the drive to SFO. She stood and took a final look at the blue sky and green fields in front of her. As always, she dreaded leaving her home and the beauty of Sonoma County, even though her family back in Waltham—a small city just twelve miles from Boston—would greet her with love and open arms. This trip was one she dreaded more than most, though. A long-lapsed Catholic, she loathed the thought of the funeral mass she'd have to attend. Far worse, she'd promised to bring Charlie's ashes with her.

CHAPTER TWO

Debra handed Genie an expertly folded cotton sweater. "The weather is supposed to be warm for the next few days there," Debra said, watching as her friend jammed the sweater into the suitcase.

"Warm and humid, I'll bet," Genie said, her mouth turning down. "Early April in New England: it's either still snowing or suddenly too warm. Once the funeral is over I'll be out of there, thank God. I'm only going for Mrs. Flaherty's sake. She loved Charlie and he'd have wanted me to do this. And of course, my brothers think I need closure. Can you believe they actually used that word?" She zipped up her case and forced a smile. "Sure you don't want to drive down to the airport with us? There'll be plenty of room in the limo."

Debra returned Genie's smile. "No, I think Ragsie and Sean will want you all to themselves."

"Coward!" Genie said. "They've always been a little afraid of you, Debs. It would be fun to see them try to act casual around you for an hour and half."

Debra stood and put her arm around Genie. "You're dreaming, my friend. You'll be driving in rush hour traffic from Santa Rosa to SFO. No way you'll do that trip in under two-and-a-half hours. If you're lucky."

Her cell phone trilled and Genie rolled her eyes. "If that's them telling me they're late," she said as she pulled the phone out of her jeans pocket. "Hello...oh, Marty, hi. No, I haven't left yet, but they should be here any minute." She listened, then said, "Thanks. I appreciate it. I'll call you when I get back."

Debra zipped up the suitcase and said, "He's really watching out for you, isn't he?"

Genie nodded. "He loved Charlie, too. They were friends, and of course, now Marty and I have something in common." Genie frowned, then shook her head. She wasn't going to start rehashing the past. Marty's wife had died recently after a long illness and she and Charlie had circled the wagons, trying to keep Marty from getting too lonely. Since Charlie's death, Marty had tried to do the same for Genie.

She looked out the window. "Uh oh, here they are. At least they're in a Town Car, not a stretch." Genie bit her lip as she saw her brother Ragsie get out of the back seat and straighten his suit jacket. When Genie was little she couldn't pronounce her brother's real name, Darragh, so she called him Ragsie. The name stuck, though it didn't suit him, especially not now. In his late fifties he was tall and heavily muscled, though his jaw was going soft, his hair finally thinning. He was more than a little pompous at times, but Genie could forgive him that. He was a decent man, devoted to his family and hard-working. Still, he and Sean would be full of advice for her all the way to Boston, everything they said under the heading of "for your own good."

She took a deep breath and faced Debra. "I guess it's show time."

Debra pulled Genie's suitcase off the bed.

"No," Genie said. "Don't bother with that. Ragsie will want to carry it." She sat on her bed and shot Debra a weak smile.

"Would you mind letting him in? I just want to sit here a little longer."

Debra ran her hand lightly across Genie's cheek, then headed downstairs to let Ragsie in.

Genie sat on the bed she'd shared with Charlie for more than fifteen years. She hugged herself as she remembered the man she'd held night after night, secure in the love they'd shared.

In the weeks since Charlie's death she'd found she slept better on the couch downstairs, coming into the bedroom only to get clothes from the closet. She smoothed the quilt they'd received as a wedding gift, its gold and blue rings still vibrant against a cream background. The pattern was called a double wedding ring, which struck them both as funny, since Charlie couldn't wear a ring. In his early twenties he'd damaged his left hand helping a friend move a piano, and some of his fingers were left crooked. Genie had given him a small gold Celtic knot on a golden chain to wear instead. He'd worn it till the day he died. Genie stood up and took a deep breath. She wouldn't let herself think about that day, not now.

Ragsie's deep voice rang out as he lumbered up the stairs. "Genie? We gotta go or we'll miss the plane." He stopped in the doorway. "You okay?" he said, his voice quieter now.

Genie wiped her face with the back of her hand. "Am I okay? No, not really." She stood and straightened her shoulders. "Doesn't matter, though. You're right; we'll miss the plane if we don't leave now."

Ragsie gave a curt nod and picked up her suitcase. "Is this it?"

"Yeah," Genie said. "I'll check it and just carry my purse onto the plane. Simpler that way."

"What about the, uh, you know...Charlie's um..." Ragsie shifted his feet, not looking at her.

"The ashes?" Genie said. "They're in the suitcase."

"Do you think that's smart, Genie? What if United loses the bag?" Ragsie barreled down the stairs while he talked, huffing slightly.

"They won't," Genie said. "Besides, what am I supposed to do, carry the urn onto the plane? Would it go in the bin above or under the seat, do you think?"

"No need to be a smartass," Ragsie said. He bent to give Debra a kiss on the cheek as he walked through the front door. "Thanks for taking care of our girl, Debs."

Debra frowned as Ragsie went outside. "Are you sure this won't be too horrible for you?" she said, drawing Genie into a tight hug.

Genie held on a moment longer. She didn't want to go, didn't want to leave her home and her friends. Finally she pulled back a little and said, "It's only a week," she said. "I can handle anything for a week." She gave Debra a quick kiss on the cheek and hurried out the door.

Genie got into the backseat with her brother Sean; Ragsie sat up front. "Will we get to SFO in time?" Ragsie asked the driver.

"No problem," the driver said. "I never miss."

To emphasize the point, he peeled out, and the car gave a little shimmy as it raced down Genie's quiet street. Her neighbors wouldn't like that one bit. In a few minutes they were speeding south down Highway 101, leaving Sonoma County behind. The drive would be a long one if they didn't talk. Sean and Ragsie were notoriously taciturn so it was up to Genie to get the conversation started.

"How was your hotel?" Genie asked. She'd offered to have them stay overnight at her house, but they'd refused, saying she needed her privacy.

After a long pause, Sean said, "Did you ask Ragsie, or me?" He was a couple of years younger than Ragsie and had kept his rangy physique, though his hair, what was left of it, was pure grey.

Genie smiled and said, "You, Sean. Tell me about the hotel."

Sean shrugged and said, "Fine. It was just a Hilton. You know how they are." He looked down at his hands and shrugged again.

Genie sighed. "Yeah, I guess I do." She looked out the window. The hills on either side of the freeway were covered in grapevines, their leaves a tender green. After a while she let her thoughts drift, which wasn't wise. She thought of Charlie, of course. A few weeks ago she'd had to go down to San Francisco to identify his body in the hospital morgue. Debra had been with her. The setting was horrific, stainless steel everywhere, Charlie's body on a plastic sheet. But Charlie looked—she hated to think this, but it was true—he looked peaceful. More peaceful than a man who'd just been shot down on the street was likely to look.

"It'll be okay, Genie," Sean said, leaning close to her. He handed her a tissue.

Genie had been crying without realizing it again. She'd been doing that a lot lately. The principal at her school had been wonderful and had put Genie on compassionate leave through the end of the school year. Less than two months, but still a kind gesture. Everyone had been so kind. Even her brothers were here out of kindness.

She wiped her eyes and said, "You know, you guys didn't have to come all this way to get me. I would have been fine flying to Boston on my own. God knows I've done it often enough."

Sean put his arm around Genie and said, "We had to come, Genie. After all, we're your big bros!"

After that, the silence in the car was an easy, familiar kind. Just as the driver predicted, they arrived at SFO in plenty of time. After checking Genie's bag and going through TSA, Ragsie led them directly to the United lounge.

"We only have half an hour before the flight's called," Genie said. "We can just sit by the gate."

"I paid for first class, and I'm going to get it," Ragsie said. "Besides, it's too noisy out here."

Ordinarily Genie would have agreed. The incessant announcements and inane one-sided phone calls annoyed her whenever she flew. But this time she'd have preferred the diversion of other travelers to the quiet of the lounge. She followed her brothers to the elevator and was soon seated on a low, grey leather chair, a bowl of bar mix and a glass of Chardonnay on the table beside her. Ragsie sat opposite her and chugged a Diet Coke. Sean took his time at the food counter, and finally joined his brother and sister.

"What the heck do you have there?" Ragsie said. "You know they'll feed us on the plane, right?"

Sean shrugged. "I'm hungry now," he said. He polished off a couple of mini-sandwiches and some cookies, then scooped a large handful of crackers into his mouth.

Ragsie rolled his eyes. "You never stop eating. How you haven't gained weight is beyond me."

Sean winked at Genie and said through a mouthful of crackers, "You're just jealous."

Genie smiled. Sean and Ragsie were grown men, but they still teased each other as they had when they were young. Unfortunately, they also still saw her as their bookish and naïve younger sister. That explained why they'd come out to California to bring her back to Boston when she could very well have gone by herself.

As if reading her thoughts Ragsie said, "It will mean a lot to Mrs. Flaherty that you're bringing Charlie home. She's ninety years old, for Chrissake. At her age, she nearly dropped dead when she heard the news about him. She's been hanging on since then for the funeral."

Genie didn't say what she was thinking. Mrs. Flaherty—"Nanny Pat"—had lived next door to the Maguire family, and Charlie had grown up thinking of her as the grandmother he'd never had. She'd always been cordial to Genie, at least to her face. But Genie had heard Nanny Pat run down every member of her own family and all her neighbors when they weren't around. Charlie was the only person she loved utterly, and she spoke about him in almost laughably glowing terms. Pat had been there the night Charlie's father had died, and she'd heard Charlie promise him that, when his day came, he'd be buried next to his parents at St. Eulalia Cemetery in Watertown, Massachusetts. Of course, she never let Charlie forget that, and when Charlie had been killed, she'd prevailed upon Genie's brothers to "bring Charlie home," Genie's wishes notwithstanding.

Rather than have her brothers lecture her about Nanny Pat, who would likely outlive them all, Genie had agreed to go back. At least she'd be able to spend time with her sister Meara, the youngest of the family. As for "bringing Charlie home," well, she was carrying an urn to bury next to Mr. Maguire, and that would have to satisfy Nanny Pat.

CHAPTER THREE

The takeoff had been standard and first class was only half full. Now Genie had to spend five hours with her brothers in close proximity, Ragsie on her right by the window and Sean on her left across the aisle. Ragsie had switched from Diet Coke to Jack Daniels, while Sean drank a Bud. Genie nursed a sparkling water while she waited for lunch to be served. She'd noticed that the two seats directly behind her were empty. After lunch she'd pretend she needed a nap and slip into the available window seat. If she didn't, Ragsie and Sean would fill the time by interrogating her about her plans and telling her what to do. They were acting out of love, they always had and always would. But that kind of love could smother her.

Ragsie nodded as the flight attendant served him his steak. Genie took a look at the brown mass on his plate and was glad she'd ordered the cold chicken salad, but Ragsie tucked into his food with his usual enthusiasm. Sean, ever the charmer, had wangled two meals—one chicken, one steak—from the flight attendant. As she set the meals down on his tray table, Sean looked up and smiled. "You're saving my life, dear," he said to the woman. "I was about to keel over from hunger."

The flight attendant gave him an indulgent smile and patted his arm on her way back up to the galley. "Can't have that, now, can we?"

Sean looked over at Genie and Ragsie. "What?" he said, his eyes wide as he looked around at the empty seats. "The food would have gone to waste otherwise."

It didn't take Ragsie or Sean long to finish their meals, and once the trays were cleared, Ragsie got down to business.

"So," he said, shifting around to face Genie, "What's the last you heard from the police? Do they have any more information about the guy who...you know...who killed Charlie?"

Genie pushed her salad aside. "I haven't heard anything for a couple of days. All they know is that he was shot. They have videotape of someone near the scene, but they still haven't found Charlie's necklace. They think maybe someone sold it for drugs." She surprised herself by sounding as strong as she did. A week ago Ragsie's question would have had her wailing.

Sean leaned into the aisle. "That's true," he said. "But still, wasn't the guy who did it supposed to be in some gang? Skinheads or something?"

A wave of nausea rolled over her, and she grabbed the armrests. She wasn't so strong after all.

"You don't look so hot, Genie." Ragsie waved over the flight attendant. "Miss, I think my sister needs some help."

Genie shook her head. "I'm fine," she whispered.

"Can I bring you something?" The flight attendant said. "Some ginger ale maybe?"

"Okay, thank you," Genie said. The three of them kept silent until the flight attendant had set the drink down in front of Genie. Genie took a sip, then closed her eyes and said. "I'll tell you both what I know, then I'm going to sit in the row behind us and get some sleep. Please don't ask me questions. I can only do this if you promise to let me talk and get it out in one go."

"Sure, Genie," Sean said, chastened.

Genie looked at Ragsie. "You too?"

Ragsie nodded.

She took a deep breath and said, "The police think they recognize the man who shot Charlie. He was a young guy, a petty criminal: trespassing, pot possession, that sort of thing. But he tried to give the impression of being a lot more dangerous, like he was part of the Aryan Brotherhood or something. His head was shaved and he had all sorts of tattoos. The police said he'd never been really violent before, though, so they were surprised to see him on the tape. Apparently he decided to up his game."

She took another sip of ginger ale and said, "The police think that because he left Charlie's money and license at the scene, he might have killed him as part of gang initiation. Just snuff out a life and hey, welcome to the party." She reached into her purse for tissue and wiped her eyes.

Sean and Ragsie sat silent, miserable at being unable to help her.

Genie managed a weak smile. "That's really all I know. The necklace was the only thing missing, and the police said it might just have been lost on the street somewhere. That's not such a nice part of town."

Ragsie cleared his throat. "You said that Charlie had been called down to a meeting in San Francisco? But there really wasn't a meeting that day, right?"

"Apparently not," Genie said. "You know that Charlie was working to get President Obama reelected. There are lots of groups in the Bay area who support his reelection, so it was hard sometimes for Charlie to keep people straight. Anyway, he got a text that morning asking him to go down to Glide Memorial Church for a planning meeting. But no one's been able to figure out who sent it. I hate to say it, but there are some real flakes in that Occupy group. It wouldn't surprise me if one of them texted him then just forgot about it."

"Yeah," Ragsie said. "San Francisco has always been ground zero for airheads. No offense, Genie."

Genie gave him a tired smile. "None taken. I've never held it against you that you voted for McCain in 2008. And you're probably on the Romney bandwagon this year."

Ragsie patted her arm. "Guilty," he said. He leaned over and kissed her cheek. "Why don't you go back there and get some sleep, sis? You look pooped."

Genie got up and sat in the window seat, using her sweater as a pillow against the wall. She felt a blanket being placed over her shoulders. Opening her eyes, she smiled up at Sean. "Thanks," she whispered.

Sean bent and kissed the top of her head. "Get some z's, kiddo. We'll be home soon."

Home. Her brothers would never accept that she had found a home in California, where she'd lived for many years. Her parents had been the same way, always holding out hope that she'd return to Massachusetts. Only her sister Meara understood why Genie had left, and why she'd never go back. It had nothing to do with her family, or the weather, or the carved-in-flint spirit of New Englanders. Victor Pulnik was the reason, and she'd found happiness only by putting a continent between the two of them.

Genie settled back, trying to find a comfortable position. She pushed all thoughts of Victor from her mind, or tried to. The truth was, he always lurked somewhere on the edges whenever she went back to Boston. He traveled extensively as a professional photographer, or at least he used to. Would she happen to run into him at the airport?

When she'd fled to California after he'd nearly destroyed her, she'd imagine encountering him and freezing him with a look. Or perhaps she'd tell him what a shit he was, tell him he had a hole where his heart should be. But after she'd met and fallen in love with Charlie, Victor didn't loom as large. Charlie was unlike Victor in every way, and his love for Genie had made her stronger.

She'd come to pity Victor a little. After all, he'd endured a grim childhood, raised as an only child by an angry, resentful father, and that would have damaged almost anyone. With his cold heart, Victor had probably led a lonely life since she'd last seen him. He was best forgotten, she'd told herself. But Charlie—her loving Charlie—was gone now, and at her core, she still feared a chance encounter with Victor. So, as always, she prayed that she wouldn't see him, that tall man with the wide, Slavic cheekbones and eyes like green ice.

1975-1979

CHAPTER FOUR

Genie fiddled with the combination on her locker, finally getting it open. She shoved her books inside and pulled out her purse. She was running late, and by the time she got to the cafeteria she'd have only a few minutes to scarf down her lunch. Debra would definitely wait for her, but the other girls would probably already have gone outside to the little patio where the smokers hung out. She slammed her locker shut and nearly collided with a tall boy who stood only a foot away.

"Oh," Genie said, "Sorry." He didn't move. He was so tall that she had to tip her head back to make eye contact. "Uh...did you want something?" His hair was short and sandy blond, different from the long locks or shaggy curls of most of the boys in the school. He was thin but not gangly; his shoulders looked strong. And his eyes... his eyes were the light green of a honeydew melon. She didn't remember ever seeing him before, and as a senior, she knew just about everyone in her class.

The boy said nothing and seemed not to hear her at first. Then a small smile crept over his face. "You're Aideen, right? You're in my chemistry class, I think."

Genie took a step back. No one ever called her by her given name. Come to think of it, though, when the new Chem teacher was taking roll the first day he did say Aideen Halloran, not Genie. But why didn't she remember seeing this boy?

"You're in my chemistry class?" Genie's face felt hot. She couldn't place him.

The boy stuck his hand out, "Victor Pulnik," he said. "Maybe you don't remember seeing me 'cause I was at the back station wearing safety goggles."

Genie took his hand, and said, "I'm Genie. No one calls me Aideen."

Victor gave her hand an extra squeeze, then let go. "'Little fire', that's what your name means."

Genie flushed harder. This boy was strange.

"How do you know that? You're not Irish are you?"

Victor shook his head. "Czech," he said. "But even a Czech can use the library."

Genie felt a little tingle in her arms. Who was this boy?

"Genie! Where the hell have you been?"

Genie swung around to see her friend Debra stomping down the hallway, carrying a milk carton and a package of Ring Dings.

"You missed lunch," Debra said, her perfectly straight hair swinging back and forth as she hurried along. "Have this quick or you'll pass out before fifth period."

Genie turned to introduce Victor to Debra, but he was already halfway down the hall. She looked after him a moment, then faced her friend.

"Thanks," she said, popping the top of the little milk carton and chugging it. She wiped her mouth with the back of her hand and put the Ring Dings in her purse. "I can sneak these during history. We're having a film strip today."

Debra raised one eyebrow and said, "Why are you so red, Genie? Who was that talking to you?"

Genie wouldn't meet Debra's gaze. "I don't know," she shrugged.

Debra's eyes narrowed. "I know who he is. He's that new kid." she grabbed Genie's arm and pulled her along. "My cousin Lori told me about him—said he's from East Boston or Revere, one of those places. Lori said he's weird."

"How?" Genie finally looked at Debra. "How's he weird?"

Debra shrugged. "How should I know? What was he talking to you about, anyway? Did he say something strange to you? Is that why you're so red?"

Genie paused. She always told Debra everything.

Little fire.

"No," Genie said. "He just asked where the AV room was."

Debra snorted. "Told you he was weird. AV doofus."

Genie smiled, but she wasn't laughing. Her next Chem class was tomorrow.

CHAPTER FIVE

"Hey, Genie? Are you stoned or what?"

Genie put the beaker down and looked at Dave, her lab partner. Dave gave her a cross-eyed look and said, "Jeez, Genie, I've been talking to you. Didn't you hear what Boneyard said? We're supposed to write down our measurements for the precipitate reaction as soon as it happens. That was five minutes ago. You've been in outer space since you got here."

"Boneyard" was Mr. Bonnard, the chemistry teacher. He'd left the classroom a few minutes before to attend to what he described as "nature's call."

Genie shook her head and looked over at Victor again, hoping he hadn't heard Dave. Victor was working alone, writing, with his head in his hand. His sandy hair was thick and clean-looking. Like yesterday, he wore an army jacket with a black T shirt under it and white painter's pants. No one else dressed that way. The boys all wore jeans, with tie-dye shirts for the freaks, mock turtlenecks for the dweebs, and rugby shirts for the jocks.

Dave picked up the beaker and said, "I'll weigh this again. You write the numbers, okay?"

"Okay," Genie said. "Sorry I wasn't paying attention."

Dave flashed a smile, giving Genie a great view of his braces. "That's okay Genie-Beanie. You've bailed me out enough in English. I owe you, I guess."

Genie smiled. "Don't forget Latin...or French...or History."

Dave rolled his eyes. "I get it."

Mr. Bonnard came back and the chatter stopped. The rest of the class went smoothly, and Genie kept her mind on her work. When class was over, she stayed a few minutes to clean out the beaker—it was her turn—then went back to get her books. Victor was standing by the door, a canvas book bag slung over one shoulder.

"Is that guy your boyfriend? The one you were working with?" Victor stood close to her again, slightly blocking the door. He smelled like Ivory soap. He shifted the bag off his shoulder and said, "Well, is he?" Again, there was that little smile, as if he was in on a secret joke.

Genie squeezed past him and held her books to her chest. "You mean Dave? No, he's not my boyfriend. He's just a friend." She should leave; she'd be late for gym. But she couldn't make herself move.

"No boyfriend at all?" Victor leaned against the door jamb, his arms folded across his chest, sizing her up.

Genie shook her head. She wasn't used to a boy talking to her like that. The boys she knew would kid around in a brotherly, goofy way. Victor was serious, and the way he looked at her made her heart beat harder.

"How about going to the movies with me this weekend—maybe Saturday afternoon? "Three Days of the Condor" is supposed to be good."

"Isn't that rated R?" Genie said. As soon as the words were out of her mouth she could feel her face get hot. She cursed herself for her tendency to blush.

Victor smiled wider. "What's the matter, Aideen? Is that too racy for a nice Irish girl like you? Would your priest disapprove?"

"My name is Genie!" Genie started to walk away. She was breathing hard now, angry and flustered. She slipped by him, then turned around. Without thinking, she said, "I'll meet you at Cinema One on Saturday afternoon." Then she hurried down the hall to the gym.

CHAPTER SIX

Sean dropped Genie off at Cinema One. "You're sure you and Debs will be getting a ride home?" he said, peering at her through his aviator sunglasses.

Genie nodded, without looking at him. "We might go to Brigham's for a frappe afterward, so we can take the bus home."

Sean frowned. "You're going to walk downtown after the movie? Won't it be dark by then?"

Genie closed the car door and leaned in through the window. "I already have a mother, Sean. The movie's over at four. It'll still be light."

Sean revved the Camaro a couple of times, and shouted, "Just be careful, okay?"

Genie smiled. "Thanks for the ride."

Sean drove away, and Genie found a shady spot to sit. She'd had him drop her off half an hour before the movie started because she didn't want Victor to see that her big brother drove her around. She had her license, but it was a rare occasion when she'd be allowed to use her parents' car. She wondered what sort of car Victor drove. If he drove her home, she'd have him drop her off a few blocks from her house. She wasn't ready to talk about him, not to her parents, anyway.

It was late September, but still warm. The light had taken on that mellow, hazy quality as summer gave way to autumn. Genie always loved this time of year, with its warm days and cool nights. Like every New Englander, she cherished the last bit of good weather before winter came. It was football season, but Genie wasn't sorry to miss the game today. Debra had started to give her a hard time about it, but Genie had claimed bad menstrual cramps, so how could Debra argue?

She'd lied to Sean and she'd lied to Debra, too. There was something about Victor that made her want to keep their date a secret. Not that Genie had dated much. She'd been to school dances and out for ice creams with some boys, boys she'd know all her life. And those boys knew her brothers, too. Ragsie and Sean had reputations in their neighborhood and beyond. They were never in trouble, but they knew how to fight. And it was well known how protective they were of their sisters Genie and Meara.

She'd been sitting on the stone wall in front of the theater for a while and only a few people had gone inside. Maybe Victor had changed his mind. Genie hadn't worn a watch, so she walked over and looked inside the lobby. It was one fifty-five. She went back outside, and there he was, crossing the busy street to the theater parking lot. So he hadn't driven after all. Maybe his parents were stingy with their car, too.

Genie stayed where she was and watched Victor approach. He had left off his army jacket, but wore his usual black T-shirt and painters' pants. As he got closer Genie could see a sheen of sweat on his forehead.

"I'm not late, am I?" he said, holding the door open for her. This time his smile was broad.

A strange happiness bubbled up inside her. "Right on time," Genie said. She followed him, and nodded when he asked if she'd like a lemonade.

Victor bought the tickets, then got two drinks. He handed her a lemonade and said, "We'd better get inside. I think the movie just started."

The theater was almost completely dark, the screen showing a man in a trench coat on a grey, rainy day. Genie was following Victor, but her eyes hadn't adjusted to the dark yet.

"Here," Victor whispered into her ear. He took her arm gently.

She gave a little start at his touch, but then let him lead her down the steps to two seats at the center of the theater. As they sat down, gunfire started on the screen. Genie shifted in her seat. She'd never liked scenes of violence.

Victor leaned close and whispered, "Are you cold?" His breath was warm on her cheek.

It was chilly in the theater, but Genie shook her head. She took a sip of the lemonade, which tasted sour and metallic. She set the cup on the seat next to her and pulled her arms close to her body, not wanting to brush up against Victor's bare arm.

For a while they watched the movie, or Genie pretended to. Victor seemed interested, and when the characters played by Robert Redford and Faye Dunaway started to kiss, he leaned forward, just as Genie put her arm on the armrest. Seductive music played, and Victor looked over at Genie, not smiling, just staring at her.

Genie didn't move her arm and could feel the heat of Victor's bare skin through the gauzy material of her sleeve. She returned

Victor's gaze, then, suddenly self-conscious, reached over for her lemonade. For the rest of the movie, she went back to holding her arms tight to her sides, avoiding any contact with him.

When the movie was over they stood outside the theater, neither saying a word at first. Genie was grateful to be back outside, where it was light and warm, and where she didn't have to sit so close to Victor.

"So," Victor said, reaching over to brush a curl out of Genie's face, "Were you scandalized by the movie?" He was smiling that half-smile again.

Genie pulled away. "Of course not!" she said. "It was fine. I wasn't embarrassed at all. I'm not a baby, you know." It was clear he was teasing, so why was she so angry?

Victor didn't respond, but his smile had disappeared. Then he reached for her hair again, and this time she let him. "Maybe you can be my baby, Aideen? At first I didn't believe that you had no boyfriend, but I've been watching, and I guess you told the truth. That's good, because, well, I'd like to be your boyfriend." He twirled a lock of her hair gently around his finger and stepped even closer.

Genie's heart pounded. No boy had ever spoken to her like that. She'd been the type of girl boys never seemed to notice, at least, not in that way. But now Victor was looking at her like she was the only girl on earth.

"Should I walk you home?" Victor said. "My Dad never lets me use his car, so I walk everywhere. But maybe you want to call for a ride...Or maybe you'll walk downtown with me and get an ice cream. You can take the bus home from there."

"I," Genie whispered, then cleared her throat. "I'd like an ice cream," she said in a stronger voice.

Victor smiled. "Let's go, then," he said. As they left the theater parking lot, he took Genie's hand. "Your hand's cold," he said.

"Sorry," Genie said. "The theater was kind of—"

"Cold hands, warm heart," Victor interrupted. "That's what my mother used to say. Is that true, do you think?"

Genie laughed. "I guess so," she said. It was thrilling to walk with this tall, unusual boy. As they walked the two miles to Brigham's, Victor asked Genie about her family, which was large. Her grandparents lived down the street from her, and she had aunts, uncles, and cousins in Waltham and in a few of the neighboring towns. Then, of course, there were her brothers and sister. By the time they got to the ice cream parlor Genie was thirsty from talking so much.

They slid into a booth and, after they'd ordered (a large dish of chocolate ice cream for Victor, a strawberry frappe for Genie), Genie said, "I've done all the talking. What about you, Victor? Does your family all live here, too?"

Victor shrugged and said, "It's just my father and me. We lived in East Boston since I was born, and we moved here this summer."

"Your mother?" He'd mentioned his mother earlier. Perhaps there'd been a divorce?

Victor shook his head. "She died when I was five. I don't really remember her, just little things, like the way she laughed. Oh, and she'd make my favorite cookies sometimes, these crescent shaped things." He locked eyes with Genie. "You don't have to look so sad. I'm used to being on my own. My Dad works all the time, and after my mother died a neighbor looked after me. Once I went to school, though, I was able to take care of myself until my father got home at night." He put his hand over Genie's. "It's been a long time since my mother died; I can barely remember her, really. It seemed normal to me to grow up the way I did. I guess you don't miss what you never had. That doesn't mean I don't like hearing about your family. It sounds great."

When their ice cream arrived Victor tucked into his right away. Genie tried to take a sip of her frappe, but found it hard to swallow. How could Victor have grown up so alone? She imagined him coming home from school to an empty apartment, no mother to ask him how his day had been or to fix him a snack.

When Victor finished eating he looked up and said, "Don't you like it?"

"I like it," Genie said. "I just guess I'm not that hungry."

Victor reached over and slid the glass to his side of the table. "Can't let this go to waste," he said, putting the straw in his mouth.

Genie couldn't take her eyes off him. His thin lips worked at the straw—the same one she'd just used!—as he sucked up the thick, pink liquid. When he was finished he gave one last pull on the straw, making a rude noise, while he crossed his eyes.

Genie laughed. It was a relief to see Victor do something silly. She looked over at the window to see their reflections. A laughing, long-haired young girl and a tall, handsome boy. He wants me to be his baby, she thought. Then she saw that the sun was setting.

Genie stood and said, "I have get going. The bus will leave soon."

Victor said nothing, just looked up at Genie a moment. Then he stood and said, "I'll walk you over."

Genie nodded and started toward the door. Before she could grab the handle, the door opened and her friend Debra came in, accompanied by four other girls. Debra was talking to a girl behind her and didn't see Genie at first. There was no way for Genie to avoid her, though.

When Debra finally turned around she said, "Genie! I thought you had cramps—I mean, I thought you weren't feeling well." Then she saw Victor standing close behind Genie. "Oh, I get it," she said in a flat voice. Her lips were pressed together into a frown.

Genie had never lied to Debra before. They'd grown up next-door neighbors and best friends, and confided all their secrets to one another. But Victor was a secret she hadn't wanted to share.

Victor leaned forward and said, loud enough for Debra to hear, "Come on, Genie. You've got to catch that bus, remember?"

Debra didn't let Genie by at first. "You don't have to take the bus. Marcy'll drive us home, if you don't mind waiting until we've had our ice cream."

Genie shook her head, not meeting Debra's eyes. "No, I guess I should go now. I told my parents I'd be home in time for dinner."

She squeezed by Debra and the other girls, and couldn't miss the shocked expression on Marcy's face. When they were out the door, Victor took her hand again. Genie didn't feel as happy as she had before, though. Now she was one of those girls who chooses a boy over her best friend. She and Debra had talked about girls like that, who always ended up being dumped by the boy after they'd cut their best friends out of their lives. But what would happen if Peter Gould, the boy Debra had been drooling over since their sophomore year, ever asked her out? Debra would do the same thing, Genie told herself. She'd lie to me if it meant she could go out with Peter. Almost convincing herself, she looked up at Victor and smiled.

CHAPTER SEVEN

It was Christmas, a day Genie's family celebrated in a big way. Grandparents, aunts and uncles and countless cousins would make the rounds of each other's houses in the days leading up to the holiday. On Christmas day they got together to exchange gifts then eat a big lunch. Genie's pile of gifts under the tree was always huge, not to mention the stocking filled with fancy chocolates and fruits. She had been going out with Victor for almost three months, but had only told her mother about him just before Christmas. When her mother insisted on having him come to their celebration, Genie worried that Victor would be overwhelmed by all her family and their celebration. Victor wouldn't have experienced anything like that before.

"Christmas is just another day," Victor had said a week before their winter vacation, when Genie asked him how he and his father marked the holiday. "My Dad will probably just go to his shop like any other day and work on an old car. He always gives me the same thing: a twenty dollar bill."

Victor pulled Genie closer. As always, they'd left school after last period and gone walking together, just the two of them. Now they were sitting side-by-side in a booth at Woolworths, nursing cups of coffee. The sleet had started an hour before, cutting short their walk. Genie snuggled up to Victor and said, "Do you give him anything?"

He shook his head. "I never give him gifts anymore. When I was a kid we made pine cone candle holders with red candles at school.

I was probably seven or eight, and I was so excited about it. All he did was laugh and say that the candle might come in handy if we had a blackout. The next day I found the pine cones in the trash."

As bad as she felt about Victor's bleak Christmases, she'd still hesitated to ask him to her house. Her huge family could get boisterous and a few uncles could be counted on to ask nosy questions. Her parents tended to be quiet and accepting, but Genie was worried about her brothers, especially Ragsie. He was five years older than Genie and already married, with a baby. A big man with a booming voice, he was used to speaking his mind. He'd likely interrogate Victor, not unkindly, but to make the point that he was watching out for his sister. And speaking of little sisters, Meara, the youngest and four years Genie's junior, was unpredictable. She could be counted on to say just the wrong thing, not to be malicious, but out of an abundance of candor. Meara had recently discovered fashion magazines, and Genie wouldn't put it past her to ask Victor why he wore white pants in the winter.

Still, when her mother said she should bring him to dinner, she couldn't say no. Shona had lit up when Genie had told her that Victor was coming. "I can't wait to meet him!" she'd said. "Won't his parents miss him, though?"

Genie, used to lying about Victor by now, said, "No, they celebrate on Christmas Eve."

Christmas morning Genie helped her mother in the kitchen, then raced upstairs to shower and wash her long hair. It would take a good hour for her to put it in curlers and dry it in the bonnet hair dryer she shared with Meara. Victor had said once how much he loved her thick, curly hair, which had come as a relief to her. When she was younger she'd tried ironing it straight and had burned her scalp. While she sat under the dryer she carefully applied a little mascara and inspected her face for blemishes. She smoothed on some light pink lipstick—Victor had said he hated girls who wore too much makeup—and blotted it with a tissue.

As she was brushing out her hair, her mother called, "Genie! Your friend is here."

Genie grabbed the little box with Victor's gift, which she slipped into the pocket of her red jumper. She took one last look in the mirror and straightened the white, lacy collar of her blouse, then ran down the stairs, taking them two at a time. She didn't want Victor talking to any of her family if she wasn't around.

Victor stood between Genie's father and her brother Sean. He was wearing a blue blazer, white shirt, and a red- and grey-striped tie, and, most unusually, grey flannel pants. Genie had never seen him dressed this way, and she was dazzled. "You look beautiful, Genie," Victor said.

"You too," Genie whispered.

Sean, his shaggy hair hanging past the turtleneck of his Aran sweater, laughed and said, "Don't ever call a guy 'beautiful', Genie. You'll make him feel like a girl." He elbowed Victor and said, "Right, Vic?"

Victor's eyes narrowed for a second, then he smiled and said, "Right, Sean!"

Genie went to Victor and held his hand, determined not leave his side for the rest of the day. She introduced him to her Aunt Dot and her young cousins Ruth and Andy, six-year-old twins. Ruth stared up at him and said, "Are you a giant?" after Victor said hello, and Andy started giggling. Genie smiled, but when she saw the frown on Victor's face she took his hand and led him away. Fortunately her mother called everyone to the table just then.

Genie had asked her mother beforehand to have Victor sit next to her, so as everyone took their places, Shona said, "Now, Victor, come sit right here beside me. I want to make sure you get enough to eat; those sons of mine will take three helpings before anyone gets a chance." She smiled and patted Victor's arm as he took his place beside her. Genie sat on his other side and gave her mother a wink.

For a while there was not much conversation; everyone was too busy eating. Genie made sure Victor got a chance to try everything.

"This turkey is great, Mrs. Halloran," Victor said as he reached for the platter in front of him. He'd already had two helpings of mashed potatoes and gravy and a huge portion of stuffing. Genie had never seen him eat so much.

Sean, sitting next to his father at the other end of the table, leaned over and said, "Hey, Vic! Don'tcha get enough to eat at home?"

Victor dropped the serving fork and put his hands on his lap, his face pale.

Shona reached over and placed two pieces of turkey on his plate, saying, "Sean, mind your manners. Victor is our guest and he's paying me a compliment by enjoying my food." She smiled at Victor and said, "Isn't that right?"

Genie leaned closer to Victor.

After a pause, Victor said, "That's right."

Shona patted his arm again and said, "Sean, you just eat your dinner and let Victor eat his."

Ragsie cleared his throat and said, "Hey, we'd better finish soon. The Bruins game starts in twenty minutes."

After that the conversation turned to sports: the lousy play of the Patriots, the hopes for the Red Sox next year, and the Celtics' season so far. Genie kept her eye on Victor, who said nothing. He'd stopped eating. Her brother Sean had been trying to be funny, but he'd nearly ruined everything. After lunch she'd apologize to Victor.

When they'd finished eating, the male members of the family went to the basement to watch the Bruins play the Canadiens. Enok had asked Victor to join them, but Victor had said he wasn't much of a hockey fan. Shona and her sisters headed toward the kitchen with the girl cousins. When Genie tried to follow, Shona said, "No, dear. You and Victor go sit in the parlor. I remember when Enok was courting me that's what we'd do." Her mother had obviously taken a liking to Victor.

Genie was relieved that the meal was over. She looked forward to being alone with Victor, away from the prying eyes of her family.

"I'm going to sit in the parlor, too," Meara said. "I want to read my new book, and Daddy's chair is the best place to do it." Meara shot Genie a sly look and started to skip toward the parlor.

"No, you don't," Shona said. "You come into the kitchen and I'll tell you all about your Aunt Dorothy when she was a girl and how she pestered me and your father when we were dating, which I'm sure is what you plan to do with your sister and Victor. In fact, Dot's in there now. She can tell you herself."

Genie waited until the kitchen door had closed and said, "Would you like to sit? Or maybe you've had enough of my family for one day...I'm sorry about Sean. He's harmless, but kind of a big mouth."

Victor took Genie's hand and gave her a quick kiss on the cheek. "It doesn't matter. Let's go sit. I haven't given you your present yet."

Genie felt for the small velvet box in her pocket. She'd had her great-grandfather's silver pen knife engraved with Victor's initials. She'd kept the gift a secret from her family even though the knife was hers to do with as she pleased. Her grandmother, who had gone back to Ireland after her father had died, had given Genie the knife when she'd turned ten. All Genie's siblings and cousins had been given one memento, though they'd never actually met their great-grandfather, who'd stayed in Ireland his entire life.

"Let me give you this first," Genie said. "You've got to keep it a secret, though."

"A secret gift?" Victor laughed.

Genie pulled the box out of her pocket and said, "Here."

Victor opened the green box and pulled the small knife out. He smiled and said, "Hey, my initials!" He turned the knife over and pulled out the blade, then slowly put it back.

"Do you like it?" Genie said. "It's antique...from Ireland!"

Victor pulled Genie close and kissed her lips softly. "I love it," he said. He set the knife back into the box. "Here, let me give you your gift." Victor reached into his pocket and handed her a black velvet bag. "I didn't have any wrapping paper," he said.

Genie's fingers trembled as she took the bag. "I didn't wrap yours, either," she said. She reached into the bag and took out a delicate gold chain with a tiny blue stone pendant.

"That's lapis lazuli," Victor said. "Can I put it on you?"

Genie nodded, then started to unbutton the high collar of her blouse. Why couldn't she have worn something simpler?

Victor put his hand over hers and said, "Let me."

Genie looked over toward the kitchen door. What if someone came out and saw them?

"Don't worry," Victor said, smiling. His long fingers undid the first button, then the next, then the next. When he had unbuttoned the fourth button he reached around the back of her neck and fastened the necklace. He kept his hand there for a moment, then slid it around to her collarbone.

"You're beautiful, Aideen," he whispered.

Genie's heart was pounding. As Victor traced his fingers along her bare skin, she found it hard to breath. She was afraid, but she didn't want him to stop. Then he ran his hand under her blouse, skimming over her left breast, then her right.

"Victor, we can't," she said. "Not here!"

"Shh," he said, "Just a little longer." He hooked his index finger under the top of her right bra cup and touched her nipple, ever so lightly.

His skin on hers, his hand touching her in such a private place, brought on a feeling she'd never had before. She was light-headed, and a strange, warm tingling started between her legs. She knew they'd gone too far, and she put her hand on his.

"We have to stop," she said, sitting up straighter and buttoning her blouse.

Victor smiled and leaned over and kissed her on the cheek. He whispered, "I want to do that again, Aideen. I want to touch you everywhere. You'll let me, won't you?"

Just then the kitchen door burst open and Genie's mother came in carrying a casserole dish wrapped in aluminum foil.

"Oh, you two are so cute!" she said. "Little angel kisses on the cheek."

Genie stood up. "Mom!" she said, smoothing down her jumper. "What's that?"

Shona said, "It's for Victor to take home. I thought maybe his parents might like some ham and turkey. We have too much."

Victor looked at Genie briefly. What had she told her family about his living situation?

"That sounds great, Mrs. Halloran. I don't know if I can take it, though. I walked over here, you know."

"That's all right, Victor. You live downtown, don't you?" Shona gave him a bright smile. "Ragsie lives down that way, off Moody. He's leaving now and can give you a ride."

Meara had come out of the kitchen and was standing behind Shona, making kissy faces at Genie.

Victor smiled at Genie, then at Shona, and said, "I guess I can't say no to that."

Shona turned to Meara and said, "Go get Victor's coat, dear."

"I'll follow you," Victor said.

As Victor walked away, Shona caught Genie's eye and mouthed, "SO CUTE!"

If you only knew, Genie thought.

Ragsie and his wife Susie were standing by the door, surrounded by the rest of the family. Aunt Dorothy handed the baby back to Susie reluctantly.

"Come on, Victor," Ragsie said, his voice booming as usual. "We've got to get little Noel to bed before he goes berserk."

"Okay," Victor said. He turned to Shona and gave her a little bow and said, "Thank you, Mrs. Halloran, for a wonderful dinner."

Enok put his arm around Shona and said, "We're so happy that our Genie has met such a nice, polite young man. And so clean-cut." He roughed up the top of Sean's head. "Not like this hippie, here."

Victor smiled and followed Ragsie out the door. As he walked down the steps toward Ragsie's car, her turned and gave Genie a little wave. She felt for the necklace under her blouse and waved back. She couldn't wait to see him again.

CHAPTER EIGHT

Back at school after Christmas vacation, Genie had a hard time concentrating. College acceptance letters wouldn't come out until spring, and Genie's parents had their fingers crossed that she'd be accepted by the University of Southern California. A childhood friend of Enok's had gone to school there after the war and had loved everything about Los Angeles. He and his wife had never had children, so he'd promised that if Genie was accepted there, he'd pay for all four years. It was either that or a local community college for Genie, because her parents had no money for a private college. Genie had applied as early as possible, excited at the prospect of traveling to California and attending such a big school. That was before she'd met Victor, though.

Now she spent her days watching the clock during class, then joining Victor in line for the school bus that went downtown. Sometimes they'd walk for hours, following the Charles River all the way to Newton and back. When it snowed they'd take the train to Boston and walk around the North End. On warmer days they'd catch the Blue Line out to the beach. They'd sit close together on the train, and Victor would sneak his hand under her coat and sweater. Genie would look around to make sure no one could see, but she never stopped him.

One day in late February Genie looked out the classroom window daydreaming about Victor, only partially aware of the Spanish lesson going on. It had started snowing in the morning, and by early afternoon the wind had picked up. Perhaps they could go to the library for the afternoon. Genie smiled at the thought of actually going to the library; that had been her alibi for weeks whenever her parents asked her where she'd been in the afternoon. It didn't matter what they did, though, as long as they were together.

When Genie met Victor at the bus parked in front of the school, he smiled and said, "I have a surprise."

They sat holding hands until the bus dropped them off near the City Hall.

"Are we taking the train?" Genie asked. She'd pulled her scarf up over her nose and mouth, but the wind whipped snow and ice pellets at her exposed cheeks.

"It'll be too windy in Boston," Victor said. "I want us to go someplace else. We can run from here. Let's go!" He tugged on her hand and they hurried down Main Street a few blocks. The snow was piling up fast and much of the sidewalk hadn't been shoveled yet, forcing them out onto the street occasionally.

"Where are we going?" Genie shouted.

"Almost there!" Victor said. He looked down at Genie and laughed, his cheeks a bright pink.

When they got to Bacon Street they turned right and went down an alley toward a small apartment building.

"Is this where you live?" Genie said as they opened the door to the narrow hallway. It was dim inside, the only light a naked bulb hanging from the ceiling. She brushed the snow off her coat sleeves and stomped her feet to shake loose the slush.

Victor fished a key out of his pocket. "This is it."

"But you told me your father doesn't like it when you bring friends home." Genie had heard a few stories about Mr. Pulnik, about his temper and angry outbursts. Since his wife had died, Victor told her, his father had tried to keep the world out, staying huddled at home when he wasn't working in his repair shop.

Victor fitted the key in the lock to a door on the right. He turned and said, "That's the surprise, Genie. He's at work. He changed hours with his helper for the next month cause the guy's wife just had a baby."

Victor went inside, shrugging out of his coat. Genie stood in the doorway. She'd never been completely alone with him.

Victor turned and put his hand out. "Come on. Let me show you around."

He switched on a light and led her into the cramped living room. On one end a dark sofa and chair hunched over a low wooden table. Newspapers were stacked in piles on the floor and on the furniture. A single bookcase stood against the wall, crammed with books and magazines. On the wall next to it was a crucifix, and beneath that a calendar. A tattered green shade nearly covered the sole window.

"The kitchen's in here," Victor said.

Genie held tighter to his hand. She'd never been in an apartment before. All her friends lived in houses, like she did. In the kitchen a fluorescent light sputtered over the stove. The window in this room had no shade, and it looked out on a small parking area where a few cars sat, their roofs and hoods capped with snow. An oilcloth-covered table was jammed into the corner, its surface nearly hidden under more newspapers, a plastic holder with a few paper napkins, and glass salt and pepper shakers.

"If you need the bathroom," Victor said, pointing through the kitchen door.

Genie shook her head.

"Oh, my room's there," he said, pointing to a closed door on one side of the bathroom. "And that's my father's room."

Genie peeked around Victor to see a room filled with stacks of papers. On the floor sat three or four steel tool cases, some open, some with hammers and wrenches piled on top.

Genie's mother had told her that whenever she was invited to someone's house, it was only polite to find something to compliment—a lovely figurine; a bright, clean kitchen; a comfortable chair—anything that would show that she appreciated the person's home. But this apartment was so dark, so cluttered and dingy. Her mother would have opened all the windows and taken a mop and Lysol to it. "Does your father collect tools?" Genie finally said. "He seems to have a lot of them."

Victor gestured for her to follow him back to the living room. "I wouldn't say he collects them, exactly. But he finds them at flea markets and places like that. Sometimes he sells them...Hey, would you like some tea—or hot chocolate?"

"Hot chocolate, please," Genie said.

He went ahead of her and dragged the piles of newspapers off the couch and put them on top of the pile on the chair. "My father reads a lot," he said. "Sit down and I'll bring out our drinks."

While Victor worked in the kitchen, Genie looked at some of the newspapers and magazines. A few were in English, but many others were not. Only a few of the books in the bookcase had English titles. The calendar showed a photo of Valvoline antifreeze. Mr. Pulnik must have gotten it at work. She wanted to straighten the dark plastic window shade, but didn't want Victor to think she'd noticed something wrong.

"Hey, relax," Victor said. He carried a mint-green jadeite cup in each hand, and set them down on the small coffee table. "Let's warm up." He put his arm around her and handed her a cup. He looked so happy to have her there.

Genie felt ashamed of herself. So what if Victor and his father lived in an apartment and not a house? She took a sip and said, "Mmm. This is great."

Victor pulled her closer, gently putting her cup back on the table. "I've dreamed of this, you know. It's always so lonely for me here, whether my father's here or not. And now you're with me, and I can hold you and kiss you..."

He put his hand on Genie's cheek and turned her face up to his. She closed her eyes and parted her lips slightly. "You're my baby," he whispered as he put his lips on hers. His tongue was in her mouth, and his hand was inside her sweater. "I want to see you," he said, his breath hot in her ear. "Can I?"

Genie nodded and pulled her sweater over her head, then folded her arms across her pink and white bra. She felt self-conscious at the size of her breasts, which were smaller than most girls'.

Victor put his hands on her wrists and said, "Let me see you." He reached around to unhook her bra, twisting the little metal hooks into her back.

48

Genie smiled and said, "Here, let me." Her hands were shaking as she reached around and unfastened the bra. She couldn't look at him; she could barely breathe. What they were doing scared her and thrilled her at the same time.

"There's my good girl," Victor said. He put his index fingers under the straps of her bra and slipped it off her shoulders. Then he quickly pulled his T-shirt off. He put one hand on Genie's breast, and took one of her hands and put it on his chest. "Come here," he said, pulling her close.

Genie's heart pounded as her breasts touched Victor's bare skin. It was hard to think, hard to speak. Victor pulled her closer, his arms around her back. "I love you, Genie." His words were muffled as he ran his tongue along her throat, and down one breast. When he put her nipple into his mouth, Genie panicked. She sat up straight and reached for her bra, holding it in front of her.

Victor looked shocked. "What's wrong? Did I hurt you?"

Genie reached around back and hooked her bra, then pulled her sweater back on. "You didn't hurt me, Victor. It's just that this is... you know...I've never done anything like this before."

Victor smiled. "I hope not," he said as he put his shirt back on. "Don't worry, Genie. I'd never do anything you didn't want me to do. It's just that, well, you're so beautiful and touching you feels so wonderful. We can slow down, though, if you want."

Genie didn't know what she wanted. "I'm sorry," she whispered, looking down at the couch. "I don't want to seem like a prude."

Victor put two fingers under her chin and raised her face up to his. "Nothing to be sorry for. You love me, don't you?"

Did she? She thought about him all the time. He made her feel special...she even felt beautiful when she was with him. It was clear how much he needed her. What else could love be?

"Yes, Victor," she said. "I do love you."

CHAPTER NINE

Every day after that was the same. Genie and Victor would go to his empty apartment and spend the late afternoon together, then Genie would rush to the bus to get home in time for dinner. Victor had to work at his father's shop on the weekends, so those weekday afternoons were precious. Genie became bolder with Victor and learned what pleased him, proud she could make him so happy.

It was Friday, well into March, and a blizzard was predicted. Genie prayed that school wouldn't be cancelled, and practically skipped out the door when it wasn't.

"Give us a call if they let you out early!" Genie's mother shouted after her. "Ragsie will go and get you in his truck."

"Don't worry," Genie shouted over her shoulder. She walked down the little hill toward the high school. She lived less than a mile away, so she didn't qualify for the bus the way Victor did. It was cold and the clouds were low and dark. A few tiny flakes drifted down and she hurried along, trying to stay warm. As long as she got to school she'd be able to take the school bus with Victor to his apartment. She'd find a way to get home for dinner in time, she told herself. Nothing mattered as long as she could be with him.

The school was buzzing with excitement. The weather reports predicted a foot of snow; surely the principal would let everyone out early. By eleven a.m. there was at least half a foot on the ground, with no letup in sight. The announcement came over the P.A. at eleven-fifteen. Classes were cancelled for the rest of the day, and the bus students were to go to their buses right away. Genie dashed to her locker and grabbed her coat, meeting Victor outside.

"Can you believe it?" Victor said. "We'll have the whole afternoon together."

Genie looked up at the sky and let the snowflakes fall on her face, then clambered onto the bus behind Victor.

When they got to Victor's apartment he made tea, which they drank along with the lunches they'd brought to school. Victor cleaned up after they'd finished and said, "Come with me. I have something to show you."

Genie followed him into his bedroom. They'd only just started spending time there. Genie had been nervous at first, but it meant so much to Victor for her to be there with him.

He led her into the room and said, "Now you just sit down here." He set her on the edge of the bed and went to his bureau. He slid something out from under a book, then sat down next to her.

"Genie," he said. "You know I love you, right?" He gazed at her with a serious expression, and held her hand.

"Yes," Genie whispered.

Victor kissed her cheek, then turned her head toward him and kissed her lips. "I got these for us," he said, slipping a small box into her hand.

Genie looked down at the box. "Trojans?" she said. She looked more closely at the box. "These are condoms."

Victor nodded. "We're ready, Genie. I know we are. You trust me, don't you?"

Genie's breath stopped in her throat. Three girls in her class had gone all the way and gotten pregnant, one of them had even gotten married. Seventeen years old and already a wife and mother. Of course, she'd had to drop out of school. Genie loved Victor, and she'd dreamed of being with him that way, but those had just been dreams. What would her life be like if she got pregnant? She'd heard rumors about girls whose boyfriends hadn't use condoms correctly. What would her father say, or her mother? Would they disown her like Marian Fritti's family? She looked around her. What would it be like to live here, in this gloomy place?

"What's the matter?" Victor said, his voice rising. "Are you afraid? Don't be. I'll be careful."

She stood up and said, "Victor, why can't we keep on doing what we've been doing? We're only in high school still, and, well, I don't know that I'm ready to do this."

Tears welled in Victor's eyes as he stood and held her hands. "I can't believe you don't trust me, Genie. I thought you of all people would understand how much this means to me, how much you mean to me."

Genie had never seen Victor cry before, even when he'd told her stories of his lonely life growing up with his distant, unloving father. His childhood had been horrible, and it was only when he'd moved to Waltham and met her that he'd felt like he belonged. It was easy to see how much this meant to him.

"I know, Victor." Genie stood up to wipe a tear from his cheek. "It's just that I'm surprised. Can I think about this a little?"

There was a loud roaring sound outside, maybe a plow or sander.

Victor's head snapped around and he said, "Shit! It's my father! Come on, I have to get you out of here."

He shoved the condoms into his pants pocket and pulled her arm. "Get your coat," he said as they ran through the living room.

Genie picked up her coat and book bag and hurried out the door after Victor, who had her boots in his hand. "Hurry and put these on," he said when they'd reached the little lobby.

Genie had her boots on and was winding her scarf around her neck when the outside door opened. A large man wearing an old parka over a coverall came in, shaking the snow out of his hair.

"What the hell are you doing?" he said, his voice rough and heavily accented. "And who is this?"

Victor smiled and said, "Hey, Pops. What are you doing home?"

"Gonna make some money with Joey's plow. He broke his leg last week and can't drive." He came closer, breathing hard and glowering at Genie. "Who are you?" he said.

Genie couldn't make herself say a word. Mr. Pulnik was just as tall as Victor, but he was much heavier, with a beard and thick black eyebrows.

"This is Genie," Victor said. "She stopped by to give me a book I'd left at my desk. We got out of school early and I ran out without it. She was just on her way to the bus now."

"Bus, huh? You sure that's true about the book? Maybe you two were up to something?" Mr. Pulnik said. "Where do you live, Missy? Some fancy place, I bet."

"She lives in Lakeview, Pops. It's not fancy there." Victor's voice shook. He turned to Genie and said, "You'd better get going, Genie. That snow's really coming down. They might not run the buses much longer."

Genie stood motionless. Mr. Pulnik didn't even know her but he seemed to hate her. She'd never had an adult look at her that way.

Mr. Pulnik pulled the door open and said, "Yes, Missy, you be on your way now. Thanks for helping my son. He's not too bright, always forgetting things, right, Victor?" He pronounced it 'Wictor'.

"Thanks again, Genie," Victor said. "Have a good weekend."

Genie finally managed to move. "Okay, 'bye," she mumbled as she walked out the door. Tripping down the steps, she started walking faster, eager to get away. As she hurried to the bus stop, she could feel the tears coming. Victor had to live with his awful father...he was all alone, except for her. And she'd rejected him that way. She barely felt the snow as it pelted her face. She could see the bus coming and raced through the slush and icy puddles. If she missed this one, she'd have to wait another hour. She got to the stop just as the bus pulled up, and hopped on board, her coat and boots dripping.

When she got home Genie trudged up the front stairs and took her boots off in the entryway.

"Is that you, Genie?" her mother called from the kitchen. "Where've you been? Didn't school let out early?"

Genie unwrapped her scarf and put it on the radiator with her mittens. She hung up her coat and came into the house.

Her mother came out of the kitchen, wiping her hands on her apron. "Where were you, honey?" She looked closer and said, "Are you all right? You look like you've been crying."

Genie wiped her hand across her face. "I'm okay," she said. "It's just the cold. I had to wait for the bus a while. They closed the library." Not a lie, exactly.

Shona came closer and put her hand on Genie's cheek. Frowning, she said, "Why don't you go upstairs and get changed. Your jeans and socks look wet. I don't want to you to catch a cold."

Genie couldn't meet her eyes. "Okay, Mom," she said as she went up the stairs to her room.

Meara was sitting cross-legged on her bed, hunched over a book. Without looking up she said, "Why did you lie to Mom?"

"What do you mean?" Genie went to the closet and pulled out a sweater and jeans, then sat down and took off her wet socks.

Meara looked up. Her chin was quivering, a sure sign she was angry. "You lied to her about the library. It wasn't open at all today. Our teacher told us that this morning because we were supposed to meet there after school for our history project. You lied, Genie."

Genie put on dry socks and pulled on the sweater. She didn't know what to say.

"You know what?" Meara pushed her book aside and sat on the edge of her bed. "I talked to Debra the other day. She says that you never go to Debate Club after school anymore, and you stopped working on the yearbook committee, too. Debra said she sees you getting on the bus with Victor now. Where do you go with him? You've been lying to Mom about that, too." Meara's heart-shaped face was pale and her blue eyes swam with tears. "You never used to be like this, Genie. You never used to lie."

Genie looked out the window. It was getting dark. "I'm going out to shovel so Dad doesn't have to when he gets home. Do you want to come?" Her throat was closing up; she'd be in tears soon herself.

Meara picked up her history book and lay back on the bed. "No, you go ahead. You can get all the brownie points for being such a good daughter."

Genie stood in the doorway a moment, then went downstairs, grateful to get away.

CHAPTER TEN

The next morning Genie spent a few hours in back of the house, shoveling out the long walkway and double set of stairs to the driveway. Working hard helped keep her thoughts at bay, but images kept coming back: Mr. Pulnik glowering at her, Victor holding the pack of condoms, and most troubling, Meara near tears as she demanded to know why Genie had lied so much. She kept her head down, determined to finish the job. When she'd finally cleared every bit of snow, she smacked the shovel on the pavement, releasing the built-up icy slush.

She pulled off a mitten with her teeth and wiped her nose with a tissue she'd stashed in her coat pocket. Looking up at the crystal blue sky, she took a deep breath of the cold, clean air. Meara had gone to her friend's house a few streets over, so Genie could hide in her bedroom a while and try to think of how to make things right with Victor. As she wriggled out of her messy boots in the back porch, her mother said, "Genie, could you come in here, please?"

Genie went through the kitchen and into the living room, where her parents sat side-by-side on the couch. Their faces were drawn, and her mother was biting her lower lip. Something was wrong. Had Meara told them about her?

"What is it?" Genie said in a soft voice.

Her father held up an envelope. "This just came for you," he said. "It's from USC."

She hadn't expected to hear from the school before April. Was it a bad sign? "Can you open it, Dad?"

Enok nodded and ripped open the envelope. He unfolded the paper and squinted to read. "Dear Miss Halloran... It is with great pleasure that we inform you of your admission to the University of Southern California—"

"Thank God!" Shona yelled as she jumped off the couch and put her arms around Genie. "I'm so proud of you, Genie," she said, pressing her face to Genie's.

Enok put his arms around the two of them. "I can't believe it, dear," he said. "Genie, you'll be the first one on either side of the family to go to college. And a good school, all the way across the country, thanks to Danny. I'll have to call and let him know he's about to part with some big money—over three thousand dollars a year, I hear."

Shona pulled away and said, "He'll be thrilled to do it. You know that, Enok."

Enok wiped his eyes and smiled down at Genie. "I wish I could be the one paying your way, sweetheart. But then you'd only be going to a community college."

"Lots of people go to community college," Genie said. Victor was probably going to Bunker Hill Community College. That's what he'd said, anyway.

"Not you, though," Enok said. "Why, Frank Gifford went to USC, you know. And even Neil Armstrong—the first man on the moon."

Genie laughed. "You've been doing your research." She took the letter and went to her room, where she read it all the way through. It was hard to believe that in just a few months she'd be flying to Los Angeles. She'd told Victor about USC months ago, but he'd never brought it up after that. Maybe he'd be able to come out to visit her there once she settled in. They could go to the beach all the time and lap up the sunshine when everyone back home was shoveling snow. She looked out the window at the bright white landscape and smiled.

CHAPTER ELEVEN

Monday was predicted to be warm and windy, and the snow was melting fast by the time Genie got her coat from her locker on her way to the bus. She hadn't seen Victor during the day but she went to meet him at the bus stop all the same. She'd tucked the acceptance letter from USC in her jeans pocket, excited to show it to him.

She stood in line waiting for the bus to roll up but Victor was nowhere to be seen. When the bus came she kept letting other students get ahead of her in line, hoping he'd appear.

"Well?" the bus driver called down to her, "Are you getting on, or not?"

Maybe Victor was sick. She hadn't heard from him all weekend, but that wasn't odd. He worked on Saturdays and Sundays, and he never called her from his house.

The driver started to close the door.

"Wait!" Genie said, and climbed the steps into the bus. She took a seat near the front and craned her neck back toward the school as they drove away, but she never did see Victor. Riding the bus without him felt strange and she wondered what she should do once she was dropped off downtown. She nodded to a few of the other students she recognized, but sat silent and looked out the window. The streets were wet with melting snow and pedestrians picked their way through the puddles at the intersections. When the light turned green on Main Street, a man shook his fist at a car that had splashed him as it sped through a pool of icy water. Genie was grateful that she had her boots on, despite the warmer temperature.

When the bus stopped at Center Street Genie got off as she'd always done with Victor. She'd considered waiting ten minutes for the city bus, which would take her back home. Maybe Victor was sick, though, and could use some cheering up. She'd just say a quick hello, then be on her way. Trudging along the sidewalk, Genie did her best to stay away from the street. Her corduroy jacket—a much-loved hand-me-down from her brother Sean and too big for her—would be no match for a spray of slush.

By the time she got to Victor's building the backs of her legs were wet up to her knees from all the water she'd kicked up. But her jeans would dry. She was more worried about what was going on with Victor. Standing outside the building, she looked around for Mr. Pulnik's truck. The small parking lot was empty except for the old Plymouth that belonged to Mrs. Arena, who lived upstairs.

Genie pulled the outside door open and walked into the dim lobby. It felt strange to be there by herself. She knocked softly on Victor's door, then, when there was no answer, knocked a little harder. If he wasn't home, she'd just get the bus. Maybe he'd be in school tomorrow.

"Who is it?" Victor said finally. His voice was muffled.

"It's me, Genie," she said, trying to sound cheerful. "I just came by to say hello. Are you sick?"

There was a pause, then Victor said, "No. Go home, Genie. I'll see you in a few days."

"Why? What's the matter, Victor? Are you sick?"

Another pause, then the door opened a crack. Victor stood in darkness and said, "No, I'm not sick." He sounded as if he had a cold. Or maybe he'd been crying.

Genie pushed the door open wider, then reached for the light switch and stepped into the room. "Oh my God, Victor! Your eye!" As she took a step toward him, she tripped over a hammer. There were tools all over the floor and on the coffee table. "What's going on here? What happened to you?"

Victor put his hands in his pockets and said, "My father beat the shit out of me, that's what happened." His left eye was swollen and dark purple. He turned away and said, "You should go, Genie. I don't want you to see me like this. I don't want anyone to."

"Why? Why did he hit you?"

Victor closed the apartment door and sat down on the couch with his head in his hands. "Because you were here the other day. He doesn't want anyone in the house, ever. Especially girls, or as he calls them, 'little whores'. That's what he called you. After you left he went nuts, screaming at me and punching me. I tried my best to fight him off, but he's so strong." His shoulders started to shake and his breath came in choked wheezes. "I couldn't go out like this. I couldn't go to school."

As he sobbed, Genie put her arm around his shoulder. Her mind was a jumble of pity and anguish for Victor and shame for herself. Victor had told her how he'd grown up, but the grim life he'd talked about had never seemed real until now. Her family life wasn't always peaceful, but no one had ever been violent. Her father might occasionally utter an oath under his breath, but he'd never call girls such names. What would he think if he'd known she'd been called a whore?

"Can't you get some help, Victor? Maybe the guidance counselor at school?"

Victor ran his hand across his nose and gave Genie a strange look. He sat back on the couch and looked at the ceiling. "What would I say to Miss Grundig? All she knows about is SAT's and college admission forms. You're the only person who can help me, Genie. You're the only one who loves me."

Genie did love him and was desperate to comfort him. She took hold of his hand and said, "It's beautiful outside. Nice and warm. Do you want to get out of here and go for a walk?"

Victor shook his head.

Genie longed to get out and breathe some fresh air. It was so depressing in this dark, disheveled room. "Why are all these tools in here?"

"My Dad was sorting them last night. He's going to sell some of his older stuff, I guess." He gave Genie a sad smile. "Do you want some tea?"

Genie, eager to get out of the room, jumped up and said, "I'll make it."

As she turned on the water to fill the kettle, Victor called from the other room.

"Hey, what's this?"

Kettle in hand, Genie went back into the living room.

Victor held the letter from USC.

"Oh, I was going to show you that; it must have fallen out of my pocket. It's my acceptance letter from USC."

Victor's face was frozen in a half-smile. "Acceptance letter?" he said, his voice faltering. "You're not going, though. You can't go. You'll get into Bunker Hill, no problem. We can commute together."

Genie put the kettle down and stood with her arms folded in front of her. "We talked about this, Victor. I have to go. It was all settled when my father's friend promised to pay. My family wants me to go."

Victor put the letter down and stood up. He was pale, which made his eye look even more livid. "Do you want to go, Genie? Do you want to be three thousand miles away from me? I just told you that you're the only person who loves me. You can't leave me." He took a step toward her.

A chill crept up Genie's spine. He looked so angry. "It won't be forever. And anyway, it's not till September," she said. "You could come out to California to visit. We'd have fun."

"No," Victor said in a flat voice. "You said you loved me, Genie." He was clenching his fists.

"I do love you," Genie said, snatching the letter and backing toward the door. She'd leave and let Victor cool down. When he came back to school they could talk things over.

"But if you love me, you belong to me. You're supposed to stay with me. We'll go to the same school, then we'll get married. You're never going to leave me, Genie."

Genie took a few more steps. The door was only a few feet away.

"Are you leaving?" Victor said. "I thought you'd stay a while. But I guess that was a lie, too." He reached down and scooped up a large, heavy-looking wrench.

Genie took another step toward the door, but Victor grabbed hold of her arm.

"What are you doing, Victor? Let me go!" Her heart pounded against her ribs. His expression was horrible.

"No, Genie. You can't leave me. Not in September, and not now. I'd rather die than let you go. I'd rather you were dead, too."

"Victor!" Genie screamed. "Let me go!"

He lifted the wrench above him, and she twisted away, pulling her arm out of the sleeve of her jacket. The wrench connected with her shoulder blade, not her head. Victor staggered from the force of bringing the wrench down and tripped over a lug nut on the floor. Genie ran and opened the door.

Victor was trying to get up, but slipped on the carpet. "Genie, get back here," he bellowed.

Genie was already down the hallway. She flew through the front door and ran down Main Street toward the Waltham Supermarket. There'd be people there and she could call for help. As she ran away from Victor's building she looked over her shoulder a few times, but he wasn't following her. By the time she got to the market, her shoulder screamed with pain. Digging into her jeans pocket, she found a dime. With shaking hands she called the only number she dared.

After a few rings, someone said hello.

"Debra," Genie said. "Is that you?"

66

There was a long pause.

"Debra, it's Genie!"

A sigh, then, "I know who it is. I'm sort of surprised you called me. After all, I'm not your lover boy."

Genie squeezed her eyes shut. "Debra, please just listen. I'm at the Waltham Supermarket. I had to get away from Victor."

"What's the matter, did you have a lover's spat?" Debra's voice was cold.

"Debra," Genie said, her voice shaking. "He tried to kill me. He hit me with a wrench. If he finds me—"

"Stay in the store," Debra said. "If you see him, tell someone to call the police. I'll be there in ten minutes." The line went dead.

Genie didn't hang up right away, just held the receiver and looked around her. She had two nickels left, and if she saw Victor, she'd call the police herself.

CHAPTER TWELVE

"Why don't you let me take you to the Emergency Room, Genie?" Debra was driving her mother's VW bug and shifted her glance back and forth between Genie and the road.

Genie took a shallow breath. Breathing too deeply hurt. "I just want to get home," she said. "Mom and Dad won't be back until late; they're visiting Aunt Rita. If I can just go lie down, maybe have an aspirin, I should be okay."

"What about the police?" Debra said. She took a left turn slowly, not wanting to jostle Genie. "He tried to kill you, Genie. What if he tries again?" She put her hand on Genie's knee and gave it a squeeze. "I can't stand knowing he hurt you."

Genie was embarrassed on top of being afraid. She'd hurt people, too. One by one, she'd cut them out of her life. Debra, for example, who hadn't hesitated a second when Genie needed help. She was ashamed when she thought of all the lies she'd told her friends, all the ways she'd deceived her family.

When they got to her house, Debra ran around to the passenger side and helped Genie out of the car, being careful not to touch her shoulder.

Genie winced, but said, "I'm all right."

The two girls walked slowly up the front stairs. When they got to the top, the door opened. Meara was standing there, her eyes huge. "What's wrong with you?"

"Victor hit her with a wrench," Debra said as she helped Genie inside. "He was aiming for her head, but hit her shoulder instead. He tried to kill her."

Meara's hand flew to her mouth. "I'm going to call Ragsie right now!"

Genie grabbed Meara's hand and said, "No! Don't tell anyone. If Ragsie and Sean find out what Victor did, they'll kill him. They'll end up going to jail. Dad, too. You know that. Promise me you won't tell anyone, Meara, please."

Meara reached over and gently unbuttoned the top buttons of Genie's blouse. Pulling the blouse off Genie's shoulder, she gasped when she saw the angry-looking welt. "Do you think something's broken, Genie?" she whispered. "Does it hurt a lot?"

Genie put her good arm through Meara's. "I'll be fine," she said. "I'm going upstairs to lie down for a while." She looked over at Debra. "Will you come up with me?" she said.

"Of course," Debra said and kissed her cheek.

The three of them went upstairs to the room Genie and Meara shared. Meara pulled the pillows off her bed and arranged them on Genie's so that she could keep her shoulder comfortable. Genie settled down, relieved to be home. If she could just rest a while, she'd be fine. Being with Meara and Debra made her feel safe.

Meara turned back to get a blanket and froze. "It's him," she said, pointing toward the window. "Victor's walking down our street."

"I'm going to call the police," Debra said.

Genie reached out and held onto Debra's arm. "Please don't. I don't want my parents to find out."

Debra looked hard at her friend. "You're not making any sense, Genie. He just tried to kill you, and now he's followed you home. He's dangerous."

Meara went into the spare bedroom—the one her brothers had used when they lived at home—and came out with a baseball bat. "He's a coward, Debs. I bet I can take him myself." She stood holding the bat over her left shoulder—all five-foot two, one hundred pounds of her—with an expression that could kill.

The doorbell rang.

"I don't want to talk to him," Genie said. "Maybe if we don't answer, he'll leave."

"Screw that." Meara stomped out of the room, with Debra right behind her.

Genie got up slowly and tiptoed down the hallway, stopping at the top of the stairs. She'd call the police if Victor said anything threatening, but she couldn't bring herself to face him. She held her breath as she listened to what was going on downstairs.

"Meara," Debra said. "Stay behind me and let me talk to him."

"No way, Debs," Meara said.

Genie heard the chain slam closed before the door opened.

"What do you want?" Meara said, her voice low and penetrating.

"Genie," Victor said, his voice quavering. "I have to talk to her. I have to apologize."

Genie's throat constricted. He sounded so miserable.

"Genie's not home," Debra said. "Her mother took her to the emergency room. You should leave, Victor."

Victor's voice got louder and more tremulous. "The emergency room? Did she tell her mother what happened? Does anyone else know about—"

Meara cut him off. "She told my Mom that she fell down the stairs. Genie hasn't told anyone besides Debs and me what you did to her, you fucking coward. She's trying to protect you, though why, I don't know. But if you ever get near her again, ever try to talk to her again, I'll tell my brothers. You've seen them before, right? If they knew what you did to her, they'd pull your arms off and stick them up your ass, you piece of shit, and then they'd really go to work on you. Now get the hell out of here before I break my promise to Genie and give Ragsie a call."

The door slammed and Genie ran back to her room and looked out the window. She saw Victor loping away, his head down and his hands in his pockets. A sudden weakness made her knees wobble, and she sat down on the bed. A minute later, Debra and Meara were back upstairs.

Meara's pale face was splotched with patches of red, proof that her temper was fully engaged. "That creep," she muttered as she set the bat against the wall. "How could you have gone out with him, Genie? He's such a... such a weenie."

Debra laughed. "Meara Halloran, after the language you used downstairs, the best you can come up with now is 'weenie'? I never knew you had such a mouth on you."

Genie sat back against the pillows, then winced at the pain. She had to smile, though. "Meara learned the art of swearing from our brother Sean."

Debra put her arm around Meara and gave her a squeeze. "You're an A student, Squeaks."

Meara pushed Debra away gently. "I told you guys not to call me that any more. I'm thirteen, not six, you know."

"You're a brave girl," Genie said, trying to find a comfortable position. Her shoulder was throbbing. "You're brave, and you're a wonderful sister. And Debra, you're a great friend. You're both so loyal. And I...I've been anything but loyal, anything but a friend." She wouldn't let herself cry, but held a hand over her eyes. "What am I going to do? How do I avoid him? We're in some of the same classes. He'll follow me around, I'm sure of it."

Debra sat beside Genie and said, "Don't worry. You have a lot of friends at school, and so do I. If I tell them to keep an eye out for you—"

"You can't tell anyone what happened!"

"I won't, Genie," Debra said, lacing her fingers through Genie's. "I'll just say that you want to keep your distance from him. He won't bother you at school. I guarantee it."

CHAPTER THIRTEEN

Later that night, after everyone had gone to bed, Genie moved onto her side and did her best not to disturb her shoulder. She hadn't gone down to dinner earlier, telling her mother that she wasn't feeling well. Meara had sneaked her a dinner roll and an apple, but she'd only had a few bites. As she lay in the darkness she kept seeing Victor's face as he'd raised the wrench over her. She could have been killed. Her parents would have been devastated...all her family would have been. She moved a little more and gasped at the sharp pain.

"Genie, are you all right?" Meara whispered.

Genie bit her lip, trying to keep from whimpering. "I'm...I'm okay. Maybe I should have some more aspirin." She switched on the lamp by her bed and took two aspirins with a quick sip of water. "I'm sorry if I woke you."

Meara sat up and said, "You should finish that roll. Mom says that taking aspirin on an empty stomach is bad for you. Besides, you must be hungry, right? I can get you some milk. Plus Mom made a spice cake. Want some of that?"

Genie shook her head. "No thanks. I'll finish this roll, though. Then you should go back to sleep. I'll be fine."

Meara got up and walked over to Genie's bed, perching lightly on the side. "This doesn't bother your shoulder, does it?"

Genie took Meara's hand and said, "Did I ever tell you what a wonderful sister you are?"

Meara rolled her eyes. "I'm not so wonderful. I've been mad at you for a long time, Genie. You've been acting so different. And pretty soon you'll be gone to California and it'll just be me here with Mom and Dad." A tear slid down her cheek, and she ran her hand roughly across her eyes.

Genie's throat tightened. "I've been selfish, Meara. This thing with Victor got me all mixed up. It was like he was my whole life, and being with him was the most important thing."

"More important than your family or your friends?"

"I never thought of it that way, but maybe that's how I felt. I wasn't thinking straight, sneaking around all the time."

Meara handed her the roll. "Maybe you snuck around and lied because you knew that being with him was wrong. I could have told you that. When he was here at Christmas he was such a phony to Mom, but really he seemed to not like any of us."

Genie took a bite and thought. "I never saw that, but you're probably right." She lay back and took a deep breath. "Well, I have three more months of school, and I'm going to make the most of it. I'm not going to see a lot of my friends again after graduation and I want to spend time with them while I can. You too, Squeaks...I mean, Meara."

Meara went back to her own bed and Genie turned out the light. "Genie," Meara said after a moment. "Are you scared about moving away from home? You'll be so far away."

"I'm excited about it," Genie said. "Not too scared now, but maybe I will be when the time comes."

"I want to travel, too," Meara said. "My dance teacher told me that I might be able to get a scholarship to a school in Philadelphia, or even New York. If I joined a troupe, I could travel all over the world."

"You'd want to do that?" Genie smiled. Her little sister had big dreams.

Meara yawned. "Of course," she said. "First I have to get out of stupid junior high, though." She yawned again. "I'm going to sleep now. You should, too. And don't worry about that creep Victor. Debra said she'd make sure he didn't bother you."

Genie closed her eyes and felt her body relax. She was soon asleep.

CHAPTER FOURTEEN

Meara was right. Victor never bothered Genie at school because he never came back. At first, Genie thought he might return after his black eye had faded. But weeks, then months went by, and he never appeared. There were rumors that he and his father had moved back to Czechoslovakia, which was ridiculous. Even if they were allowed back in, Mr. Pulnik would never have wanted to go. He hated the government there and was proud of becoming an American. But Mr. Pulnik's shop had changed hands and was now called 'Andy's', according to Debra's brother.

Even though Victor had probably moved away, Genie never got over the feeling that she'd run into him. She made sure to keep busy with the extracurricular activities she'd ignored when she and Victor had been together. It was easier not to give into feelings of dread when she was surrounded by her friends.

When graduation rolled around, Genie finally relaxed a little. She was on track to start school in early September and looked forward to being far away, even though she'd miss her family and friends. She and Debra went to a graduation party for their friend Dave, whose parents were bereft at the thought of him going to school in Oregon. It had been a while since she'd been to Dave's house, where she'd always felt welcome. Dave's mother, Mrs. Bluestone, was a kind, if overly attentive, hostess.

"Genie, dear," she said, holding out a tray of hot dogs. "You've hardly eaten a thing. Your mother is going to be worried sick if you lose any more weight when you're out there in California. Come on, have a hot dog, and don't say you're too full."

"Thank you, Mrs. Bluestone," Genie said. She could take a bite or two and just toss the rest when Mrs. Bluestone wasn't watching.

"Leave Genie alone, Ma," Dave said. "She's not that skinny. You're just picking on her cause she's going far away like me. Far out west, where kids can't get a decent meal for days and days." He wiggled his eyebrows at Genie and said, "Okay, Genie, I've distracted her. Make your getaway!"

Mrs. Bluestone swatted Dave's arm, and he kissed her on the cheek.

Genie wandered over to where a few of her friends sat on lawn chairs arranged in a circle. The sun was close to setting, and the evening was warm. Genie sat back in an Adirondack chair and closed her eyes, listening to her friends joke and rag on one another. A sweet sadness came over her. She might never see some of them again, and she was grateful to be with them now.

"Hey," Paul said. "Is that a firefly over there?"

Genie opened her eyes, surprised to see how dark it had become. She joined the others who had wandered over to the tree-filled hilly space that abutted the Bluestone's yard. The little creatures flashed on and off in a silent light show.

"I remember catching those for school," Debra said. "When was that, Genie? Eighth grade?"

One by one, the others went back to where they'd been sitting, all except for Genie, who watched in amazement as the beetles sparked their own light and danced through the dark. They seemed drawn to the trees, and soon disappeared among the higher branches. Genie was about to turn back to join her friends when she saw it, something white among the trees at the top of the hill. Genie's heart pounded. It was a tall man wearing white pants. He stood there, looking at her. Victor had come back.

"Debra!" Genie yelled, pointing to the hilltop. The man ran away.

By the time Debra got to Genie, he'd disappeared. Genie was gulping for air and shaking. "Can you get me home, Debra? I don't want the others to know."

Debra pulled Genie's face toward her. "Know what, Genie? What happened?" She stared hard into Genie's eyes.

"I saw him," Genie whispered. She pointed again. "Victor! He was up there, just looking at me."

"Are you sure?" Debra frowned. "It's awfully dark up there."

"I'm sure," Genie said.

Debra wasn't convinced, but clearly Genie was. As she walked her home, she kept reassuring her. "I heard he ran away from home, Genie. His father took off after him."

"Maybe," Genie said. "But he could have come back."

"I doubt it. Either way, he won't follow you to Los Angeles. You can be sure of that."

Genie nodded. She was counting the days until she could fly away. If she stayed, she'd always be looking over her shoulder. She was afraid of him, but not for the reason that Debra or Meara thought. He regretted hitting her; she believed that. The more time she'd spent away from him, though, the more she realized how much he'd controlled her and shut her off from everyone else. She'd loved him, and she knew he'd loved her. But it wasn't the kind of love you saw in movies, or heard about in songs. It was a dark love, and Genie didn't want it in her life. If Victor ever found her alone, he'd lure her back, she was sure of it.

CHAPTER FIFTEEN

Los Angeles was a different world for Genie, and not just because it was so far from home. Palm trees graced the stately USC campus and the scents of gardenia and jasmine filled the air well into the winter months. Although Genie never joined a sorority she enjoyed walking up and down fraternity row, looking at all the huge houses with the Greek letters out front. Genie loved everything about USC, even when the smog clamped down on the city and stung her eyes. She and her friends went to the beach nearly every weekend, and she even managed to get a slight tan. She could feel herself relaxing, changing.

In her junior year she started dating Jake. A rugby player, he had dark hair with bright blue eyes. His family lived in San Diego, and he'd taken Genie down there a few times. Jake had plans to join the Army after school and later to serve in the diplomatic corps. Although he had serious plans for the future, he was easy-going and fun to be with. He and Genie had an understanding that theirs would be a college romance, with no real plans beyond. That was fine with Genie. After her experience with Victor, the last thing she wanted was a serious boyfriend.

One warm day in December, when the rest of the group was trying to surf, she walked to the water's edge alone. It was late in the afternoon, and the sun shone golden on the dark waves. She reached into her pocket and pulled out the lapis lazuli necklace Victor had given her. Without even looking at it, she pitched it into the water, then turned and walked away.

Later on Genie and her friends sat around a fire pit on the beach. They'd eaten pizza and were working their way through a case of beer. Jake had taken the empty pizza boxes up to the trash cans by the parking lot. When he came back he sat behind Genie, putting his arms around her.

"Hey," he said in a soft voice, "are you okay?"

Genie leaned up against his chest and said, "I'm fine. Why would you think there's anything wrong?"

"You've been kind of quiet tonight. Plus, I saw you earlier, when the rest of us were surfing. You were standing in the water, and it looked like you threw something. Do you want to talk about it?"

Genie hadn't told Jake about Victor and she didn't plan to. "It was just a penny, you know, for good luck," she said. "It's silly, I know. But I've been doing it since I was a kid." She sat up and looked around the fire at her friends. "Hey! Any more marshmallows left?"

• • •

Genie had known from the first that she wanted to major in English, and was never disappointed by her classes; even the class on English in the Middle Ages, which meant slogging through "The Canterbury Tales," delighted her. By her sophomore year she'd decided to become a teacher. The way she saw it, she'd be able to pass her love of English onto generations of students.

As much as she loved Los Angeles, though, she wanted to go back to Boston after graduation. Her favorite professor at USC had offered her a place in the graduate program and a job as her teaching assistant, but when the letter from Boston University came, she decided she'd enter graduate school there. Los Angeles had given her a lot: a wonderful education, new friends from all over the country, and an appreciation of life beyond Boston. More than anything else, though, California had offered her a safe harbor, far from Victor and his violent ways. She'd always love Los Angeles, but the tug of her family and the life she'd always known was strong. By the end of June she was back in her family's home, making plans for graduate school.

2012

CHAPTER SIXTEEN

It was late when the taxi pulled up in front of Meara's house, the house Genie had grown up in. It had been passed on to Meara after she'd nursed both parents in their final illnesses.

They'd dropped off Ragsie on the way, so it was Sean who carried Genie's big suitcase up the steps. The light came on and Sean gave Genie a kiss on the top of the head. "You okay, kiddo?" he said.

Genie nodded. "I'm fine, Sean. Go on home to Donna."

The door opened and Meara reached out and grabbed Genie's arm, pulling her in for a hug. "Genie!" she said softly, "Genie, you're here." She hung on, long enough for Genie to start to relax after her trip with her brothers.

Genie pulled back and stroked Meara's long hair, the black shot through with grey now. Her little sister had just turned fifty. "You look beautiful," Genie said. She waved goodbye to Sean and followed Meara into the house.

"Look at this place," Genie said. "We were here for such a short time at Christmas that I didn't really have a chance to look around."

Meara gave her a big smile. "A lot can happen in five years," she said. "When Mom couldn't go out anymore I became quite the DIY goddess, courtesy of online shopping. Of course, I got a lot of help from Frank."

Frank Tomlinson had grown up a few doors down from the Hallorans, and like Meara, had come home to care for his mother. He was a graphic designer, not a surprise for someone who had always won the art prizes in school. He was good at his job and was able to work from home.

"Frank was always such a nice boy," Genie said, collapsing on the pearl-colored shabby-chic sofa. When Genie had grown up in this house, the living room furniture was dark, with lace curtains on the windows and portraits of JFK and Pope John XXIII on the walls. Now the room was furnished with light woods and cream and beige upholstery. A huge blue and fawn Persian Nain rug—one of the many treasures Meara brought back from her decades-long wanderings—took pride of place on top of the natural maple floor.

Meara sat in an overstuffed chair opposite Genie, laughing. "That nice boy is fifty-one, Genie." Suddenly serious, she leaned forward and said, "How are you, really? On the phone the other day you sounded pretty good. Did the boys nag you all the way across the U.S.?"

Genie shook her head. "They were fine. It was so nice of them to come out to get me, even if it wasn't necessary."

Meara frowned. "I think it stinks that you had to come here at all. Don't get me wrong, I love seeing you. But you and Charlie had planned to do things differently. That old bat put the screws to Ragsie and he folded."

"Ah, Nanny Pat," Genie said, leaning her head back and closing her eyes. "She's an old lady, Meara, and I know that the one person she ever truly loved in this world was Charlie. He would have wanted to do something for her."

"All those years in California have mellowed you, sister," Meara said. She looked at her watch and yawned. "I know it's still early for you, but midnight's past my bedtime. Plus we have a date at the funeral home at ten a.m. Beatrice will be there. She's pretty broken up about Charlie."

"He loved her, too." Beatrice was Sean and Donna's adopted daughter, and secretly Genie's favorite. Genie gave Meara a sad smile. It had been a long day in a series of long, miserable days. She stifled a yawn. "You go ahead. I'll make myself a cup of tea and decompress."

After Meara went upstairs Genie sat for a while with her hands in her lap. As she walked to the kitchen she started to feel annoyed. It was bad enough to have to come back for a funeral service, but that damned funeral home set her teeth on edge. She'd been to O'Rourke's, the so-called "Irish" funeral home, more times than she could remember. The last time had been for her mother's wake. And now she had to go through the charade of planning a funeral and burial for her dear Charlie, who hadn't gone to church since he was seventeen and had little use for what he called the "Death Industrial Complex." They'd made their own plans long ago, and Genie would keep her promise to him, no matter what anyone else thought was right.

Later, she crept up the stairs, not wanting to wake Meara. She still couldn't get over how different the house was from when she'd grown up. Meara had knocked down walls and opened up the spaces on both floors, transforming the small, dark house built in the early twentieth century. Genie slipped into the bathroom, amazed to see a spacious shower and a separate deep soaking tub. She took a quick shower, then went to the bedroom she'd shared with Meara. That, too, was almost unrecognizable. Instead of the two twin beds jammed against opposite walls, an elegant queen-size bed with a delicate scrollwork iron headboard dominated the room. A bedside table held a modern and efficient reading lamp, a vintage-look clock, and a simple water carafe and glass. Meara had worked her magic in this room, too. She deserved to live in this beautiful place, Genie thought. Meara had spent years with their parents as, first Enok, then Shona, endured debilitating illnesses. Although Ragsie and Sean did what they could, they had families and businesses to look after. Genie visited from California occasionally, but never stayed very long. Meara's siblings knew she had shouldered the burden of their parents' care, and they would always be grateful to her.

Genie turned off the light and lay in bed. As her eyes adjusted to the dark, she watched the light cotton curtains blow in the mild spring breeze. A sound she'd grown up with drifted in through the open window: the ceaseless traffic on Route 128, a north/south state highway located a mile or so away. When she was a girl she'd listen to the far-off whine of the cars and trucks and wonder about where people were going so late at night. Exhausted by the day, she let the familiar sound lull her to sleep.

CHAPTER SEVENTEEN

Despite being on California time, Genie found herself in the kitchen at seven the next morning, her laptop open on the table. In the last few years she had started writing young adult romances, and to her surprise, a couple had been published. Since Charlie's death she hadn't even thought of writing, but she'd taken the laptop with her in the hopes that she'd start again.

She made coffee while Meara showered, amused to see that her sister had started using Peet's coffee, a brand beloved in the Bay area. Once the coffee was ready, Genie went to get milk, but what she saw on the refrigerator door took her breath away. Nestled among the magnetized mementos from Nantucket and other New England vacation spots was a photo of Meara, Genie, and Charlie. It had been taken a years before, when she and Charlie showed Meara around Sonoma County. Meara stood in the middle, with Charlie and Genie on either side of her. All three were beaming, their arms around each other. They looked so happy.

Genie clapped her hand on her mouth and stifled a moan. She reached back toward the kitchen table and guided herself toward a chair, holding her head in her hands.

"Genie!" Meara said, running into the kitchen. "What is it?"

Genie shook her head, unable to speak. Meara sat next to her and leaned up against her shoulder, rubbing her back. "Oh, Genie," Meara said, "What you've been through this month. I'm so sorry."

Gradually, Genie calmed down. She wiped her face with the back of her hand and gave Meara an embarrassed smile. "Sorry. Not the best way for you to start your day, I'm afraid."

Meara took Genie's hand and kissed it. "I'm fine. It's you I'm worried about. You've endured something that would break most people. And now you've been dragged out here."

Genie got up and ripped a paper towel off the dispenser by the sink and blew her nose. "I don't care about that so much. This will mean a lot to Nanny Pat." She sat down and looked at the mug she'd set down on the table. "I made coffee." She raised an eyebrow. "I see you've switched from Dunkin Donuts, finally."

Meara nodded. "Yes, you were right about Peet's," she said. "Let me get some milk." She put her hand on the refrigerator door, then stopped and said, "Oh, God, Genie. I'm so sorry. I should have taken this down." She started to take the magnet off the door.

"No, don't take it down," Genie said. "It's a beautiful picture. I remember that day. We'd taken you wine tasting in the Alexander Valley."

"That would explain my red face," Meara said, as she brought the milk over to the table, then got the coffee pot. She sat opposite Genie and poured her a cup of coffee, then one for herself. Taking a sip, she glanced over the top of her mug. "Are you sure you're okay going to O'Rourke's? Ragsie will take care of everything for you if you ask him."

Genie rolled her eyes. "That's exactly why I'm going. I want to keep the maudlin crap to a minimum. Do you remember how Tommy O'Rourke nixed the music we wanted for Mom's funeral? She wanted "What a Wonderful World," and Tommy said some shit about Holy Mother the Church not allowing secular songs at a funeral. So we ended up with the usual Ave Maria. Ugh. The one song Mom really loved he wouldn't allow."

Meara shrugged. "Not his call, Genie. He's only doing what the Catholic Church demands. I agree, though. It would have been nice to have what Mom wanted at her own funeral."

"That's why I'm going to be at O'Rourke's today. No music at the funeral, no sermon, no prayers at the wake, no freakin' collage of old photos with "Danny Boy" playing in the background." Genie drummed her fingers on the table.

Meara smiled. "Tommy won't make much money on this funeral."

"Yup. It'll be the stripped-down version, for sure." Genie got up and put her mug in the dishwasher. Looking at the clock she frowned and said, "Well, I'd better get ready."

"Do you want to go for a walk this afternoon?"

Genie smiled. "I'd love to, but don't you have classes later?"

Meara ran a small dance studio downtown, something she'd done since Shona's death.

"Sandy's going to cover for me for the next few days," Meara said. "She's a peach."

Genie crossed her arms and beamed at Meara. "You know what, Meara? You should be very proud of yourself. You've got a successful business. And this house...you've made it beautiful."

Meara said, "I've been fortunate. But what about you? Isn't your latest book going to be made into a movie?"

Genie shrugged. "Philip keeps trying. He's a great agent, but he's about as grounded in reality as my books."

Meara got up and poured the rest of the coffee into the sink. "Real or not, those books are something else, Genie. They're positive and old-fashioned in a good way. And you've done pretty well for yourself, right?"

Genie nodded. "I've been lucky, too, Meara. Or, I used to be." She looked over at the photo. "Once I met Charlie, everything changed for me. The world became a beautiful place."

Meara put her arm around Genie's shoulder and said, "I know. He was a wonderful man, Genie. I loved him, too."

"And he loved you." Genie took a deep breath. "Okay, I gotta stay strong and get through this morning. Where will we walk later?"

"How about Prospect Hill Park? We should get some nice views today."

Genie kissed Meara on the cheek and said, "You're on. I'll even race you to the top."

CHAPTER EIGHTEEN

The day of the funeral dawned cloudy and raw, with a sleety rain mocking the daffodils and tulips that had bloomed in the warm days before. Genie kept her head down during the mass, trying her best to ignore the anguished mutterings of Nanny Pat beside her. The older woman was tiny, with a nearly wrinkle-free face. Her white hair was done up in tight pin curls, and her thick-lensed glasses made her blue eyes look huge. She wore an old but well-preserved London Fog raincoat and clear plastic overshoes.

"That boy," Nanny Pat said under her breath as the priest went through the age-old ritual on the altar. "That boy was like the shining sun, so cheerful and kind. How could he be gone now? Lord God, how could you have taken him from us? He didn't de-serve to die like that, all alone on the street, so far from his home. Shot down like that, so terrible!" She blew her nose and pulled a rosary out of her purse, but didn't start a decade. Instead, she kept up her sotto voce mourning, swaying slightly as she spoke.

Genie dug her nails into the palms of her hands to keep herself from saying something. She leaned forward and looked toward Ragsie, who stood on the other side of Nanny Pat. He had his eyes closed and was mouthing the words of the prayers along with Father Burton. Genie stared at him, willing him to open his eyes. Finally, she reached around behind Nanny Pat and gave Rag-sie's sleeve a tug.

Ragsie opened his eyes and mouthed "What?"

Genie pointed to Nanny Pat, who gazed at the ceiling. "Tell her to stop!" Genie mouthed.

Ragsie's eyes popped, but he nodded and leaned over to whisper something in Nanny Pat's ear.

Suddenly the old woman stopped and made the sign of the cross with the crucifix of her rosary, then started whispering the familiar prayers.

Genie mouthed, "Thank you" to Ragsie, and gritted her teeth. Only a little more to go, she told herself, then a trip to the cemetery, where the urn she'd brought from California would be buried with Charlie's parents.

Mercifully, the rain had stopped by the time the mass was over. Genie got into the O'Rourke Town Car with Meara and Ragsie. Sean, God bless him, had offered to drive Nanny Pat to the cemetery. When the little funeral procession entered the cemetery, Genie grabbed Meara's hand and squeezed hard. She'd need every bit of her strength to get through the next few minutes.

The sun started to shine weakly through the clouds as the mourners got out of their cars. Genie and the others followed the priest up the little hill to the gravesite of Charlie's parents. She handed the urn to Tommy O'Rourke, who set it on the green Astroturf covering the grave. Keeping her eyes on the urn Genie bit the inside of her cheek as the final prayers were said. To her surprise, a bagpiper came up the hill and started to play "Down by the Glenside," an Irish rebel song, not a tune that would have been approved by 'Holy Mother the Church'. She smiled. She had no idea who'd arranged for the piper, but it would have pleased Charlie to kick against the rules one last time.

After the service, Genie put her arms around Nanny Pat. "Charlie loved you. He'd talk about your peanut butter cookies all the time, and loved it when you read him poetry. You were so important to him."

The older woman looked up at Genie, her eyes swimming behind the oversized lenses. "So were you, dear. He told me once that you made him happier than he ever thought he could be. Never forget that." She kissed Genie on the cheek.

Beatrice walked by holding a rose in her hand. Nanny Pat said, "Isn't that the Indian girl your brother Sean adopted? My, she's a brown little thing, isn't she?"

Genie counted to three before she said, "Actually, Beatrice is from Guatemala. Sean and his family are so lucky to have her."

Nanny Pat clucked, then crooked a finger toward Meara's friend Frank. "You can take me home now," she said.

Frank winked at Genie and helped Nanny Pat back to the car.

Genie stood by the grave a little longer, glad to feel the sun warming her face. She told herself that Charlie wasn't there; she'd never leave him in this sad place. Meara joined her, looping her arm through Genie's. "Shall we go now? There'll be people coming to the house, remember?"

Genie nodded. It would be good to have a cup of tea with old friends.

CHAPTER NINETEEN

A week after the funeral, Genie was back home. She sat on the patio watching the hummingbirds fight over the feeder, swooping and buzzing in their gravity-defying flight. "Meara!" she called, "Come outside and watch these acrobats!"

Meara opened the French door and joined Genie on the outdoor sofa. She put her sunglasses on and leaned back with a contented sigh. "I'm so glad you talked me into coming back with you, Genie. I may never leave."

Genie laughed. "As I recall, it was you who said you needed to come here. Something about keeping an eye on me. I certainly don't need to be observed, but I am glad you're here."

"It's only for a few days," Meara said. She stretched her arms over her head and sighed again. "I just want to make sure you're really okay. If I have to stay in this gorgeous place to do that, I'm willing to make the sacrifice."

Tramp sauntered from the side of the house and stood in front of Genie, staring at her.

"Yes, what may I do for you?" Genie scratched under the cat's chin. The cat leaned into her hand, then walked in a circle around Genie's feet, settling down on top of her bare toes.

Meara reached over and stroked the lustrous black fur on Tramp's head. "He's got you well trained, I see."

Genie nodded. "I think he's wondering where Charlie is. Those two were best friends." She slid her feet out from under the cat and got up. "Would you like some lunch?" Her lips quivered, but she tried to smile.

Meara jumped up. "Put your shoes on. I'm taking you out somewhere nice."

Genie took a deep, shaky breath. "Yeah. Let's get out of here."

• • •

For the next few days, Meara and Genie fell into an easy rhythm of hikes, shopping at farmers' markets, and dinners prepared in Genie's well-used kitchen. Both women knew that Genie would be lonely after Meara left, but Meara had seen what she needed to. Genie's support system was strong: from Debra and her family, to Genie's coworkers at school, to the people who'd worked with Charlie at Mercy's Family. Marty Edmund, the chairman of the board for Mercy's Family, was especially close. After his wife had died the year before, he'd leaned on Genie and Charlie. Now it was his turn to be there for Genie. She was surrounded by people who loved her. She had started writing again; that would help, too.

Genie had prepared roast chicken and root vegetables for Meara's going away dinner. They sat in the small dining room, with candles casting a warm glow. Tramp, somehow knowing he had to keep Genie in his sights, lay on a chair nearby.

Genie poured two glasses of cabernet. Meara raised her glass and said, "To Charlie."

"To Charlie," Genie whispered. She said a little prayer to herself, as always, whenever her husband's name was mentioned. "You

97

know," she said as she filled Meara's plate, "it would be no problem for me to drive you to the airport tomorrow morning."

Meara shook her head, her mouth too full to let her answer right away. She dabbed at her lips with the napkin, then said, "I told you, Ragsie insisted on a limo. He's paying, Genie. You think I'm not going to take him up on it?"

• • •

Genie was exhausted. She hadn't slept well the night before, and it had been hard to say goodbye to Meara. She'd promised to go back to Boston for a Christmas visit, her first holiday without Charlie. Right after the car picked Meara up, Debra had called, asking Genie if she felt like company. Genie had begged off, saying she'd probably take a nap in the afternoon.

And so she found herself lying on the couch, a light cotton coverlet pulled over her. She closed her eyes and listened to the far-off sounds of the kids in the playground. Tramp had found her and, never one to let a good nap opportunity go to waste, had snuggled up beside her. Genie smiled at the familiar presence against her back and drifted away.

She was back at the cemetery, standing alone at the Maguire family grave. She shivered in the sleet, pulling the hood of her raincoat close to her face. As she turned to leave, there was Charlie standing with his hands in his pockets, his curly salt-and-pepper hair ruffled by the breeze. He was looking past her and smiling, as if he'd seen someone he recognized.

Genie ran to him, overjoyed to see him again. As she got closer he put his arms out to her.

"Charlie!" Genie said, leaning into him. "You're here!"

98

Then she saw that it was Victor who held her. He put his hand on Genie's chest and pushed her away. "Of course I'm here," he said in a mild voice. "Why wouldn't I be? You're the one who doesn't belong here." He pulled a wrench out of his back pocket and held it over her head.

"No!" Genie screamed. When she woke she could hear Tramp scrambling down the hallway. She must have frightened him badly. She sat up and wiped the tears off her face, trying to calm down. She picked up the phone and dialed. "Debra," she said. "Can I take you up on your offer after all? I could use some company."

<u>1988-1989</u>

CHAPTER TWENTY

Genie sat at her hand-me-down dining room table. She loved the solid oak piece, with its drop leaves and finely milled legs. She remembered sitting at it with her Aunt Beth, drinking tea and talking about family history and whatever Genie was interested in at the time. She wondered what Aunt Beth would say about the wedding invitation she'd just opened. Her former boyfriend (and almost fiancé) was marrying someone named Suzi in the spring. Good luck to Suzi, Genie thought.

Matt, or as it said on the invitation, Matteo Francis Lorusso, was a nice man: good-looking, smart, and successful, and Genie had enjoyed dating him for a couple of years. Mama Lorusso, however, was another matter. She'd hated Genie on sight and never missed an opportunity to get a dig in. Genie had tried her best to ignore her, but as she and Matt became more serious, Mrs. Lorusso upped her game. Matt got put in the middle and, over time, his Mama's boy tendencies became pronounced. It got so bad that Matt, who'd asked Genie to live with him, retracted the offer the day the move was supposed to happen. His mother had told him that she'd be mortified if her friends knew her son was living in sin. Rather than upset Mama, he'd let Genie scramble to find another place to live. Having given up an apartment she'd loved, she'd had to move in with her parents while she looked for a new place. Matt had offered to pay for storage of her furniture but she'd declined, telling him he should use the money to buy a spine.

The one good outcome of the Matt fiasco was that she'd found her current apartment, the first floor of a large, beautifully restored house in Cambridge. She slipped the invitation back into its envelope and made a mental note to buy something nice at Crate and Barrel, the store where Matt and Suzi had registered. It was the least she could do for Suzi.

She shivered and got up to close the window. When she'd come home from school the fall sun had been warm, but it would be dark soon. Some of her teacher friends were coming to dinner, and Genie still had to buy food. She grabbed her favorite flannel-lined denim jacket and headed to Formaggio's, where she bought fresh pasta, cheese, and bread, along with olives and prosciutto. As she walked back home balancing a couple of bags, she gave an awkward wave to her landlady, who was sweeping the sidewalk in front of the house. Mrs. Ellery was a nice woman, if a bit obsessed with keeping her property immaculate. Genie didn't mind. She was neat by nature, and loved calling the impressive old house her home.

She hustled into the kitchen, popped her new Tracy Chapman CD into the player, and started cooking. Before long the doorbell rang, and Tess, Mike, and Celine trooped in. It was Friday night, the best night of the week for students and teachers alike. Genie and her friends tucked into the food and laughed and commiserated about the school's vice principal, their promising and infuriating students, and the general state of being single in their early thirties.

"What about you, Genie?" Celine said, helping herself to another piece of bread. "You almost got hitched once. When are you going to give it another go?"

Genie laughed. "I'm perfectly happy the way I am right now. It's been a year since Matt and I split up, but you know, there's a lot more to life than dating."

"Just don't wait too long," Mike said. "If I hadn't convinced Tess to date me, I'd still be a loser hanging around in bars."

Tess folded her arms. "You still hang around in bars, Mike. You're gonna meet your buddies at Sully's after dinner tonight."

Mike put his arms around Tess and gave her a big, loud kiss on the cheek. "Well, yes, I'll be at Sully's, Tessie, but the boys and I will be talking about you the whole time! They're so envious of me. And of course, they all want to get to know your beautiful friends Genie and Celine."

Tess gave him a playful push and wiped the side of her face. "You goofball!"

Mike gave her a killer grin. "You got a thing for goofballs, Tessie. Admit it."

Genie smiled and took it all in. Yes, being in a relationship would be nice, but she could wait, despite what her brothers and parents said. She'd just turned thirty and would love to have a husband and children, but she knew what could happen when a romance went sour. Meanwhile, she had her friends and family. She loved her job, and she was even starting to write, though she'd told no one about it. One day the right guy would come along; she was sure of it.

CHAPTER TWENTY-ONE

Genie walked into her classroom and sat at her desk with a big smile on her face. The students trickled in, buzzing about their plans for the short Thanksgiving break. Outside the skies were a dull November grey, and the trees shivered in the wind, leafless and bare, but inside the mood was cheerful. She waited until all the tenth-graders were seated. Their conversations petered out as one-by-one they saw their teacher, the usually no-nonsense Miss Halloran, sitting with her hands folded on the desk, still smiling.

No one spoke for a little while until a voice piped up from the back. "What gives, Miss H.? Didja win the lottery or something?"

Genie laughed and said, "Not exactly, Larry." She stood up and pulled a piece of paper out of her pocket. "I think this is even better."

The students whispered to each other.

Genie put an index finger to her lips and the class quieted. "You all remember that short story writing contest, the one sponsored by the Boston Literary Society?"

"Who could forget? You forced us all to write a thousand words! My wrist still hurts." Larry said, shaking his hand. Every class had a boy like Larry. Good-natured and smart, but unable to rein in his wise-guy personality.

Genie smiled again, her eyes sparkling. "Sorry about your wrist, Larry. But it wasn't all in vain, you know. You came in third."

"What?" Larry looked confused. A few students laughed; most of them clapped, though.

Genie held her hands out in front of her and motioned downward. "Wait," she said, laughing. "I have more to tell you."

The kids leaned forward.

"In the history of the contest, no school has ever had two students place in the top three. Well, Waltham High has two: Mr. Larry Weldon, and in first place..." She paused, drawing out the anticipation and eliciting groans from the kids.

Genie walked down the row and stood in front of the desk of the shyest student she'd ever met. "Ellie," she said, handing the slight girl the letter, "you won first prize."

The classroom exploded in applause, and poor Ellie McKenzie turned scarlet.

Genie walked back to the front of the class and said, "Okay, quiet down. You can give Ellie and Larry your congratulations later. I know we're all very proud of them. The winners will receive scholarship money. They're also invited with their parents to the awards lunch at the Parker House Hotel right after Christmas."

"Are you going, too?" one of the other boys in the back shouted. Larry had been rendered speechless.

"I wouldn't miss it," Genie said. She sat down and opened her lesson plan book. "Okay, enough excitement for one day." She looked up with a sly smile and said, "Who'd like to scan a poem for me? Maybe some Yeats..."

A few boys grumbled.

Genie ignored them. "'When you are old and grey and full of sleep'...C'mon, kids. I know this is your favorite!"

When class was over, Ellie tried to make a quick break for it, but a group of girls caught up with her. The excited little bubble tripped out of the room, followed by the rest of the class. Larry lingered in the doorway with a frown on his face.

Genie looked up and said, "Well, Larry, aren't you happy?"

Larry dug his toe into the floor. "I guess," he said. He looked at her with a scowl. "But I thought only one story could be submitted. Isn't that the rule? Why did you send my story in with Ellie's?"

Genie put her elbow on her desk and her chin on her palm. "The rules say that a teacher may send in any story she thinks is well-written. There's no stipulation as to how many. And your story was well-written, Larry. Obviously." She got up and sat on the corner of her desk. "Aren't you happy about this? Won't your father be pleased?"

Larry's face lit up. "My Dad'll shit a bri—I mean, yeah, he'll be happy. He might not believe it, but he'll be happy."

Mr. Weldon had recently lost his wife, leaving him with Larry and six other children to raise on his own. Larry's story, while not addressing his mother's death directly, had clearly been influenced by it. Genie had pondered whether or not to submit the story given that, but she knew it was good. Now that his work had been chosen by the Literary Society, maybe Larry would take himself and his schoolwork more seriously.

"And he'll attend the lunch with you?"

Larry smiled. "He will. Grams will babysit."

"Good," Genie said. "Your whole family will be very proud, I'm sure."

"Thanks, Miss Halloran," Larry said. He smiled shyly; the wise guy had disappeared. "Have a great Thanksgiving."

"You too, Larry," Genie said. She watched her student stride down the hall, calling out thanks to his friends.

CHAPTER TWENTY-TWO

It was the Saturday after Christmas, and New Year's Eve would be Wednesday night. That meant another few days of vacation, but Genie was up early. The Boston Literary Society lunch was scheduled for noon, and she was going over her notes for the short speech she'd been asked to give. By nine she'd showered and dressed and put the coffee on. She'd have a quick bite before she left; she'd be too keyed up to eat lunch. When she went out the front door to get the paper she was pleased to see a bright blue sky. Snow had been forecast, but they'd only had a light dusting overnight. Genie wouldn't have to shovel herself out.

Sitting down with a cup of coffee and toast, Genie opened the Boston Globe. There, on the front page, under the fold, was the headline: "Two Waltham Students to be Honored for Winning Stories." As she pulled the paper closer the phone rang. Genie went into the kitchen and could hear talking before she even put the receiver to her ear.

"... see the Globe? The literary guy is calling you a mentor and an inspiration!"

Genie laughed. "I just got the paper, Mom. I haven't had a chance to read the article yet."

"Oh, Genie. Your father is so proud. He's already called everyone we know. I'm proud of you, too, honey." Shona was sniffling a little.

Genie blinked hard. Whenever her mother cried, she cried, too. But she didn't have time to reapply her makeup. "Mom, be proud of my students, not me."

Shona sniffed again. "Well, they wouldn't be where they are now without you, Genie. And I'll be proud of you if I want to be."

"Okay, Mom." Genie picked up her coffee cup and dishes and put them into the sink. "I gotta go now. They want me to be there early. I'll call you tomorrow and tell you all about it."

Half an hour later Genie was on Storrow Drive on her way to the hotel. The Saturday traffic was light, so Genie had a chance to look over at the river. There were a few sculls zipping down the Charles, and bundled-up runners jogged along the Esplanade. Genie felt a pang of regret. She'd much rather be outside today, but she had no choice. She had to be there for her students and her school.

Leaving her car with the valet, Genie walked through the lobby of the venerable Parker House hotel. The rich wood paneling and thick carpet barely registered; she was preoccupied with her speech. She quickly found a sign directing guests to the ballroom on the mezzanine. How many people were coming to this lunch, anyway? she wondered. Having been a teacher for so long, Genie wasn't shy about speaking to a group. But maybe she'd underestimated the size of this gathering. She tried to ignore the nervous flutter in her stomach and kept walking.

Outside the ballroom stood a short woman with oversized glasses. She held a clipboard and appeared to be looking for someone, standing on her tiptoes and craning her neck. Thinking she might be able to direct her to Marian Livingstone, her contact at the Literary Society, Genie approached. As she got closer, she saw the nametag pinned to the woman's jacket.

"Ms. Livingstone?" Genie said.

The woman blinked at her. "Oh, please tell me you're Aideen Halloran."

"Everyone calls me Genie." Genie extended her hand. "You're Marian, right?"

"Yes! And I'm so glad you got here when you did. My boss—he's the chairman of the board of the society—decided he had to have a chat with you before we get started with the lunch. He has tickets to the Celtics game later and, well, you don't want to hear this...Would you mind spending a few minutes with him? He's right over there."

Genie looked into the ballroom and saw a tall, grey-haired man speaking to a couple of women. All three wore dark blue blazers.

"Come," Marian said. "I'll take you over to Bill...I mean Mr. Frizzell. He's a real Boston Brahmin, you know. Very proper. But nice."

Genie followed Marian into the ballroom, which had been set up with large tables. Salads, baskets of bread, and water glasses had already been set out, reminding Genie of every wedding she'd ever attended. Soon she was introduced to Mr. Frizzell, and spent the next few minutes answering his questions about her pedagogical philosophy and her opinion of "The Satanic Verses." To her relief, people started to trickle into the ballroom, taking seats at their assigned tables.

Marian came rushing over and said, "Bill, I'm afraid I'm going to have to steal Genie away now. We have to get her lav mic attached and tested."

"Miss Halloran," Frizzell said, bowing slightly, "It's been my supreme pleasure to talk to you. I must say, I was more than a little surprised when I saw the quality of work of your students...after all, one would have expected to read such stories from Milton Academy or Groton School students. But to have two of such high quality from a public school in Waltham? Well, it speaks to your dedication and, if I may say, your surprisingly sophisticated approach."

Genie dug her nails into the palm of her hand to keep herself from laughing at his pomposity. Though she'd never say it, her brother Sean's famous phrase, "Thanks a pantload!" popped into her mind. Instead she said, "Er, well, it was nice to meet you, too." She turned to the other woman and said, "I'm all yours, Marian."

Soon Genie was seated on the dais, her mic attached to the lapel of her black velvet jacket. She took a sip of water and watched as the crowd grew larger. At one point she saw her student Larry enter the room. Her heart dropped to see that he was alone, but then he motioned toward the door. Two little girls wearing matching white and red dresses came toward him, followed by an older woman carrying a toddler. Behind her were three boys ranging in age from eight to thirteen being shepherded by a middle-aged man in a suit. Larry's whole family was with him. Genie resolved not to look in his direction while she spoke. She wouldn't be able to talk with a lump in her throat. Soon the room was full and lunch began. When Genie rose to speak she winked at Ellie, who sat at a table near the front.

By two o'clock the ceremony and lunch were over and Genie spent a few minutes chatting with Larry's father and Mr. and Mrs. McKenzie, Ellie's parents. Bill Frizzell was in deep conversation with the parents of the boy who'd taken second place, a student from Phillips Academy. They seemed aggrieved, but perhaps Genie was just imagining that. She left the ballroom with a smile on her face, proud of Ellie and Larry and pleased with herself, too. The rest of the day was hers, and she looked forward to spending it in her sweatpants, under her favorite afghan, with a P.D. James novel.

CHAPTER TWENTY-THREE

As she stood by the hotel door Genie rooted around in her purse for the valet ticket. She felt a slight touch on her elbow and swung around, sucking in her breath when she saw who stood there.

"Genie...is that really you?" It was Victor. He spoke in a gentle tone, smiling slightly. He'd changed a lot since Genie had last seen him. He'd filled out, and his hair was longer and darker blond. He wore a suede jacket, white shirt, and jeans, and held an expensive-looking leather satchel. A small Leica camera hung from a strap around his neck.

"I, ah, yes," Genie said. Her face felt hot and she wished she hadn't put her coat on in the ballroom. "What are you doing here?" It had been more than twelve years since that awful day. She took a step back, adrenaline racing as she remembered what had happened between them.

"I saw you by the door and just wanted to say hello." Victor's smile faded. "But maybe I should have just left you alone. I don't blame you for not wanting to talk to me, even after all this time. What I did to you—well, there's no forgiving some things. I was pretty screwed up then; you were right not to have anything to do with me afterward. I just never got a chance to tell you how sorry I was for hurting you like that. It's too late, I guess." He hung his head and turned to go.

Genie bit her lip. She'd often wondered what had happened to Victor and how his life had turned out. Clearly, he'd grown up.

"Wait," Genie said. She cleared her throat. "It took guts to come over and talk to me, Victor. I respect that."

Victor's face lit up. "You're the one with the guts, Genie. I mean, given what happened that day. Some girls would be calling the cops right now."

Genie laughed. "I doubt that, Victor. You look pretty respectable."

"Yeah. I stopped wearing painter's pants a long time ago." Victor smoothed down his jacket sleeve. "Now I dress for success, or at least, better than I used to. You look great, Genie. I love your hair like that."

Genie reflexively touched her head. She wore her hair chin-length now and let the natural curl do its thing. "Thanks," Genie said. She looked into Victor's eyes, remembering how she used to feel about him. A second later she looked away. "So...anyway...why are you here?"

Victor touched the camera and said, "I was meeting with a client. He's got some properties on the waterfront and needs photos. I guess he plans to build out there."

"You're a professional photographer? That's great." So he had done something positive with this life.

"But what about you?" Victor said. "I remember you said you wanted to teach."

Genie smiled. "And that's just what I do. In fact, I just attended a lunch honoring high schoolers who won awards for their short stories. Two of my students were winners."

"Doesn't surprise me at all. I'm sure you're a wonderful teacher." Victor looked around and said, "Do you think we can go have a quick drink to catch up? I'd love to hear more about what you've been doing."

Genie wouldn't meet his eyes. "I don't know if that's such a good idea, Victor."

"No?" Victor's tone was light. "Oh, hey, you're not married are you? I'm not trying to put any moves on you, Genie. It's just that it's been a long time, and…I guess I'd understand why you wouldn't be jazzed to talk to me."

Genie hesitated. "No, I'm not married," she said. She thought a moment longer. After all, they were in a big, public place and it was the middle of the afternoon. She had nothing to lose by talking to him, and she'd keep it short.

"Okay," she said, "but I have to leave by four. I'm meeting a friend later." A friend could be a man…just because she wasn't married didn't mean she wasn't dating. Well, she wasn't right now, but Victor didn't have to know that.

"Great," Victor said. "The bar is right through here. Or we can go to the restaurant if you're hungry."

Genie was hungry. She hadn't eaten since she'd had those two bites of toast. But sitting down to a meal wasn't a good idea.

"I'll just have a Coke," she said. "The bar is fine." She followed Victor through the lobby and into a snug, well-preserved bar and sat on a leather wingback chair.

Victor sat opposite her and signaled for the waiter. When their drinks arrived, a beer for Victor and a Coke for Genie, Victor sat back in his chair and pulled the camera off his neck. He set it down on the table just as the waiter brought a small snack bowl.

"Hey, Genie," Victor said. "Those look like Cheez-Its. Do you still like them?"

It was all Genie could do not to scoop a big handful out of the bowl. Instead she took a couple and popped them into her mouth, nodding. "Anything crunchy is okay with me," she said. "I just have to watch out. I could eat a box of those bad boys some days."

Victor tilted his head, eyeing her. "You don't look like you have a problem. You look great, in fact." He leaned forward, his hands on his knees. "Tell me more about those kids you teach."

He'd asked the right question. Genie had no problem talking about her students. She loved teaching and was proud of what she'd accomplished in the six years since graduate school. As she warmed to her subject, she talked freely, happy to discuss the kids she'd known. Victor smiled and nodded, taking an occasional sip of his beer. After a while she realized she'd done all the talking.

"But what about you, Victor? I never saw you again after that day. Someone told me your father sold his business. Where did you go?" It seemed unreal to be sitting with him after so long. Maybe this was the right thing to do, though.

Victor gave a little laugh. "Are you sure you want to hear this? And anyway, you probably want to get going soon."

Genie looked at her watch and was surprised to see it was three thirty. "I still have a little time." She settled back in her chair.

Victor took a final sip of his beer, then set the glass down slowly. He sat back and took a breath. "I told my father what I had done to you. His reaction surprised me. I thought he'd go nuts and beat me to a pulp."

Genie flinched.

Victor shook his head. "He didn't, though. Instead he said we had to go away. I think he was afraid you'd call the police. You have to remember where he grew up and how scary the police were there. Anyway, the next day he called someone who'd said he was interested in the shop and my father told him he could have it at half of what it was worth if he paid cash. A guy showed up that night with an envelope, and the next day we were on the road, headed west. Turns out my father's brother had settled in Montana. I didn't even know I had an uncle. In a few days we arrived at this big cattle ranch where my uncle Tomas was the manager. Of course, everyone called him Tom."

Victor smiled. "Tom was the exact opposite of my father, easy-going and friendly. He put me to work right away fixing fences and baling hay. My father took over for a mechanic who had just left. It was great. I loved the place and didn't even mind when I had to ride out after cows that wandered away."

"So you were a cowboy?" Genie said with a laugh.

"Yes, ma'am," Victor said, tipping an imaginary Stetson. "But not for long. The guy who owned the ranch—his name was Will Colley—asked my uncle about me. He was worried about my education and thought I should be in school, or at least doing more with my life. One day he asked me up to his house and showed me into his study. There were beautiful black and white photos all over the room—pictures of the ranch, the sky, even the ranch hands—just stunning and simple compositions. When I asked about them he said he'd taken them himself and offered me a used Nikon, if I was interested. Not too long after that he came out to where I was trying to photograph a hay baler. It was right around sunset and I was having a problem with the light.

We talked, then pretty soon I was following him around while he did his photography—I even went on a trip into Yellowstone with him once. He taught me a lot."

"So how did you become a professional photographer?"

"I guess I can thank Will for that," Victor said, leaning back and stretching his long legs. "He called a friend of his at the Missoulian—that's the newspaper in Missoula, Montana. Then he mailed him some of my photos, and the next thing I knew I had a job offer. I was nineteen and living on my own in a little apartment. I learned a lot in the next year or so, and some of the guys on the paper helped me out, too. By the time I was twenty I knew this was what I wanted to do with my life. I couldn't stay in Montana forever, so I split and traveled. A lot."

"Where'd you go?" Genie shook her glass and drank some Coke-flavored water.

"Where didn't I go?" Victor said. "All over Asia, South America, Australia and Tahiti, Europe—pretty much anywhere you can think of. I was able to freelance for American magazines and newspapers. I also got some gigs from French and German publishers."

"And are you still living abroad? Why are you in Boston?" Genie could never have imagined Victor living such a glamorous life. But why not? She knew nothing about this man sitting across from her. She'd only known him as a confused boy.

Victor steepled his fingers and said, "I live here, Genie. I moved back about two years ago. My studio is downtown...Jenton Way. I live right above it."

So Victor lived only a few miles away from her. The news rattled her a bit.

"Oh, wow," she said. "Why did you come back? I mean, you could live anywhere, right?" She could feel heat creeping up her neck and hoped she wasn't blushing too badly.

"I could, and I did," Victor said. "But this is where I grew up, and I guess I'm trying to put down roots. After all, I'm thirty now." He looked briefly into Genie's eyes. "All that traveling was fine, and I still take the occasional assignment in Europe, but I want to establish a life here. Hey, I even teach photography to kids at the Y."

Just then the waiter came back. "Would you like another drink, sir?" he asked.

Victor looked at his watch. "Holy cow," he said, straightening up. "Genie, didn't you say you needed to leave by four? It's four-fifteen." He turned to the waiter and said, "No, thank you. Just the bill, please."

For just a second, Genie thought she might say she could stay. Realizing how awkward that would sound she gathered her coat and bag and stood up. "Wow, Victor, this was, well, a big surprise. A nice surprise, though."

Victor pulled a twenty out of his wallet and slid it under his glass, then stood and helped Genie on with her coat. He took a step back and said, "You know, I dreamed about this moment." He chuckled. "No, I don't mean that literally. I just mean that...you know...there have been so many times I've thought about you and wished I could tell you how sorry I was, how sorry I am, for what I did that day. There's no excuse; I was just so afraid of losing you. I guess that's why I traveled all the time. If I stayed away from Boston I thought maybe I could stop thinking about my life here. But no matter where I went, I never stopped regretting what I did. I'm glad your life has turned out so well."

"I'm happy for you, too," Genie smiled up at Victor, truly pleased to have heard about his success.

When they got to the lobby, Genie reached into her bag, this time locating the valet ticket right away.

"Well," she said, "I should really go. Do you have a car? Can I drop you somewhere?"

Victor shook his head. "I walked over here. It's not far." He took a deep breath, then reached into his pocket. "Genie, here's my card. I know you probably aren't interested, but I'd love it if you came to see my studio sometime." He held the card out, waiting for Genie to take it. "You don't have to...It's just that I'd love you to see what I've been able to accomplish. There's really no one left here who'd care."

Genie took the card and put it in her pocket. "What about your father? Has he seen it?"

Victor frowned. "No, he died a long time ago. My uncle, too."

"I'm sorry," Genie said. He must be lonely with no family; she couldn't imagine life without hers. She took the card out of her pocket. "Jenton Way. Where's that?"

"It's a short walk from the Aquarium T stop, or a little longer if you get off at Haymarket. Why? Do you think you might actually come?"

Victor had no one from his past to share his success, and he seemed contrite about his behavior. Genie could afford to be generous; after all, she had family and friends and Victor had none.

"Sure," Genie said. "I've never actually seen a professional photography studio."

It was as if the sun had burst through the clouds. Victor smiled broadly and said, "Can you come Monday? I'll be finishing up around four, then I can give you the grand tour—or, maybe you have school..."

Genie shook her head. "I don't go back until Friday, if you can believe it. They're opening school for one day, then closing for the weekend."

"So, Monday, then?" Victor took the valet ticket and said, "I'll take care of this for you."

Genie slid the ticket out of his hand. "No, thanks. I'll do it." She wrapped her scarf around her neck and said, "See you Monday." A few minutes later she saw that Victor was still watching from the lobby as she drove away.

CHAPTER TWENTY-FOUR

By Monday afternoon Genie was on the verge of calling Victor to say she couldn't come. She'd called Meara, who was living in Greece, thinking she might have good advice. But she couldn't bring herself to say anything about Victor. Meara would have told her she was crazy to even consider seeing him again. Maybe she was. She went into the kitchen and picked up the receiver, then dialed Victor's number. By the second ring she hung up. After all, there'd probably be other people at the studio. All she had to do was look around, tell Victor he'd done well for himself, then leave. She'd be home in time to make herself some spaghetti and salad.

The weather was unseasonably warm for late December, about forty-five degrees, so she decided to walk to Harvard Square to get the T. A good half hour in the brisk air would push all her misgivings aside. The sidewalks would be slushy and wet, so she stuffed her jeans into her Bean boots. She put on her parka but kept it open, checking the pocket for subway tokens. Her black turtleneck would keep her neck warm, so she didn't bother with a scarf. She grabbed her small red shoulder bag and went out the door. As soon as the fresh air hit her she felt better. This would be an adventure, something she could talk about with her teacher friends later in the week. They'd never heard of Victor before, so they wouldn't scold her like Meara or Debra would.

The T station was not too crowded, and as Genie waited for the red line train that would take her to Haymarket she indulged in a little game she'd played when she was younger. She looked down at the ancient, filthy tracks and watched for movement. The mice that lived in the subway stations were the same dark grey as the tracks, so spotting one required patience. Before she saw any movement, though, she felt the telltale rush of air that preceded a train. A moment later, she entered the car, sat down and closed her eyes, listening to the rattle and roar of the train as she headed to the Haymarket stop.

Back on the street, she pulled her collar up against the freshening breeze and walked down Congress Street. The wind blew straight off the water, damp and biting at the same time. She cursed herself for not wearing a hat, but it would have pushed her hair down and flattened the curls. She shook her head. It was stupid to worry how she looked, and even more stupid, probably, to be heading to Victor's studio.

There were a few Christmas lights still shining on the trees near Post Office Square; they'd be gone right after New Year's Eve. She hurried along, her head down. At Franklin she took a left, then, there it was, Jenton Way. The narrow brick street was lined by tall buildings with huge windows, most of which were dark. She came upon a small doorway in the deep shadows of the building opposite. With no light overhead it was hard to read the lettering over the buzzer, but she could just make it out: Pulnik. She paused. She could leave now and pretend she'd never come. What was Victor going to do? He'd never pursue her, she was sure about that. The next step was hers.

She pushed the button and there was an immediate harsh buzz. She opened the door onto a gloomy hallway illuminated by a few flimsy light fixtures. Straight ahead stood a freight elevator. She pressed the call button, and when the car dropped into place, she pulled up on the strap to open the top door, then pushed down on the bottom door. She pressed the up button inside the car, which jerked a bit, then ascended.

Moving up the elevator shaft she could hear loud, regular thumps. As she got closer she realized it was music. "House Nation" blared as the elevator settled into place on the third floor.

A short balding man with three cameras slung around his neck pulled the door open and smiled. "Hey Vic!" he shouted. "Your little friend's here."

He waved her forward, a strange smile on his face. He leaned toward her and yelled in her ear. "Vic's just finishing up. Want a drink?"

She shook her head and walked out. The music was loud, its clanging rhythm cutting through her. Victor knelt on the maple wood floor, his back toward her. There were bright lights to either side, and in front of him were two tall women, their arms entwined, holding each other tight. One wore a shiny vinyl halter dress and high boots, the other was nearly naked, wearing only a lacy red thong and high heels. The shutter clicked fast, and Vic swiveled his torso up and down, while the two women stood motionless, their faces blank.

Suddenly the music stopped.

"Hey, Vic. I said your friend's here. It's time we wrapped this up. Those two will want overtime in another ten minutes." The man with the cameras walked across the room and handed the nearly naked one a little blue robe.

Victor got up, the camera dangling from his hand. "We're done, girls. Time for you to leave," he said, sounding more bored than rude.

The woman took the robe and, without much hurry, put it on, not bothering to belt it. Her breasts were large and creamy white, tipped with rosy nipples. Genie reflexively stood straighter. The other model walked toward her, the heels on her shiny boots tapping on the floor.

"So you and Vic went to high school together," she said. She was smiling down at Genie, her glossy red lips pulled back to show perfect white teeth. "I can't imagine him as a schoolboy. I'd have guessed he hatched from a shell—like a lizard or something." Up close, Genie could see that, despite the smoky makeup and false lashes, the woman's eyes were rather small. Given the way the vinyl fabric of her top strained against her breasts, though, it was likely that her eyes were not what got her hired.

The other model, finally closing her robe, hurried past them toward a rack at the back of the room. "Vic, do you ever turn on the heat in this place?" She dropped the robe and pulled a sweater on, then stepped into a tight pair of jeans. She struggled with her red moonboots, then grabbed a hooded down coat. "I'm outta here. Are you coming Alessandra? We're supposed to meet those guys at seven."

Alessandra stayed by Genie a minute more, staring at her. "I hope you know what you're getting into, honey," she said in soft voice. Then she stalked away, grabbing a leather coat from the rack. She wound a bright blue scarf around her neck and said, "See you, Tony. Later, Vic. Thanks for introducing us to your friend."

It was quiet once the two women had left. Tony spent a few minutes putting the cameras in their cases. Victor handed him his Hasselblad and turned off the light kits. He walked over to Genie, his eyes bright. "You came," he said, smiling.

"I said I would," Genie said. Victor wore a dark green V-neck sweater, black boots, and acid-washed jeans. Genie had noticed the other day that he dressed more fashionably than he used to in high school. But there was something else. The melancholy, solitary boy she'd known was gone. This Victor, this "Vic," seemed too sophisticated to be impressed by the beautiful women who modeled for him. His studio, a huge open space, was filled with expensive photographic equipment. The speakers that had rattled her bones were nearly four feet tall and had to have cost thousands. Victor had come a long way from the dark, crowded apartment on Bacon Street.

He ran his hand through his hair and looked away. "Uh, I got my dates mixed up, by the way. I thought I'd be doing a different kind of shoot today. Something not so, I dunno...sexy."

Genie wouldn't admit to being embarrassed. "Do you do this kind of work a lot? I've seen some photos like this in Vogue,"

Victor laughed. "Believe me, I've never worked for Vogue, though I don't mind being a second-rate Helmut Newton every once in a while. The money's good. A lot of this stuff ends up in Italy and even Eastern Europe, if you can believe that."

"I guess..." Genie had no idea what Victor was talking about. She looked around, aware he was watching her.

"Would you like a little tour?" Victor put his hand on the small of her back and said, "I can show you some photos you might like...something a little more wholesome than this shoot." He walked her over to a few wide steel cabinets and pulled out a drawer that held a large flat binder. "I do a lot of work for manufacturers. You know, machine parts and that kind of thing. He opened the binder and flipped through a few pages of gleaming metal parts—stainless steel engine components and brass cam wheels—all resting on a black background.

"What's this here?" Genie said, pointing to some tiny letters on the lower right of each photo. She squinted, then looked up. "V P...your initials!"

Victor went to another cabinet and retrieved another binder. "I do more than machine parts and half-naked women," he said with a smile. "I took these photos in Paris," he said, slowly turning the pages.

Genie recognized some of the buildings in the photos—the Eiffel tower and the Arc de Triomphe—but there were many street scenes and gardens she could not place.

Victor kept turning the pages. "You've been to Paris?" he murmured.

Genie shook her head. "Never. But I'd love to someday."

Victor closed the binder and gave Genie a thoughtful look. "Paris would suit you, I think. It would appeal to your delicate soul."

"My what? What do you mean?"

Victor shrugged. "I don't know...it's hard to explain. It's just that, since I first met you I always felt that you had an unusual sensibility; not fragile, but delicate. Paris is like that, too." He held her gaze, then pushed the drawer closed. Breaking into a wide smile he said, "I'm getting hungry. How about you?"

Genie glanced at her watch. It was close to seven. Had she really been there so long?

Victor tapped her arm. "Come on, Genie. Let me buy you dinner. It's the least I can do for dragging you down here. You like Italian food, right? We can go to Ristorante Antonina in the North End. It shouldn't be too crowded on a weeknight."

She was hungry, and she did love Italian food. Would going to dinner with Victor qualify as a date, though?

"Don't say no. You'll love their Chicken Marsala. Or, how about some shrimp scampi, heavy on the garlic?" Victor raised an eyebrow.

She'd planned on making spaghetti with sauce from a jar for herself. Chicken Marsala sounded a lot better. "Sure," she said. "But let's go Dutch, okay?"

Victor walked to retrieve Genie's parka and grabbed a black lambswool jacket for himself. "Absolutely not, Genie. You're in my town, so I pay. You can invite me to Cambridge sometime and pay for me." He helped Genie into her coat and turned off most of the studio lights, then followed Genie out the door.

It was dark outside, and Genie was surprised to see a light snow falling. She wished now that she'd brought a hat.

"I'm parked back here," Victor said, leading Genie around the corner to a small alley. He approached the passenger door of a dark, low-slung sports car. "Miss Aideen," he said, opening the door with a flourish.

A chill gripped Genie, and it had nothing to do with the weather. No one ever called her Aideen, no one but Victor, the boy who'd tried to smash her head with a wrench. She didn't move.

"What's wrong, Genie?" Victor said. His smile faded.

"You called me Aideen," she whispered. "It just sounded strange."

"I'm sorry, Genie. I didn't know it bothered you. I won't do it again." He pulled the door open wider. "Please get in. I promise you'll like your dinner." He held up his right hand and gave her the three-finger Scout salute.

Genie giggled. "You were never a Boy Scout," she said.

"I'll enlist tomorrow if you'll have dinner with me tonight," Victor said. "Come on, Genie. Please?"

"Okay." Genie got into the car. She'd eat dinner, then go directly to the T afterward. She had to be smart, had to watch out for herself.

In no time they were in front of the restaurant. A valet opened the door for her and Victor tossed him the keys. Once inside, Genie realized how hungry she was. The smell of grilled meat and tomato sauce made her mouth water. Fortunately, with the restaurant more than half-full, the noise of the happy diners covered the sound of her stomach growling. They were shown to a small table near the window.

When the waiter handed them their menus, Victor said, "Do you carry Super Tuscans?"

The waiter shrugged. "We have a Brunello di Montalcino. Is that okay?"

"Fine," Victor said. "Bring it to the table and open it, please."

The waiter shrugged again and went away.

"What was that about?" Genie said. She'd never heard of a Super Tuscan before, and couldn't imagine what it was.

Victor looked up from the menu. "Oh, I didn't even ask if you liked wine. If you don't we can get something else," he said.

Genie liked wine, but her taste, which ran toward Ernest & Julio, was clearly not as sophisticated as Victor's. She nodded, and said, "I like it. I just never heard of...what did you call it? Super what?"

"Super Tuscan. It's red wine from Italy." He put the menu on the table and said, "Here he comes. Give it a try and see if you like it."

The waiter arrived with the wine, two glasses, and a corkscrew. He opened the bottle and set the cork in front of Victor, then poured out a small amount of wine. Victor took a deep sniff then tipped the glass and drank. He nodded curtly and said, "Fine."

"D'ya wanna order now?" The waiter said. He was very young and quite handsome, with dark eyes and black, curly hair.

Genie smiled at him. She'd grown up with so many cute Italian guys, and of course, she'd dated Matt Lorusso for years. The waiter had come from the same mold. "May I have the Pappardelle Bolognese, please?" she said, handing him her menu. That was almost spaghetti and sauce, but so much better than the meal she'd planned for herself.

Victor frowned at the menu, then said, "We'll start with the antipasti. And I'll have the Saltimbocca." The waiter left, and Victor poured Genie a generous glass of wine, then one for himself. Holding his glass out, he said, "Cheers, Genie."

"Cheers." Genie took a sip. It was a revelation: smooth and rich, not at all like the more astringent wines she was used to. "This is great!" she said as she took another sip. "How do you know so much about wines?"

Victor ducked his head and chuckled. "I think I picked it up by osmosis. Some of my clients are high-rollers, and when they like my work they'll occasionally ask me out to a fancy restaurant. That's one of the perks of the job, I guess." He leaned forward and smiled. "I'm glad you like it. I hope you'll like your meal, too."

"I'm sure I will." Genie sat back in her chair and looked around at the small restaurant with its brick walls and old wooden floor. Outside, the snow fell, the wind swirling icy circles. Inside, though, it was warm and cozy. She was glad she hadn't given in to her earlier doubts. There was nothing wrong with having a nice dinner with Victor. That's all it was: just dinner.

When the food came they ate and talked about the state of the world, politics, music, and movies. Genie was impressed when Victor told her he'd attended and taken photos at the Winter Olympics in Calgary earlier in the year. They avoided discussing the past. Though nothing could change how Victor had acted when they were younger, it was clear he'd changed. He was more relaxed now. He'd found his place in the world and wore his success well. As dinner was winding down Genie had refused coffee and dessert, but Victor ordered an espresso, which he polished off in two quick sips.

"I'd never get to sleep if I did that," Genie said. "One cup of coffee in the morning: that's my limit."

Victor rolled his eyes. "Sleep is overrated."

Genie stood and pulled her parka off the back of the chair. "You're self-employed, Victor. I'll bet if you had to be up for your job at six a.m. you wouldn't drink coffee at night, either."

Victor put money down on the table and slipped into his coat. "You're probably right. Plus, you're a teacher. You have to be somewhat alert to do your job." He adjusted his scarf and said, "But you don't have to go to work for a few more days. Plenty of time to sleep in if you want to."

When they got outside the snow was falling heavily. Genie didn't look forward to trying to find a cab to take her home from the Harvard Square T station. But she'd walked that distance in the snow before. She could do it again if she had to.

The valet pulled up with Victor's car, and Victor handed him a tip.

"Well," she said, extending a gloved hand to Victor, "Thanks for dinner. It was delicious."

He took her hand and said, "Where are you going? I'll drive you home, Genie."

Genie pulled her hand away. "No, it's fine. The Haymarket T is just over there."

Victor took her arm and gently ushered her over to his car. Opening the passenger door, he said, "You're not even wearing a hat. You'll probably have to walk home from Harvard Square and you'll freeze to death."

Again, she hesitated. The snow was falling fast now, heavy and wet. Her hair was already dripping, and she'd only been standing outside for a couple of minutes.

Victor ran his hand lightly over her head, wiping away the snow. "You'll catch pneumonia, Genie. A horrible substitute teacher will take over your classes and your students will all become juvenile delinquents. They'll drop out of school, get hooked on crack, and die young. All because you wouldn't let me drive you home. Do you really want that on your conscience?"

Genie rolled her eyes. "All right, I'll take a ride."

"Thank God," Victor said, putting his hand over his heart. "Those kids won't die an early death after all." He got into the car and maneuvered through the narrow, car-clogged streets of the North End. The windshield was fogged up, and Victor swore under his breath as he adjusted the blower. The snow was coming down hard; Genie would have been soaked inside of five minutes if she'd attempted to walk home from Harvard Square. The drive took barely any time at all, and soon they were sitting in front of Genie's house.

"Well," Genie said, "Thanks again, Victor. This was nice." She put her hand on the door handle.

"It was." Victor looked out the windshield and tapped the steering wheel with his fingertips. "Um...I know it's short notice, and I'm sure you have other plans, but..." He looked at her and shook his head. "No, it's crazy. You wouldn't be interested."

"Interested in what?"

"There's a party at this guy's house in Brookline. He's kind of a business associate of mine. It's on New Year's Eve. I wasn't going to go, but I thought if you were interested, then maybe..."

Victor's eyes found hers, and then she felt it. Her heart tripped a hard double beat. She should say no. She should get out of the car and walk away.

"Well, I'm having dinner with my parents that night. They don't go out much anymore and my brothers will be with their own families."

"Will dinner be late? I mean, if you're free by nine or so, that would be great. And the party isn't anything formal. You can just wear a dress, but nothing too fancy. And it might be fun. I should say, it will be fun for me if you come."

Later she'd blame the wine, but she knew that wasn't true. She wanted to see him again. "Okay," she whispered. She cleared her throat and said, her voice louder now, "I mean, yes, if you want to pick me up at nine, I'll be ready." She pulled the door handle and jumped out. Leaning into the car, she said, "Thanks again for dinner."

Victor smiled. "It was my pleasure. See you Wednesday at nine."

Genie watched him drive away and stood out under the street lamp a while. She could hear the snow dropping onto the tops of the cars parked nearby. It was a mistake to have agreed to see him again, but she was going to do it anyway.

CHAPTER TWENTY-FIVE

It was nearly nine, and Genie had tried on three different necklaces. She wore a simple black velvet sheath dress and low heels and hoped that she wouldn't be underdressed. The sparkly long gold chains were pretty, but they might be too much. Genie caught a glimpse of herself in the mirror and made a face. "You're being an idiot, Genie," she muttered. She settled on the strand of cultured pearls she'd received from her parents when she'd graduated from USC.

The doorbell rang just as she'd fastened the clasp. Genie peeked out the front window to see Victor standing on the porch, his breath visible in little puffs. The weather had turned viciously cold, and Genie wished she could wear a sweater over her sleeveless dress. She went out into the small entryway and opened the front door, smiling at Victor and saying, "Brr. Come in. It's freezing out here."

She led Victor inside. "Can I get you anything before we go?" She took his coat and laid it over the back of a chair, catching a whiff of the fresh, cold air and something else...a scent of leathery cologne.

"I don't need anything," Victor said. His gaze slid from the top of her head to her feet. "Wow, don't you look delicious?"

Genie's hand went to her necklace. "I wasn't sure what to wear. You said a dress..."

"You look perfect." Victor was wearing jeans again, this time with a white shirt and dark tie. His jacket was black or very dark blue. He crossed his arms and said, "I hate to say it, but we should probably get going. I told my friend Mark that we were coming and he made me promise we'd get there before ten. He's hired some musicians and I think he wants to have lots of guests so he can get his money's worth."

"Okay." Genie ran to her closet and pulled out her coat and a long, silk scarf Meara had sent to her for Christmas. She looped the scarf around her neck and started to put on her coat.

"Here," Victor said, standing behind her. "Let me help." He held the coat out for her to slide her arms into the sleeves, then pulled the coat around her, his face nuzzling the back of her neck. "Mmmm...you smell fantastic."

Genie tingled at his touch, then her nerves kicked in. She giggled and said, "So do you!"

Victor shrugged. "Drakkar Noir. It's kinda new."

For a moment, neither one of them spoke, then Genie looked at her watch. "It's already after nine. Didn't Mark want you to show up right around now?"

"You're right." Victor waved Genie ahead of him. "It won't take us long to get there."

• • •

Twenty minutes later they were driving through Newton and into Chestnut Hill. Genie was holding a paper with directions to the house. "It says to take a left onto Heath Street at the next intersection. Your friend's house is on the right."

Victor turned and slowed down as he came upon a house set far back from the street. There were cars parked in the circular driveway and many more on the street. "I guess this is it," he said, craning his neck to look up at the house.

Genie peered out the window and nearly gasped. The house—more like a mansion—was huge, with an imposing main hall and wings off to either side. "Did you say your friend lived here alone?"

Victor leaned over to look out Genie's window. He gave a low whistle and said, "That's what he told me. He could fit half of Newton in this pile. What a show-off." He opened the driver's door and said, "Ready to see how the other half lives?"

He got out and walked around to Genie's side. She shivered again. "I guess I knew that people lived in places like this. I never thought I'd get to see the inside."

Victor took her hand and they walked up the driveway. "Don't be too impressed. Mark got kicked out of Harvard and even his old man's money couldn't get him back in. Daddy disowned Mark after that."

"How could he afford a place like this, then?"

"Stocks...arbitrage..." Victor shrugged. "I don't really know what he did, but a few years ago he made a killing. Not sure what he does now. He might not have been Harvard material, but he was smart enough to stay out of jail."

The door opened before they rang the bell. A middle-aged woman wearing a black dress and white apron stood in the doorway. "Good evening," she said. "May I take your coats?"

Victor and Genie exchanged smiles and handed their coats to the maid. They walked through a large entryway dominated by a glittering crystal chandelier, where the mirrored walls reflected the light and made the room seem even larger. Genie caught a reflection of herself that appeared to multiply into infinity. For a moment she panicked and wished she could leave, but it was too late. Victor held out his hand and led her toward the sounds of laughter and music.

At the end of the entryway a hall split off in either direction. It was clear from the noise where the party was. As they stood in the doorway of an enormous room filled with people Genie noticed right away that most of the women wore fancy party dresses, many of them strapless, lacy confections. She smoothed the straight skirt of her black velvet sheath, hoping that she'd see other women wearing similarly conservative clothes.

"Vicky!" A young woman wearing a short red dress with a poufy skirt and plunging neckline staggered toward them.

Victor held onto Genie's hand. As the woman got closer she stumbled and Victor reached for her arm.

"Mmm, Vic," she said, nuzzling up to him. "You're such a gennelman."

"Thanks, Suki," Victor said. He mouthed, "Sorry!" to Genie. Helping Suki stand up straighter, he said, "Maybe you should sit down somewhere. You look like you had a little too much."

Suki sniggered. "You're right, Vicky. Too much vodka. Too many 'ludes, too. Too, too much everything."

Genie tried to step behind Victor when Suki said, "Who's this, Vic? Is this your new girlfriend? She looks so cute in her little black dress. So classy. What's your name, honey?"

"Leave her alone, Suki," Victor said. He took her by the arm and tried to walk her toward a loveseat along the wall.

Suki pulled her arm away and said, "No, I want to talk to your friend. I bet she's real smart. Mark told me you were bringing a teacher. Are you a teacher, honey?"

Suki leaned closer to Genie and smiled broadly. Her eyes were unfocused and she smelled of cigarettes. "C'mon, Teach. What's your name?"

Genie tried to step away, but Suki took her hand. "My name's Genie," she said.

"Genie!" Suki put her arms around Genie and kissed her cheek. Genie leaned away, and when Suki lifted her head she said, "You use Oil of Olay! I haven't smelled that since Granny kicked the bucket." Her laugh was hoarse, a smoker's laugh.

Genie's face felt hot. Knowing she was blushing just made things worse.

A tall man strode over and pulled Suki away. "Stop scaring the guests, Suki. Go sit down." He gave her a none-too-gentle shove and propelled her toward the loveseat.

The man turned to Genie and said, "Sorry about that. Suki is actually sort of fun when she's not messed up." He put his hand out and said, "I'm Mark Stanton. You must be Genie."

Genie took his hand. Mark wore an open-collar pink shirt and jeans. He was probably about thirty-five, but his hair, which he'd slicked back, was receding, and his jaw had a softness to it. If he didn't watch it he'd become jowly before long.

Mark brought Genie's hand to his lips and kissed it.

"Jesus, Stanton," Victor said. "What's with the Rudolph Valentino act?"

Mark shook his head. "Victor, my friend. I'm just appreciating the presence of your refined friend. She really stands out in this crowd of bimbos. And, if I may say so, she's a pleasant departure from your usual ladies."

Victor shook his head. "Don't listen to him, Genie. Mark always seems like an asshole when you first meet him. Once you get to know him, though, you realize he really is an asshole."

Mark gave Victor a mock bow. "A pleasure as always, Victor. Please, you and Genie get yourselves a drink. We have everything. And, if you'd like something other than a drink, go find Moe. He's around somewhere. He can hook you up with just about anything you like."

"We'll stick to Champagne, thanks," Victor said.

Mark ambled away, his hands in his pockets. He was soon surrounded by a few other slick-looking young men, some of whom smoked cigars, tilting their heads back to blow away the smoke.

Victor took Genie's hand. "I'm sorry," he said. "That's just how Mark is. Except for a few years of having to hustle after his Dad gave him the boot, he's always lived the high life. It's probably warped him."

Genie tried to smile. "How do you know him? And, uh, Suki? From all the people waving at you, it seems like you know a lot of people here."

Victor rolled his eyes. "I can't say for sure. Some of them I know socially. I think I met Mark at a charity event, if you can believe it. They're not bad people, Genie, but I can see this really isn't your scene. Do you want me to take you home now?"

Genie shook her head. "Not right away. I don't want to seem rude. Maybe we can just get a glass of Champagne?"

"Great idea." Victor put an arm around Genie and kissed the top of her head. "We won't stay too long, though."

They made their way to a bar set up on the opposite side of the room. The bartender poured them two flutes of Champagne, and Victor suggested they sit in a slightly quieter corner nearby. Genie took the chair against the wall and Victor sat across from her. He held out his glass and said, "To a happy 1989." He smiled at her and leaned forward. "I'd be happy if I thought you'd be in my life again."

They clinked glasses. Genie took a sip of wine, aware of Victor's intense gaze. Things were happening fast, but no matter how nice Victor seemed it didn't change the way he'd behaved years ago. There was something about him now that was different, though. "I think we can both be happy," Genie said.

Victor leaned closer and Genie did the same.

"Pulnik! Why are you hiding back here?" A red-faced man in a tux clapped Victor on the shoulder. Behind him were three other men, all wearing tuxes with no ties, their collars open. One had a cigar stuck in his mouth, another held a bottle of Champagne by the neck.

Victor turned around and said, "Hi, guys. Look, I'll catch up with you later, okay?"

The one with the bottle took a large swig and said, "What's the matter, Vic? Don't want to introduce us to your classy lady friend? I seem to remember you weren't so standoffish last year. And you certainly weren't squiring this one around." He turned to the others. "You remember who Vic was dating last year? What was her name...some Russian chick, right?"

"That's enough, Brad," Victor said. He set his glass down and stood up. "Why don't you guys find somewhere else to hang out?"

The four of them laughed. The one with the cigar looked at Genie and said, "You'll have to excuse us, Miss. I'm afraid my friends and I are somewhat the worse for drink."

Two of them smirked and elbowed each other. "You're pouring it on a little thick, aren't you Trent? After all, she might look classy, but we all know the kind of girl Vic dates, or should I say, hires. I doubt she offends easy."

Genie stood up and pushed past them, then made her way as fast as she could through the crowded room. When she got to the doorway she set her glass down, then ran down the hallway. She ignored Victor's calls and looked around for the maid who'd taken her coat. She'd get out as fast as she could and try to hail a cab somewhere, even if she had to walk a few miles to do it.

She opened a door and found a room with racks of coats. She'd find hers and leave right away. Flicking through the fox fur and minks, she found her navy wool coat. Just as she was about to take it off the hanger, Victor rushed toward her.

"I just want to get out of here," Genie said as she shot her arm through a coat sleeve. "You don't have to leave, though. Stay with your charming friends, Victor. No doubt you'll want to reminisce about your ex-girlfriends, or whatever they were." She slid past him and walked toward the door.

Victor grabbed his coat and said, "Genie, I'm sorry. Those guys aren't usually so rude. They're probably high as well as drunk."

Genie turned and said, "I don't care, Victor. Why did you take me to this party? I obviously don't fit in with these people. I'm just a prim little schoolteacher in dowdy clothes. Did you bring me here to be humiliated by everyone?"

Victor took her hand, and when she tried to pull away, he held on. "Genie, you have to believe me. I never wanted to hurt you. When they sober up, they'll want to apologize, not that I'd ever let them near you again."

"This was a mistake. It was stupid to think that there could ever be anything between us again. We should have left the past in the past." Genie tugged her hand away.

Victor hurried around her and put his hands on her shoulders. Tears welled in his eyes. "Oh, Genie, please. I'm sorry. Please believe me." He ran the back of his hand across his face. "Don't give up on me. I promise you, I'd never do anything to hurt you again. Since that day I swore to myself that if I ever met you again I'd prove to you that I regretted what I did to you. There were times when I was traveling that I'd get so down on myself I really didn't think my life was worth much. I mean, what kind of guy does what I did?" His eyes were anguished. After a moment, he seemed to give up. He let go of her shoulders and sighed, saying, "I'll take you home—I'll take you anywhere you want to go."

Genie hesitated, then laughed in spite of herself. "Where else would I want to go now? It's eleven thirty on New Year's Eve. It's not like I can go grocery shopping."

Victor picked his head up and smiled. He held his hand out and said, "Home, then?"

Genie returned his smile. He wasn't responsible for his friends' behavior, after all. And he was hurting; that was clear. The past was over and it was time to move on.

They hurried down the driveway and out onto the street. Genie slipped her hand into Victor's and leaned against him. When they got to his car, Victor said, "I know it's a few minutes early, but can we pretend it's midnight?" He put his arms around her waist and pulled her close. He bent down and kissed her on the mouth, so softly.

Genie melted into his embrace. "Happy New Year," she whispered, tipping her head back. When he kissed her again, she kissed back, hungry for his touch.

"Aideen, my little fire," Victor whispered into her ear, "Aideen, I never stopped loving you. All these years I wished I could take back what I did that day."

Tears stung Genie's eyes. Victor's sorrow hurt her heart, and now they were being given a second chance. "Take me home, Victor. I want to be with you."

• • •

When they pulled up in front of Genie's house, Victor turned to her and said, "Are you sure?"

Genie leaned over and kissed him on the cheek. Then she smiled and crooked her finger, saying, "Follow me."

She raced up to her front door, with Victor right behind. Once inside, he scooped her up and said, "Uh, which way to the bedroom?"

Genie laughed and pointed. "That way!"

Victor kissed Genie's forehead, her eyes, her throat, finally her lips, then carried her down the hallway to her bedroom. Letting her down gently, he took her coat off, then his own. "Aideen," he whispered. He reached around and unfastened her necklace, placing it on the bedside table. He ran the back of his hand down the front of her velvet dress, slowly moving down her shoulder, then her breast, all the way to her waist.

Genie's heart thumped as she reached up and unbuttoned Victor's shirt. She slid her hand inside and pressed her palm to his chest and smiled. When she'd known him before his chest had been hairless, but not anymore. She stepped closer as Victor unzipped her dress, slowly...too slowly. He slipped the dress off her shoulders, and she shivered. She wasn't cold, though. She'd had lovers in college, and she'd had years of intimacy with Matt. But nothing like this. All she wanted was Victor's hands on her; she wanted him inside her. She reached over and pulled the coverlet off the bed, then took Victor's hand and slipped under the sheets, bringing him with her. "My beautiful Aideen," was what she heard, just before the world exploded.

CHAPTER TWENTY-SIX

A ray of early morning sunlight brightened Genie's bedroom. She opened her eyes and shifted slowly onto her back, not wanting to wake Victor. He slept with his arm around her waist, his mouth open slightly. Genie studied the face she'd known so well when she was a girl. But no, not this face, not really. The corners of his eyes were lined, his cheeks were scruffy with brown and grey stubble. His dark blond hair flopped over his forehead, so different the crewcut teen she remembered.

The radio came on, the local NPR station announcing that it was eight a.m. Genie reached over to switch it off, but it was too late. Victor was awake, smiling lazily.

"I'm sorry!" Genie put her hands over her eyes. "I always get up at eight on my days off. It's nice to sleep in."

Victor snorted. "Sleep in? Eight is the crack of dawn as far as I'm concerned." He pulled the covers over his shoulders and heaved onto his side.

Genie stared at the back of his head. "Uh...sorry. I'll let you sleep for a while, okay?" She started to slip out of bed when Victor flipped over and grabbed her.

"You're not getting away that easy. You woke me up, now you'll pay!" He laughed and started her nuzzling her neck, making exaggerated smacking sounds.

Genie giggled, then, as Victor's kisses became more intense, she sighed. Soon they were entangled again, and it was long after

148

nine before they finally got out of bed. Genie had offered to make breakfast, but Victor refused. He'd take her to a great place for brunch, then they'd spend the day at his studio.

Genie stood in the shower, letting the warm water sluice through her hair and down her body. She couldn't stop smiling, and even though she ached a little, she looked forward to spending more time in bed with Victor at his place. As she dressed in jeans and a white V-neck cashmere sweater she hummed along with Neil Young, playing on her stereo in the living room. She dabbed on a little blusher and lip gloss, brushed some mascara on, then ran into the bedroom to get her boots. The bed was a rumpled mess. She'd deal with it later.

She hurried into the living room and sat on chair to pull on her black lace-up boots.

Victor lay on the couch, writing in a small notebook. His shirt was still unbuttoned. Genie couldn't take her eyes off the trail of hair from his chest, down his navel and beyond. When he noticed her he sat up and snapped the notebook closed. "I didn't hear you come in."

Genie got up to turn off the stereo. "Do you take notes for your work?"

"Something like that," Victor said, buttoning his shirt. "Ready to go? I'm starving."

• • •

The next day Genie sat at her desk. She'd asked her students to read their short stories aloud and for the other students to critique them. Usually she was an active participant in this exercise, but this morning she was exhausted. Victor had dropped her off at her apartment at one a.m. and she'd barely gone to sleep before the alarm woke her at six. Thoughts of Victor, his hands on her breasts and thighs, his mouth bringing her to climax, played over and over in her mind. She sat there, the voices of her students barely registering.

"Miss Halloran! Yo, Teach!"

The students' laughter shook Genie out of her reverie.

Larry stood in front of her, holding a vase filled with at least two dozen red roses. "Miss Halloran, I've been calling you. The vice-principal just brought these flowers. She said they're for you."

Genie's face burned. "Oh, thank you, Larry. Please put them down here."

As Larry walked back to his seat he said, "Gee, Miss Halloran, you were really out of it just then. You must have had a good Christmas vacation."

The class burst into laughter again. Genie knew it was pointless to pretend her behavior hadn't been odd. "You're right, Larry. Very perceptive of you." She got up and came around to sit on the side of her desk. "I hope all of you had a good vacation as well. Now who wants to read next?"

When class was over, Genie looked for a card among the roses but couldn't find any. It didn't matter. She knew what Victor was saying to her through those beautiful flowers. She drew them to her and inhaled their fragrance, then sat with her hands folded, waiting for her next class.

• • •

Victor came to her that night and stayed the weekend, leaving late on Sunday night. That set the pattern for their relationship in the coming weeks, with weekends of eating, watching movies, and long stretches in bed. During the week, Victor might come by and take Genie out to dinner one or two nights, but he'd never stay over. They rarely went to his place, and that suited Genie. The living space above his studio was stark, with a small utilitarian bathroom, a large bed and a dorm-size refrigerator and micro- wave. When Victor stayed with her, Genie loved making him extravagant dinners and cozy breakfasts to make up for the lonely meals he had at home.

One Sunday morning in March Genie poured a second cup of coffee for the two of them. Victor looked up from the business section of the New York Times and said, "That was a great break- fast, babe. If I don't watch it, I'm gonna get fat on those pancakes of yours."

He patted his stomach and Genie reached over for his hand. "Somebody has to make sure you eat enough. And you're a long way from fat, Victor. I'd say you're nearly perfect."

Victor opened his mouth in surprise. "Nearly perfect, you say? You might change your tune when you find out what I did."

Genie put her elbows on the table and leaned forward, her chin on her folded hands. "What did you do?"

Victor shook his head, "I don't know if I want to tell you now. After all, I'm only nearly perfect."

Genie laughed. "Okay, you're perfectly perfect. Now tell me what you did!"

Victor raised his eyebrows and smiled, then he reached under his placemat and pulled out an envelope. He waved the envelope at Genie, saying, "We're going to Paris for your April vacation. We leave Friday night and we'll stay a week. We're flying first class, and we're staying in a suite that overlooks the Eiffel tower. Now who's perfect?"

Genie jumped out of her chair and into Victor's lap. "You are!" she said, covering his face with kisses. "I've always dreamed of going to Paris." She jumped up and started to clear the table. "Oh, I can't believe it." She ran into the kitchen with plates and utensils, then ran back saying, "April in Paris. Oh, Victor, it will be so wonderful. Oh, you're wonderful."

Victor stood up and gently took the coffee mugs out of her hand. "We're wonderful together, Aideen." He put his arms around her and kissed the top of her head. "You belong in Paris. You'll love it there."

Genie looked up into Victor's green eyes and kissed him. "I know I'll love it there. I love anywhere I can be with you."

Victor returned her kiss, and soon they were back in bed. Genie was sorry when Victor left at ten that night. She wished that just once he wouldn't leave her at the end of the weekend. It made her dread Mondays, though she loved going to her job. Still, the arrangement seemed to work best for him. He kept strange hours, often working past midnight. He never talked much about his work, saying that when they were together, he wanted to concentrate on her.

CHAPTER TWENTY-SEVEN

Genie walked into her apartment, sorting through the mail. There it was. Her expedited passport had arrived, four days before her trip. She sat down in the dining room and opened the envelope, cringing to see how strange her hair looked in the photo. When the phone rang, she slipped the passport back into the envelope.

"Hey, big sister! How are you?"

"Hi, Meara." Genie leaned back in her chair. She looked forward to these calls from her sister, who'd been living abroad for years. The last time she'd seen her was Christmas, two years before.

"Guess where I am?" Meara said, talking louder than necessary. Perhaps there was static on her end.

"No idea…Zanzibar?" Genie kicked off her shoes and tucked her legs up under herself.

"Wrongo," Meara said. "Strasbourg. I have a teaching gig here with a new dance company. I'll be here for three months."

"Remind me," Genie said. "Strasbourg is in Germany, right?"

"Ha! Typical English teacher, typical American. No sense of geography. Strasbourg's in France, although it's near the German border."

"Well, I guess I get a few points for my answer. Tell me," Genie said, patting the envelope. "How far is Strasbourg from Paris?"

"Paris?" Meara hesitated a minute. "I dunno, about three hundred miles, maybe a little more. Why?"

Genie hesitated. It would be so wonderful to see Meara after all this time. But she'd never breathed a word about Victor to anyone, certainly not to her family or Debra. Still, she'd only be three hundred miles away from her sister. "Well, as it happens, I'm going to Paris. I'll be there on the eighth of April."

"What?" Meara was shouting now. "I can't believe it. I'll take a train down there, Genie. We'll have a blast."

"Um," Genie stood up and started pacing. "It's a little more complicated. I'm going with someone...a guy."

"You have a boyfriend and you didn't tell me? How long have you been going out? When did you meet him? Is he someone I know?"

Genie could picture Meara jumping up and down. She had to tell her. "Actually, it's Victor. We've been dating since New Year's."

Dead silence.

"Did you hear me, Meara? Are you still there?"

"I heard you, Genie, loud and clear." Meara wasn't shouting; her voice was low, but sharp and cold. "I heard you, but I can't believe that you'd do something so stup— so incredibly self-destructive."

"I know how it sounds, Meara, but Victor is completely different now. He's really changed."

There was another long pause. "Nobody changes that much, Genie. You're kidding yourself if you really think he won't hurt you again."

It was Genie's turn to pause before answering. She couldn't be angry at Meara, and really, what could she expect? Meara's last memory of Victor was when he'd come to the house that terrible day; she hadn't seen how much he'd matured. Finally she said, "Look, I don't want to talk about Victor now. I'll be in Paris next week, and I really want to see you. Victor has to work part of the time, so he won't be around when we meet."

"I can meet you on Wednesday afternoon. Would that be okay?" Meara seemed to be trying to get past her anger, just like Genie. "Where are you staying?"

Genie picked up the itinerary from the dining room table. "The hotel is called Hôtel Plaza Athénée. Have you ever heard of it?"

Meara whistled. "Whatever Victor is up to these days, he must be raking in the dough. That place is wicked expensive."

"So you know it?" Genie was pleased that Meara was impressed.

"Yes, I know it. It's a famous place, very old and très chic. I'll meet you in the lobby at one."

"One o'clock on Wednesday," Genie said. "I can't believe I'm really going to see you, Meara."

Meara's laugh sounded forced. "Me neither, Genie. And I can't believe what you just told me. There's a lot about this conversation that's unbelievable. But the important thing is that we'll see each other."

"I'm so happy! I can't wait—" The line had gone dead. Meara had hung up. Genie held the receiver out and stared at it. She knew she'd have it out with Meara when she saw her, but she didn't care. She'd be in Paris, she'd be with Victor most of the time, and she'd see her sister. Things were getting better and better.

CHAPTER TWENTY-EIGHT

It was Friday and Genie was all packed and ready to go. She'd checked her purse three times to make sure she still had her passport. Victor was supposed to pick her up at five, and it was four-thirty. She stayed away from the window, forcing herself not to look for his car. By the time five o'clock rolled around, Genie was pacing. Maybe Victor had run into traffic. It was Friday, after all. Five minutes went by, then ten. Maybe Victor had had an accident.

The phone rang and Genie ran to answer it. "Victor?"

"Genie," Victor said. "I'm really sorry I'm late. I got caught up with something here at the studio."

"That's okay," Genie said. "Do you think we can still make the plane?"

"Yeah, of course. The flight's not till eight thirty. Look, I ordered a cab for you. It should be there by five thirty. I'll meet you at Logan. Tell the driver you're taking Air France. He'll drop you off at the right door. I'll be waiting for you. I'm leaving now."

Relief made Genie's arms and legs feel rubbery. "Okay," she said.

"I'm sorry about this," Victor said. "I don't want anything to ruin our trip."

"It won't. I love you," Genie said.

"You too."

Genie hung up the phone and got her coat. It was twenty past five and the cab should be out front any moment. She checked her purse one more time for her passport, picked up her suitcase and headed for the door. Next stop, Paris.

• • •

"Here, Genie," Victor said, holding out his hand. They'd taken off an hour before and had just finished their dinner.

"What's this?"

"Xanax. It'll put you right to sleep." Victor popped a pill into his mouth and chased it with Champagne.

Genie looked at the pill. "Isn't that a prescription drug? I heard it's for anxiety."

Victor turned to her and crossed his arms. "Genie, it's just one pill. Yeah, it's prescribed for anxiety and panic attacks. But it will help you sleep. Believe me, you don't want to stay awake for this flight. You'll be a zombie when you get to Paris."

"Do you have a prescription for this, Victor? You don't seem like you'd need an anti-anxiety pill."

Victor frowned and sucked in his breath. "No, I got these from a friend...just four of them: two for the flight over, two for the flight home. Although we probably won't need them going back." He picked up a magazine and slapped it down on the tray table in front of him. "Don't take it if you don't want to, but you'll be a drag if you don't sleep. We get to Paris when it's mid-morning there. Why spend the first day exhausted?"

This was no way to start their trip. Genie put her hand out, saying, "I guess it's okay." Victor dropped the pill on her hand and opened the magazine, turning away slightly. She swallowed the Xanax with some water.

Victor put the magazine down and reached over to caress her cheek. "Go to sleep, Genie. I promise we'll have a wonderful time in Paris."

Genie pushed the button to recline her seat and felt Victor put a blanket over her. She drifted off. When she woke, Victor was gently shaking her shoulder. "Wake up, sleepyhead," he whispered. "Have some coffee and a croissant. We'll be landing in half an hour."

Genie smiled and took a sip of coffee. Nibbling on her croissant, she looked out the window. She was in France, or at least, flying over it. A few minutes after the coffee things had been cleared away they landed. Genie was in a daze as Victor guided her through customs, then outside where taxis queued up. It was exciting to hear people speaking French and bustling about, everyone headed somewhere exotic. Victor pointed to their bags and told the driver the name of their hotel. Genie got into the backseat next to Victor and put her arm through his. "I can't believe we're really here!"

Victor kissed the tip of her nose and said, "Wait till you see our hotel." He leaned forward and said to the driver, "*Salut, mon ami. Puis-je avoir une cigarette, si'l vous plait?*"

The driver passed a pack of cigarettes and a lighter over his shoulder. Victor shook out a cigarette and put it in his mouth, then lit it. He handed the items back to the driver. "*Merci, monsieur.*"

He looked at Genie apologetically and rolled the window down halfway. "Do you mind?" he said. "It's a thing with me. Whenever I'm in Europe, I have to smoke."

Genie did mind, but she wasn't going to say so. "It's okay, I guess. It's not like you're in Europe all the time."

Victor laughed and took a deep drag, then blew the smoke out the window. "Not in a while. But you know, I lived in France for nearly a year. Spent some time in Germany, too."

"You never told me that," Genie said.

Victor took another drag and laughed, which got him coughing. When he stopped he regarded her with a strange expression. "There's a lot I haven't told you. After all, we, ah, said goodbye when we were seventeen. A lot can happen in thirteen years. I'm sure there's a lot you haven't told me, too."

A strange feeling passed over her, but she didn't say anything else, just watched the mid-morning traffic working its way into Paris. Narrow commercial vans and tiny trucks bearing unfamiliar logos sped by. Her mood lightened as they drove into the city itself, circling the Arc de Triomphe and down the Avenue Marceau. The day was slightly overcast, but that just made the old limestone buildings grander somehow. When the pulled up in front of the hotel, Genie took a deep breath. "It's beautiful!"

"You'll love it here," Victor said.

"I already do," Genie said as a man in a fancy uniform opened her door.

"Bonjour, Madame," he said.

Genie waited in the ornate lobby, its gilt and statuary a far cry from anything she'd ever seen in an American hotel. Victor checked them in, speaking in rapid French to the clerk. His fluent French was a surprise, and then there was the smoking. Genie told herself that Victor had been right about a lot happening in thirteen years. She still hadn't told him that she'd nearly married Matt.

Victor led her to the elevators, and a bellman followed them with their bags. Once in the room, Genie took in the sumptuous furniture, the gorgeous bedcover and pillows, the elegant grey walls. She waited until the bellman had collected his tip, then ran to the window and said, "Look! It's the Eiffel Tower!"

Victor walked over and stood next to her. "Oh, yeah," he deadpanned. "I think I've heard of that before."

Genie rolled her eyes. "Okay, I get it. I'm a typical American tourist."

He put his arms around her and pulled her close. "A very cute American tourist, though."

Genie wriggled out of his embrace. "I have to take a shower. Then I'll feel cute."

The bathroom was as luxurious as the bedroom and the lobby, with marble everywhere and a huge mirror dominating the room. Genie slipped into the shower and let the warm water relax her muscles. She'd just rinsed the conditioner out of her hair when the glass door opened. Victor stood there naked, wreathed in steam.

"You were taking forever," he said. "Would you like some company?"

"Mais oui," Genie said, dredging up one of the few French phrases she recalled from school.

Victor washed quickly, then grabbed her, pushing her against the marble wall. He lifted her slightly and was inside her before she could say anything. He'd never handled her so roughly before. Genie had a hard time breathing with the water dripping down her face, but it was exciting, too. A few minutes later, Victor turned the water off and picked her up, carrying her naked into the bedroom. Genie forgot all about the Eiffel Tower as Victor continued to make love with a hunger he'd never shown before. Afterward, they slept for hours. It was early evening when they woke.

Victor put his arm around her and said, "Well, Mademoiselle, it's nearly Saturday night in Paris. What would you like to do?"

"Eat!" Genie laughed and got out of bed. She opened her suitcase and pulled out some clothes. "Should I get dressed up for dinner?" she said.

Victor plumped the pillow under his head and said, "We won't go to a fancy place. Just a nice bistro or brasserie. You can wear jeans and a sweater."

"Great." Genie rummaged around for underwear and jeans.

"We can't go eat now, though." Victor reached over and pulled a cigarette out a pack in the table drawer. Lighting it, he said, "No one in Paris eats at six. Eight or eight-thirty is the earliest."

Genie frowned as Victor blew smoke toward the ceiling. "Where'd you get the cigarettes?"

Victor sat up and took another drag. "God, you're really bummed out by these, aren't you?" he said, placing the pack on the table. "I got them downstairs when you started your shower."

"Oh, I just wondered."

Victor extended his arm and held the cigarette out. A little ash spilled onto the blanket as he said, his tone turning gruff, "Look, I can get rid of them if it's going to be a problem."

"No," Genie said. "No problem."

Victor smiled. "Good. Go get dressed and I'll buy you a drink. We'll go somewhere where you can get a little snack, my hungry little American."

Genie's smile was tight. "Okay," she said, gathering up her things and heading into the bathroom to change and put on her makeup.

For the next two days, Genie felt whipsawed between Victor's affection and his impatience. She told herself that she was probably imagining it. After all, travel could be stressful, and this was the first time they'd gone anywhere as a couple. No matter how Victor acted, though, Genie made up her mind to enjoy Paris. They spent hours in the Louvre and walked along the Seine. On Monday Genie bought a print from one of the riverside *bouquinistes*.

"I'm sure it's not a print," Victor said when she showed it to him. "These guys source from Asia now, you know. It's just a reproduction."

Genie took the print back and looked at it again. It showed a man and woman walking in a garden. From their clothing it appeared to have been painted in the mid-1800's. "I don't care what it is, I like it. I'll frame it when I get home. It's better than a postcard or a magnet."

"Whatever floats your boat," Victor said, then put his arm around her, pulling her close.

They finished the day at a bistro in Montmatre. A tiny place with thick stone walls, the restaurant was just what Genie had always imagined when she dreamed of Paris. She and Victor shared an octopus salad, washing it down with a minerally Sancerre. As he had for the previous two nights, Victor had steak frites. Genie ventured into uncharted territory and ordered lapin a la cocotte, trying hard not to think of Bugs Bunny while she ate the rabbit dish. It was delicious. Because the night was fine, they decided to walk back to their hotel, practically rolling down the hill after all the wine with dinner and the Calvados after. Once they got to their room they fell into bed and Genie went right to sleep.

The next morning, Genie woke to hear the shower running. She checked the clock. It was only seven-thirty, early for Victor. She got up and put on a robe, then pulled a chair up to look out the window. She knew Victor would laugh at her, but she could never get enough of the Eiffel tower. Soon she'd be back in Cambridge and who knew when she'd ever get back to Paris? She's savor it as much as she could.

Victor came out of the bathroom with his jeans on and took a shirt out of the closet.

"Are you going somewhere?" Genie said.

"I told you a couple of days ago, Genie. I'm supposed to meet with a guy I used to work with when I lived here. He might be able to get me some assignments for later in the year." He pulled the shirt on and buttoned it up, scowling. "I told you that."

Genie put her hands up. "Okay, you told me. I just didn't know it was going to be so early."

Victor took out his wallet and extracted a few franc notes, which he tossed onto the table. "Here," he said. "I won't be back until later this afternoon. You might want to get lunch somewhere."

"I have my own money," Genie said, trying to keep her voice even.

Victor shrugged and retrieved his suede jacket from the back of a chair. "Suit yourself," he said. He walked over and gave her a quick kiss on the cheek, then left the room.

Genie sat back on the bed and wondered what had just happened. She got up and put on her jeans and a sweater and her black boots, then scooped up the notes Victor had left, grabbed her purse and headed toward the door. "Screw you, Victor," she said under her breath. She'd go and explore by herself, have a nice early lunch somewhere, then come back and shower. Maybe by the time Victor came back he'd be in a better mood. If he wasn't, Genie was going to have to lay down some rules for him. She hadn't come all this way to be treated like a nobody.

Walking through the extravagant lobby, Genie couldn't help but smile. The tall pillars, gorgeous arrangements of peonies and hydrangea, and oversized crystal chandeliers made it impossible for her to feel grouchy, despite Victor's behavior. She nodded to the uniformed man who opened the art deco door. Practically skipping onto the sidewalk, she headed up the Avenue Montaigne to the Champs-Elysées. She stopped at a café for a coffee and a slice of pain aux abricots. She wished she could bring home a suitcase full of the delicious apricot bread, but then where would she put all the chocolates she wanted take? After her breakfast she walked for miles, stopping in at little shops along the way.

When she returned, she was relaxed and happy; Paris had worked its magic on her again. She'd bought gifts for her mother and father. Since she'd be seeing Meara the next day, she'd bought her a gorgeous blue and purple silk scarf. She'd even indulged herself, buying a box of macarons and a small braided loaf filled with cheese and black olives. She'd take a shower and drink a glass of wine and wait for Victor, who should be in a much better frame of mind.

She poured herself a glass of Chateau Montrose and took off her sweater and jeans and stepped into the bathroom. She didn't see it at first, half-hidden under a towel. It was Victor's notebook. Genie wished she knew how to reach him, since he probably needed it for his meeting. Oh well, it was too late now. She removed the towel and, since the book lay open, couldn't help but see her name.

Genie picked up the book and held it closer to the window. Victor's spidery handwriting was hard to read, but she soon adjusted, then wished she hadn't.

Genie is easier to manipulate than I would have thought. That prim little teacher persona is no act; she really is as naive as she seemed that day when I "bumped into her" at the Parker House. Thank God I saw that article about the literary prize in the paper…I'd never have been able to pull this off otherwise.

Genie frowned and flipped a few pages ahead.

I can't wait for this to be over. Genie is acting like a little kid about Paris, and it will be damned embarrassing to be seen with her if I don't watch it. She dresses like she did in high school, like she's a lifetime customer of LL Bean. And that silly hair of hers. Definitely won't take her to any clubs. Not that Miss Early Bird would ever want to be out past ten.

A wave of lightheadedness made her stagger. She had to sit down, so she took the book out to the bedroom. She put her robe on and lay on the bed, then opened the notebook to the first page.

Today went just like I planned it. Genie totally bought it that I'd just 'happened' to be at the P.H. She was totally snowed by my apology. I should have killed the bitch when I had the chance, but now I'll keep the promise I made to myself in Concord. I won't use violence again, at least not directly. I'll use my brains and my words. They can hurt just as bad.

Victor had been in Concord? The state prison? That was impossible. Genie suddenly felt very cold. She got up and put her clothes back on and sat at the desk. She didn't want to be in bed when Victor got back. She took a large gulp of wine and kept reading. It was hard to concentrate, hard to turn the pages with shaking hands. Finally she just skimmed over the words, turning back and forth through the pages:

Genie's still as flat-chested as she was in high school…she's a surprisingly good lay, but way too clingy afterward…Mark and the guys did a great job on G. New Year's Eve. By the time they were done with her, I seemed like Prince Charming; it was almost too easy to get her into bed after that…

…I can barely get through the weekends with her, so thank God I told her I worked late during the week. Yeah, I work on getting as much action as I can away from her. It's such a relief to be with women who just want to fuck and don't expect pillow talk…

…Does she really think I care that she 'forgives' me for what I did? She's just lucky she didn't end up like that guy in the bar…

… I still can't believe she fell for that Montana shit! As if Father would have gone out West. As if I would have gone anywhere with the son of a bitch…

Genie jumped when she heard the key in the lock. Victor came in with a cigarette in his mouth and smiled to see the notebook in her hands.

"I see you found it. Good. I thought I might have covered it too well with the towel. How far have you gotten through my notes, Genie? I mean, Aideen?" Victor emphasized the last word with a goofy expression, as if her name were a joke.

Genie was too angry to cry. "I've read enough, Victor. I guess you meant me to."

"Indeed I did," Victor said, stubbing the cigarette out in the crystal ashtray. He took his suitcase out of the closet and started packing. "Aren't you interested to know what I'm doing now? You're usually quite the little chatterbox, always asking questions."

"I guess you'll tell me without my asking," Genie said quietly.

Victor stopped packing and pulled a chair up on the other side of the desk. He took her glass and drained it. "I'll tell you everything, Little Miss Halloran." He stood and brought the wine over to the desk along with another glass, then poured each of them a hefty drink.

"As you no doubt guessed, I haven't been exactly honest with you since we met at the Parker House. Take today, for example. I took the train to Rouen to visit an old friend of mine, someone I knew when I lived here before. She's a great fuck, you know. Better than you, although you're not too bad, Genie." He took a sip of the wine. "As a matter of fact, she's driving back here," he checked his watch, "in about an hour. We're going to Germany, and then I'm off to Czechoslovakia. There's a lot going on there, and I want to be a part of it."

"Germany, then Czechoslovakia," Genie whispered. She sat straighter. "You planned this all along, didn't you?"

"Bingo!" Victor leaned over and bopped her on the nose with his index finger. "Pretty mean of me, huh?" He stood up and went back to his suitcase. "Oh, by the way, you're going to have to clear out of here tomorrow morning. I've paid for four nights in this place, but no more. You'll have to find a place that's a little less fancy for the rest of your stay here. This cost me an arm and a leg, not to mention flying first class. But it was worth it. I mean, you should see your face." He pulled his lips down at the corner, then laughed.

"But why?" She'd never felt hated like this.

"You know why, Aideen," Victor said, zipping his suitcase. "You remember that awful day, when I came to your house? All I wanted to do was beg your forgiveness. I'd have done anything you wanted, even turn myself in to the police, if that's what you told me to do. I was a wreck, I was begging, and that little bitch Meara said you wouldn't see me."

"But you'd tried to kill me," Genie whispered. "I ran for my life."

"If I had wanted to kill you that day, I'd have done it. I let you get away." Victor took another drink.

Genie curled her fingers into fists. "I made Debra and Meara promise not to tell my parents or my brothers what had happened. My father..." she swallowed hard, fighting back the tears.

168

"My brothers—they would have beaten you to a pulp. They probably would have killed you."

Victor picked up his case and swung his jacket over his shoulders. "Maybe. But I guess we'll never know. Anyway," he looked down at his watch again and said, "I gotta go. Can't keep Danika waiting. She's a real tiger when she gets mad. Unlike you, my forgiving little pal."

Before she could stop him, Victor leaned over and kissed her cheek. "Enjoy the rest of your stay in Paris, Genie. Oh yeah..." He reached into his jacket pocket and tossed an envelope onto her lap. "Here's your ticket home; I couldn't strand you here, poor baby. Not first class this time, but still..." He shrugged his shoulders and smirked, then walked out, closing the door with a bang. The notebook sat on the table, the words inside left to mock her.

CHAPTER TWENTY-NINE

The next morning Genie sat in the lobby, in a chair close to the door, to wait for Meara. She hadn't slept the night before and had showered and packed at dawn. She resisted opening Victor's notebook again, knowing it would make her feel worse. She'd give it to Meara, who'd already told her that taking up with Victor again was a mistake. As always, her little sister was the wiser one.

When Meara entered the lobby, Genie jumped out of her chair and ran to her. "I'm so glad you're here," she said, hugging Meara tight.

"Genie, what's wrong? Did Victor hurt you?" Meara stood back and held Genie's arms, looking hard at her, searching for bruises or cuts. She looked over Genie's shoulder and said, "Are those your bags? I thought you were staying in Paris for another few days."

Genie hung her head and said, "I am. But I can't stay here. Victor left and checked us out of the hotel. I have to go." She didn't bother to wipe away the tears rolling down her cheeks.

"Let's go and sit down. You need to tell me what's going on," Meara said, leading Genie back to her chair.

Genie told Meara everything, and showed her the notebook. Meara glanced at the words briefly, then snapped the book closed. "That son of a bitch," she muttered. "Wait right here, Genie. I'm going to find us a place to stay."

"You don't have to stay with me, Meara. Don't you have to work?"

Meara put her hand on Genie's arm. "I don't start until Monday. And I wouldn't leave you now anyway. Give me a minute."

Meara went to the concierge desk, where an elegant young woman sat. Genie could make out a few words of the conversation. She was surprised at Meara's flawless French, but not at her confidence. She'd always been a strong person, even as a child. The concierge picked up the phone and, after a short conversation, wrote something on a piece of paper which she handed to Meara. When Meara came back, she said, "Let's go. We have a place in the Marais."

They walked to the Metro and arrived at the little hotel in less than half an hour. Their room was small, and the hotel was clearly very old, but scrupulously clean. The window opened onto a small garden where a brown tabby snoozed in the sun. Genie sat on one bed, Meara on the other, the two of them not really knowing what to say. Finally, Genie said, "Thank you, Meara. I don't know what I would have done without you."

Meara shook her head. "I'm sure I screwed up Victor's grand plan. After all, he had no way of knowing when he cooked up this little caper that I'd be coming to visit you. He was planning to leave you high and dry. You'd have figured out what to do, though."

"Maybe," Genie said. "But I would have been alone and..." she started sobbing, worn down by lack of sleep as much as anything else.

Meara jumped to her feet and said, "Okay, time for lunch. You've cried enough over that asshole. Let's go eat."

For the next two days, Meara and Genie explored the narrow streets of the Marais, dipping into the Picasso museum, and sitting in quiet cafes. Meara was much more knowledgeable about the city than Victor and an expert guide. It had been so long since Genie had spent any time alone with her sister. She usually saw her only at family gatherings and holidays, where they were surrounded by relatives. Genie was content to follow Meara around and even found she was enjoying herself.

The night before Genie's flight, the sisters lay in their beds, the room illuminated by a small gaslight in the garden.

"Genie," Meara said in a soft voice. "Are you going to be all right when you go back home? You won't let this thing with Victor get you down, will you?"

Genie thought a minute. "I think I'll be okay," she said. "It's good to know that he won't be nearby."

"You don't know that for sure. He lied about everything else; who knows if he really went to Czechoslovakia, or if he'll stay there for long." Meara shifted and folded her arm under her head. "Hasn't Debra been after you to go out to California? You told me that she said there are plenty of teaching jobs in Santa Rosa. It might be a good idea to put some distance between you and that shithead."

"What about Mom and Dad?" Genie said. "They're not doing so well these days. I see them at least three times a week, and they call me anytime they need help."

Meara exhaled loudly. "And of course Ragsie and Sean are always too busy."

"I guess," Genie said. "But they have families of their own."

"Ugh," Meara said, getting up and sitting on the edge of Genie's bed. "I've heard that from Mom for years. What about you? What about me? Don't we have lives too?"

Genie took Meara's hand and smiled. "Of course. But Mom's old-fashioned; in her mind it's different for daughters, right?"

Meara squeezed Genie's hand. "When you get back you should talk to Debra about California. Don't worry about Mom and Dad. I talked to Mom when you were in the shower this morning. After I finish this gig in Strasbourg, I'm going home. I've been away too long. I'm going to stay with Mom and Dad for a while until I figure out what to do next."

"You're not just doing this for me, are you?"

Meara snorted. "You're the one who'd make a sacrifice like that, Genie. Not me." She went back to her own bed and lay down. After a moment she said, "I've been thinking about this for a while, actually. It's been great to live abroad for so long, and I'd never trade all my experiences. But it's time to go back. Mom and Dad won't be around forever, and to tell you the truth, I've been kinda homesick lately. As for you, you should really think about California."

Genie had visited Debra and her husband in Sonoma County a few years before and had loved it. Maybe she should consider making a move. She yawned and said, "But if you come back and I go to California, I still won't see you very much."

Meara turned over and muttered sleepily, "You'll be home at Christmas, Genie. And probably more often than that..."

"I'll think about it," Genie said.

"Do it quietly," Meara said. "I'm going to sleep."

• • •

Before Genie left she showed Meara her plane ticket. It was for the last row in coach.

"I guess that's Victor's final jab," Genie said as she hugged Meara goodbye.

"Good riddance," Meara said. She put her hands on Genie's shoulders and glared at her. "If you ever talk to that asshole again—"

A cab pulled up in front of the hotel.

Genie put her hands up in surrender. "I won't! I promise." She got into the cab and waved. "Thank you for everything."

Meara blew her a kiss. Genie settled back and sighed. The trip hadn't been what she'd thought it would be, but spending time with Meara had taken a little of the sting off what Victor had done. Meara had insisted on keeping Victor's notebook, saying Genie would brood about it otherwise. She was right about that, too. Genie closed her eyes and imagined starting a new life in California. The golden state had been a refuge from Victor once. Maybe it could be again.

<u>1994-2011</u>

CHAPTER THIRTY

Genie stretched out on a lawn chair. It was Friday and the last day of school at the Jenner Academy, where she'd taught English for the last three years. She'd finally decided to move out to Santa Rosa after a year of thinking about it, and it had been the right decision. The little bungalow she'd rented near Cherry Street had everything she needed, including a front porch just big enough for two chairs. She sipped her chamomile tea and looked out at the succulents planted in the tiny front yard. It was nearly seven and still light, but she needed to shower and change. She'd agreed to meet Debra at a fundraiser for farmworkers' rights, a cause Debra and her husband Ed, a winemaker, stoutly supported. It would be nice to stay home and savor the quiet, but she'd have all summer for that.

And of course, there was her book. She'd nearly finished the second draft of the romance novel aimed at teens. When she'd been back in Cambridge she'd started it more than once, but she hadn't really dug in until she'd moved to Santa Rosa. Maybe it was being so far from home and all the expectations of her family, and, of course, the painful memories of Victor. No matter what it was, though, she was certain that the book was good. Debra knew a woman who worked for a small publishing company in San Francisco, and she'd sounded interested when Debra had talked to her about the book. Maybe, just maybe, she'd be published. She'd have the summer to put the final touches on it, then she'd send it to Debra's friend.

She checked her watch. It was time to get ready. Forty five minutes later she walked downtown to a small event space called The Barrel, where she was supposed to meet Debra at eight thirty. Soon it was eight forty-five, and still no Debra. That wasn't surprising; Debra had always had a casual relationship with time, and Genie just let it go. She decided to buy her ticket and pick one up for Debra, too. Might as well be generous as well as relaxed.

The box office line was short. "Two, please," she said at the window, sliding a ten across the counter.

A young man with a pierced septum, through which he'd fastened mini bull's horns, took her money. As he reached for the roll of tickets he said, "You Genie?"

Genie thought she hadn't heard him correctly. "Am I what?"

"Genie?" he repeated, handing her the tickets. "This chick with an amazing Boston accent called and said her friend Genie would be buying a ticket." He squinted, making the horns twist slightly. "She said you look sorta like Glenn Close in Fatal Attraction." Squinting more, he said, "Maybe the hair, but..."

Genie patted her curly bob and looked around. "That was probably my friend Debra."

"Right, that was her name," he said. "She said I should tell you she wasn't gonna come tonight. Said she had car problems and she'd call you tomorrow." He held up a finger and said, "No, wait—what she really said was 'Tell huhh my cahh wouldn't stahht...'" He laughed and said, "She's your friend, right? Are you from Boston, too?"

Genie nodded, pressing her lips together. Who was this idiot?

"You're really from Boston, too?" He giggled. "Can you say 'Pahk the cah in Hahvad Yahd?'"

"Hey!" said a man who'd come up behind Genie. "Bostonians don't appreciate being mocked like that, man. How'd you like it if someone asked you what happens to that thing in your nose when you sneeze?"

Genie let out a giggle and turned around, smiling. "For that, you get a free ticket," she said, holding out her hand.

The man behind her put his hands up, "I'd have said that for nothing. I'm from Boston too and have zero tolerance for that Harvard Yard crap."

Genie put the ticket in one of his upraised hands. He had a nice face, what she could see of it. Most of it was covered with a thick, salt-and-pepper beard. The hair on his head was even curlier than hers, but up there the salt was winning the battle.

"I insist," Genie said. "It's not often I meet someone from home out here."

He closed his hand around the ticket and said, "I accept on the condition that you let me buy you a drink. Then we can talk freely to one another and drop all the "R's" we want to."

Genie hesitated. She'd only come to this event because Debra had insisted, and now Debra wasn't even here. The guy seemed nice enough, but…

"My name's Charlie, by the way," he said, holding his hand out. "I'm from Watertown, Massachusetts. You know it?"

Genie grinned and put out her hand. "I know it well, Charlie. I'm Genie, from Waltham, Massachusetts, right next door."

Charlie smiled and shook her hand. "Come on, neighbor. Let me buy you a nice glass of wine."

• • •

Charlie and Genie ended up sharing a bottle of Ravenswood Zinfandel and talking about Sonoma County and everything they loved about it. It was good to talk to another person from home. Genie sometimes came across as too direct to people who'd grown up in California, and she found Charlie's slight Boston edge familiar and appealing. There was something else about him, a sense that he knew who he was and was sure of his place in the world. The music from the benefit concert filtered into the bar, but they didn't leave their seats until closing time.

Helping Genie with her sweater, Charlie said, "Was your friend going to give you a ride home?"

"Probably," Genie said. "That's okay, though. It's only a few blocks. I like to walk."

Charlie shrugged himself into his old Cal jacket. "So do I. But it's after eleven, and it can get tricky downtown when it's this late. Let me walk you."

"I don't want to put you out," Genie said.

"It's no problem. I live over by the hospital, so I won't have far to go. Besides, I can use all the exercise I can get." He patted his middle, which was only slightly rounded.

They stepped outside and Genie shivered a little. "I can't believe it was eighty degrees today."

Charlie smiled. "Crazy, isn't it? Once the sun goes down here—boom! The temperature drops twenty degrees in just a few hours."

Genie nodded. "One of the many things to love about this place."

They walked slowly, navigating the uneven sidewalks. When Genie stumbled slightly, Charlie put a steadying hand on her elbow.

"These sycamore roots really screw up the pavement. That and the earthquakes," Charlie said.

"It's better than snow and ice," Genie chuckled.

"You told me you loved shoveling," Charlie said, nudging Genie.

He wasn't much taller than she was, Genie realized. She wondered how old he was. He had a lot of grey hair, but his face, what she could see of it above the beard, looked young enough. His eyes, brown and kind, had a few wrinkles at the corners, but those could have come from laughter as much as age.

When they reached Riley Street, Genie said, pointing a few houses down, "That's me there."

"Great place," Charlie said. "This neighborhood is historic, you know."

"So I've heard. Of course, I grew up in a hundred-year-old house and lived in an even older one in Cambridge. There's not much around here that can compete with Boston when it comes to history."

"Genie!" Charlie said, his eyes twinkling. "You gotta let go of that New England flintiness. You're in Sonoma County now. Time to chill."

Genie laughed. "You're right. After all, you've been in California how long now? You seem pretty relaxed."

Charlie took a little bow. "Thank you. Once you've been here for a decade or so, you'll definitely start to lighten up. Of course, I'm happy to give you tips along the way."

"I just might take you up on that," Genie said. Not for the first time that evening, she felt happy that Debra had stood her up.

They stood for a moment in front of her house, neither one quite ready to say goodbye.

"You said that you like to hike, Genie. Come hiking with me Sunday morning?" Charlie asked. "I'll pack us a lunch. If we leave early we can climb to the top of Hood Mountain before it gets too hot."

Genie thought a minute. She had a good feeling about this guy. "Okay, if you let me make brownies."

Charlie clapped his hands to his heart. "Brownies! You said the magic word. Pick you up at eight?"

"Eight it is," Genie said. "See you Sunday." She gave him a wave and went to her front door. When she turned around he was still watching her, his curly hair lit by the streetlight.

CHAPTER THIRTY-ONE

At the summit, they sat on a large, flat rock and Charlie eased his backpack off his shoulders. "Man, that kicked my butt," he laughed. "Straight up, all the way. I did this hike when I was a student, but it's been a while."

Genie took off her baseball cap and wiped the sweat from her brow. "It's good we started early," she said. The grass had already turned brown as it did every summer, but there was a slight breeze rustling the oak leaves. A tiny sagebrush lizard skittered across the rock and disappeared under a nearby manzanita. Genie looked up at the clear blue sky, then out toward the south. "Is that Mt. Tamalpais?"

"Yep," Charlie said. He handed her his water bottle. They'd drunk all her water already.

She took a big gulp and said, "What's for lunch? I'm starving."

"You have a choice." Charlie rooted around in his pack and pulled out a couple of brown-paper-wrapped packets. "I've got a hummus, olive, and apple sandwich, and a turkey and Swiss. They're cut in half so we can share if you like."

Genie gave Charlie a look. "You made two different kinds of sandwiches? I was expecting maybe PB&J's."

"I'm a single guy, but that doesn't make me a Neanderthal," Charlie said, offering Genie half of the hummus sandwich. "Besides, I lived in Berkeley for a long time and took some cooking classes."

Genie took a bite of her sandwich. "Mmm. You must have been an A student. This is great."

"You should taste my pizza...goat cheese, sundried tomatoes and onion jam is my favorite." Charlie dug into the other half of the sandwich, offering Genie a plastic container of orange sections.

They ate in silence for a while, content to cool off and look at the spectacular view. Genie glanced at Charlie while he unwrapped the other sandwich, studying his face and gentle-looking hands. He looked up and smiled. "Why are you looking at me like that?"

"Sorry," Genie said. To cover her embarrassment she reached into her pack for the container of brownies. "I'm just trying to put together a picture. You came to Berkeley as an undergrad and stayed for grad school and became a professor there. Now you're up here in Sonoma County. Just wondering why, I guess." She offered him the container.

His eyes lit up as he reached for a brownie. "Why does anyone do anything?" He took a bite and smiled. "Outstanding!" he said. He held up a finger and said, "If I'm going to tell you this story, I gotta finish at least one brownie first."

Genie laughed. "Take your time," she said. "I don't want to pry, though."

Charlie finished chewing and nodded. "You're curious. That's okay, I'm curious about you, too. After all, you moved away from your friends and family, away from a place you'd lived your whole life, practically. There's gotta be a story, there too, right?" He smiled gently.

"Of course there's a story," Genie said, fiddling with a buckle on her pack. "One of the oldest. There was this guy who wasn't too

184

nice to me, and my friend Debra convinced me that a change of scene would do me good."

"And it has, right?" Charlie looked longingly at the container of brownies, but didn't take another.

"It has," Genie said. "Sure you don't want another?" She held the brownies out to him.

"Maybe when we get back down," Charlie said. He turned his face up to the sky and closed his eyes. "If I eat any more now I'll want to take a nap. Then you'd have to roll me down the trail." Without opening his eyes, he said, "So that guy who wasn't nice to you...how long ago was that?"

"Four years ago," Genie said. "I should have seen it coming, but I wanted to think the best of him." She lay down on the rock and squinted up at the sky.

Charlie turned to her and said, "If he treated you badly, that's on him, not you." He took a drink of water and said, "Love, or what we think is love, can make it hard to think rationally. Your instincts for self-preservation don't always work too well when you're infatuated."

Genie sat up and looked Charlie in the eye. "Sounds like you know what you're talking about."

He packed a few things away and shook his head. "You got me there. I lived with a woman in Berkeley for six years and thought we'd be together forever. But it didn't work out that way. She found someone else, and that was that." He stood up and held out a hand to help Genie off the rock. "Shall we start down? I'll give you the Reader's Digest version of that relationship on the way, if you're interested."

Genie smiled. "I'm interested," she said.

It was a lot easier going down, though Genie had to keep an eye on the trail to avoid tripping on the rocks. As they kicked up dust from the dry soil, she walked behind Charlie, who told her about his life in Berkeley, his decision to leave teaching and start a nonprofit to help released prisoners find jobs and housing, and Michelle, the woman who'd left him for another man. Soon they were in the parking lot. The walk down had been quick, given how long it had taken them to get to the top.

"It's a lot easier going down," Charlie said with a laugh. He bent his legs a couple of times. "Tough on the knees, though." He looked back up the trail. "I was twenty the last time I did this. I guess things can change in, what, eighteen years. Man, am I old."

Genie put her pack in the trunk of Charlie's car. "Thirty eight isn't old," she said. "I'll be thirty five later this year. And I'm not old." She laughed and slid into the passenger seat.

Charlie got into the driver's seat and buckled up. "You look ten years younger than that, Genie. Not trying to snow you."

"Just for that, you get the rest of the brownies." She smiled and looked into his eyes. She liked looking at him, liked seeing a sly smile creep across his face, liked his dark eyes and his greying curls. He looked his age, maybe a little older. But in a good, comfortable way.

On the way back they kept the conversation light, no more talk about past loves and heartbreaks. When Charlie pulled up to Genie's house he jumped out to get her pack out of the trunk. Handing it to her, he said, "Thanks for today, Genie. I hope we can see each other again soon."

"I'd like that," Genie said.

Charlie bent closer and kissed her cheek. "I'll call you," he said.

Genie waved as he drove away. It had been a lovely day. Now all she wanted was a bath. Then she'd phone Debra as she'd promised. Debra wanted details, and Genie couldn't wait to give them.

CHAPTER THIRTY-TWO

A couple of weeks later Genie stooped over a raised bed of herbs in Debra's back yard. She'd promised to help Debra weed, though gardening was not one of her favorite things. Debra's usual helpers, her twins Chad and Robert, were in Pocatello visiting Ed's parents, so she'd drafted Genie. Genie didn't really mind, though. Spending the afternoon with Debra would give her a chance to talk about Charlie, something she enjoyed. Since their hike they'd spent a lot of time together, talking about their childhoods, why they'd chosen their careers, their political views, and their dreams for the future. They often brought picnic lunches or dinners to keep expenses to a minimum. Though Genie made a decent wage as a teacher, Charlie took only a small salary as executive director of Mercy's Family, the nonprofit he'd founded. He wasn't ashamed at not having much money, but he'd been adamant about not wanting Genie to pay for things. "Save your money," he'd always say. "My mom was a teacher, and I know how hard you all work."

Genie didn't mind. There was more to life than expensive meals in fancy restaurants. And being with Charlie, no matter what they did, was always special. She had another reason for coming to Debra's house today, and was glad that Ed and the boys weren't around. She had something to say, something that made her very happy.

Debra came out with a tray of iced blackberry tea, which she set on a table under a pergola covered by a profusion of fragrant purple wisteria. "Break time!" she called to Genie.

Genie dusted off her hands and joined her friend. Debra handed her a glass of tea, saying, "You have to have one of these cookies, too. I made them last month for the twins' last day of school, but they forgot them. They've been sitting in the freezer tempting me and today I finally gave in. Take two. That'll be two less for me to eat."

"Two fewer," Genie said in a fluty voice. "Try to remember your grammar, please."

Debra dipped a finger into her glass and flicked some tea at Genie's head. "You can cram it, Miss Halloran. I'm not your student."

"You'd be in detention with language like that," Genie said, taking a cookie. She took a bite, then set the cookie down, suddenly serious. "Debs, when did you know that Ed was the right guy for you?"

Debra laughed. "Wow, way to change the subject! Are things getting serious with this Charlie of yours?"

Genie shrugged. "They might be. But answer my question, please. After all, I don't have the best track record when it comes to men."

Debra was kind enough not to agree. She smiled, then leaned back against the chair, closing her eyes. "I think I knew about ten minutes after I met him. I know it sounds like a cliché, but still... He was the best man at my cousin Tina's wedding and I was a bridesmaid. Romance was in the air, I guess." She opened one eye and frowned. "You already know about this. I remember calling you at your dorm that night."

"I remember the call, yes. But you'd just met him then and the hormones were raging. Now that you've been married all these years, do you still think you fell in love with him that quickly?"

Debra smiled. "I really do. There was just something about him. He looked so handsome in his tux, and he was so tall...It might not have been ten minutes. But by the time he asked me to dance at the reception, I was like a wet noodle in his arms. He seemed exotic...a California guy, training to be a winemaker. He wasn't like the guys we'd grown up with, or the ones I dated at North-eastern. He was—I don't know—it sounds New Age-y to say it, but he was centered. Like he knew himself and what he wanted to do in life. But there was more. He was a kind person, accepting and steady. You know what I mean?"

Genie nodded. "I do. That's exactly what Ed's like. I was so happy when I met him; I knew he'd be good for you, Debs." She leaned forward and tapped Debra's knee. "You deserve happiness, you really do. You're kind, just like Ed. You were always such a good friend to me, even when I didn't deserve it."

Debra sat up straight. "Don't get all gooey on me, Genie. You and I have always been friends, and you'll be my friend till the day I die. What happened for a few months in high school is nothing compared to all we've been to each other."

The two women were quiet for a moment, then Genie took another bite of her cookie. "Mmm, this is delicious. Can you bring some of these to dinner at my house tomorrow night?"

"Dinner?" Debra reached for a cookie. "Did I forget something?"

Genie's eyes danced as she chewed her cookie. "Remember you ordered me not to sleep with anyone until you'd met them?"

"Yes," Debra said, "Is that what this conversation has been about? You and the Berkeley professor are gonna do it, huh?"

"Ex-professor," Genie said. She sipped her tea, letting Debra stew a minute. "Seriously, can you and Ed come to dinner tomorrow night? I know you'll love Charlie, Debs. He's the real deal; I'm sure of it."

"Well, you've been seeing him for a few weeks. I guess that's long enough to at least have a hunch."

"Just meet him and find out for yourself." Genie wiped the cookie crumbs off her hands and said with a big smile, "I'm going to marry this guy, wait and see."

CHAPTER THIRTY-THREE

Genie sighed and rested her head on Charlie's chest. As soon as Debra and Ed had left, she'd led Charlie to the bedroom. They'd made love unhurriedly, leaving her feeling content and cherished. She ran her fingers through his curly chest hair and said, "Debra and Ed really liked you, I could tell."

Charlie slid his fingers through hers. "I liked them, too. But why do I get the feeling that if they hadn't liked me, I wouldn't be in your bed now?" He was smiling, but she could tell he was serious.

She propped herself on an elbow and kissed his forehead. "I knew they'd approve of you, Charlie. But Debra had made me promise that before I got involved with someone again, she'd meet him. She's been a little protective since...Well, I told you about that guy back in Boston."

Charlie reached up and caressed her cheek. "You didn't tell me much, but it must have been pretty bad for you to have moved all this way and for Debra to be so concerned." His smile disappeared. "Was he abusive to you? You don't have to talk about this if you don't want to ..."

Genie lay down beside Charlie and they looked at each other. "This night is too beautiful, Charlie. I'll tell you all about him someday, but not tonight."

Charlie leaned toward her and kissed her lips gently, then more deeply. "I can't see into the future, Genie," he said, drawing her closer. "But I promise I'll never knowingly hurt you. I'm not perfect, and I'll do dumb things. But never to hurt you."

They didn't say much more, and they were together every night after that.

CHAPTER THIRTY-FOUR

Genie sat at her desk. Class had been dismissed and the students grumbled their way out the door. She'd just assigned *Silas Marner*, a book she had given to every tenth-grade class she'd taught for the last ten years. Invariably, the class would complain about the corny old book by that George Eliot dude. A few of her more enterprising students would quickly figure out that Eliot had not been a dude, and some even came to like the book. She always assigned it at the beginning of November, timing it so that the kids finished just before Christmas break. She shied away from *A Christmas Carol,* the more obvious choice, though Christmas plays a role in Silas Marner's story. But Eliot's novel, having been written by a woman who lived contemporaneously with Charles Dickens, helped round out the students' understanding of life in Victorian times and challenged them with its unfamiliarity.

She piled papers and books into her bag and was about to leave when there was a soft knock on the door. She looked up to see Lily Wagner, a tiny, dark-haired girl who barely said a word unless prompted. Genie was surprised; Lily hadn't been in class that day. She had on her usual oversized flannel shirt and ripped jeans, but she also wore large dark sunglasses—a waifish Jackie O in grunge.

"Miss Halloran," she said in a whispery voice. "I'm sorry I missed class today. I just came to get the assignment for next week."

"Oh, Lily," Genie said, reaching for a copy of Silas Marner on the table by her desk. "You could have waited until Monday. Are you not feeling well?"

Lily stood holding her left arm with her right hand. She looked paler than usual. "I'm okay," she said. She came forward to get the book, but when Genie handed it to her, Lily fumbled and dropped it. She bent to pick it up and her glasses slid off her face. Genie hurried around to help. Before Lily could put them back on, Genie saw the left side of Lily's face.

"Lily!" Genie gasped. "What happened to you?"

Lily bobbled the glasses and nearly dropped them again. "Nothing, Miss Halloran." She put the glasses on, but they slipped down her nose. Lily's chin quivered and she said, "Please don't look at me like that. Nothing's wrong."

Genie walked quickly to the door and closed it, then put her arm around Lily and led her to the back of the classroom. By the time they both sat down Lily was weeping silently, her shoulders shaking.

Genie pulled her chair close to Lily's and gently took off the girl's sunglasses. There was a huge gash through Lily's left eyebrow, and the skin on her left cheekbone and just under her eye was a mottled purple. Genie put her hand under Lily's chin. "Who did this to you, Lily?" She spoke quietly, trying to keep her voice steady. "Please don't tell me you fell or walked into something. I think your ribs might be injured, too, by the way you're holding yourself. You can be honest with me, Lily. I want to help you."

Lily sniffed and pulled an old-fashioned bandana out of her pocket, wiping her eyes and nose. "That's what Jenna said."

"Jenna MacAllister?"

Lily nodded. "She's my best friend. She told me I should talk to you."

"What about your parents?"

Lily looked down at the desk. "I stayed at Jenna's house last night. They haven't seen me yet."

"I think they'll want to take you to a doctor and make sure you're all right. Why haven't you gone home? You can call them from here, you know."

Lily shook her head. "I can't tell my Dad. He'll freak out when he sees me."

Genie took Lily's hands in hers. "Let me take you to the nurse's office, Lily. You have to go home sometime, and your parents have to see you. I'll call them for you if you want."

"You won't tell Dad what happened, will you?" Lily's hands were icy.

"I don't know what happened, Lily. It looks to me, though, like someone hurt you pretty badly."

Lily looked away. "I knew I shouldn't have gone with him," she muttered.

"Who?" Genie whispered. She thought she knew, though. Tyler Strand, a junior who had transferred to the school recently, seemed always to be standing near Lily in the hallways and outside the school. He was big—not tall, but muscular—and wore a perpetual scowl.

Lily put her hand to her mouth as if to keep her secret. "Tyler," she said. "He got mad at me. We were out by the creek last night. I knew I shouldn't go, but he promised we'd just go for a walk. But he wanted to... you know." She shrugged, looking closer to ten than fifteen. "I said I didn't want to have sex with him. He said he just wanted to touch my..." she wiped her cheek and sniffed. "He just wanted to touch my breast." She looked up at Genie, her face wracked with fear and hurt. "I know I shouldn't have gone with him. I shouldn't have lied to my parents. I told them I was going to Jenna's for a sleepover."

"What did Tyler do, Lily? How did this happen?" Genie ran her finger above Lily's brow.

Lily held onto the desk, her knuckles turning white. "He got so mad at me. He called me a cock tease and said I should feel lucky he even paid attention to me, cause I'm so ugly. Then he picked up a rock and threw it at me. I tried to turn away, but it hit me here." She pointed to her ribs. "I started to run, but he caught me. He grabbed me by the hair and smashed my face into a tree."

Genie bit her lip. If she said anything too negative, Lily might clam up or even run away. "That must have been awful, Lily. What happened then?"

"I guess I blacked out for a little while. When I came to, I was on the ground and Tyler was gone. I walked to Jenna's house from there. She hid me in her bedroom—her parents were out last night. This morning, I stayed in her room until her parents went to work. Jenna cut school at lunch and came to check on me. That's when she told me I should come and talk to you. I was afraid in case Tyler saw me, so Jenna walked me here. She told me she'd have her brother Wade beat the shit out of Tyler if he tried anything. Wade's on the football team." Her lips twisted into a little smile. "Sorry about saying 'shit', Miss Halloran."

Genie took Lily by the hand and said, "Lily, come with me to the nurse's office. You know you're going to have to tell your parents about this sometime."

"But Miss Halloran, my father will get so mad!"

"He won't punish you, Lily. I'm sure about that."

"I don't mean that. My father hunts wild boar in the hills. He has guns. He might get so mad he'll go after Tyler. If my Dad shoots Tyler, he'll be in trouble. I don't want my Dad to go to jail."

Genie went numb. How many other girls were like Lily and herself, girls who felt more protective of their fathers and brothers than they did of themselves? She took a deep breath, then willed herself to do what was needed. For the next few hours she stayed with Lily and her parents as they visited the emergency room and spoke to a police officer. Lily had insisted she stay with her, and Mr. and Mrs. Wagner agreed. Lily had spoken to them about Ms. Halloran before, and they could see Genie's calming effect on their daughter. When Lily was discharged from the emergency room—she'd need reconstructive surgery on her face, and her ribs had been badly bruised—Genie drove herself home.

It was after ten when she got home, and Charlie was waiting for her.

"How's Lily?" he said, folding Genie into his arms.

Genie held on tight, finally letting the tears flow.

"Hey," Charlie said. "What is it? She'll be okay, won't she?" He led Genie over to the couch and sat down next to her.

198

Genie put her head in her hands and tried to calm down. "She'll be okay, physically. I worry about how she'll deal with this emotionally, though. At least she won't have to see her attacker at school." She wiped her hand across her eyes. "The police said that the boy who did this to her would probably be charged with aggravated assault. He's seventeen, so I'm not sure what that means, but I know the school will kick him out. Jenner Academy has a zero tolerance policy on violence, even when it happens off school grounds." Genie started sobbing.

Charlie got up and came back with a glass of water and a box of Kleenex. When she'd calmed down, he said, "This isn't just about Lily, is it? I know you care about that girl, but there's more going on here. Can you tell me about what happened to you, Genie? What that guy did to you... I mean, you don't have to. But I want to listen if you want to tell me."

Genie looked into Charlie's eyes. She'd only known this man a few months, but she wanted him to understand her. She told him everything—from Victor trying to kill her and her keeping it secret from her parents, to his painful betrayal in Paris. Charlie was the first man she'd confided in since then and as she spoke she felt lighter, less burdened. They talked until nearly one in the morning, then fell into bed. Before they went to sleep, Charlie suggested that Genie sign up for kick-boxing classes. He'd heard that martial arts could help women who'd been physically abused, and he wanted Genie to feel like she could take care of herself no matter what the circumstances. Genie murmured her agreement, and was able to sleep, feeling safe in Charlie's arms.

CHAPTER THIRTY-FIVE

It was a drizzly morning, the Saturday before Thanksgiving. Genie had made pumpkin bread the night before and now she wrapped the sliced loaf in waxed paper. Charlie had told her his friend Jerry had a sweet tooth, though "tooth" too neatly described his dental condition. Jerry had spent over twenty years in prison and hadn't found his way after his release. Years of hard living on the streets had robbed Jerry of many things, including his health and most of his teeth. When Charlie had learned that Jerry was showing signs of dementia he'd managed a miracle and got him placed in a small nursing home on the outskirts of Santa Rosa. Charlie had followed a life path that hadn't brought him much wealth, but he had good friends from college who had done well financially. As Charlie told them when he occasionally hit them up for money to help people like Jerry, "Fifty thousand is a drop in the bucket for you, but for them it's life and dignity. That's a pretty small price to pay for a big deposit in the karma bank." Those guys valued their friendship with Charlie enough to never say no, nor to resent Charlie for asking.

When Charlie had asked Genie to go with him to visit Jerry, she'd agreed. She wouldn't tell him that it made her a little nervous to spend time with someone whose Alzheimer's disease was becoming more severe. She was afraid she might not know how to behave around Jerry. She'd put in an appearance, be pleasant, and let Charlie do the talking. They wouldn't stay long, Charlie had said. They had plans to meet friends for an early dinner, and anyway, Jerry got tired easily these days.

As they exited Highway 101 and drove west the rain picked up. The windshield wipers in Charlie's venerable Corolla clacked back and forth, discouraging conversation. They climbed and descended gentle hillsides covered with grapevines. A few days ago those vines had glowed yellow in the unseasonably balmy weather, golden leaves covering cordons splayed out upon the trellises. Now the wet wind shook them to the ground, leaving sodden piles among the tidy rows. Genie told herself the rain was better than all the snow she'd had to shovel back home. Still, she wished the day were cheerier, given where they were headed. The only time she'd ever been to a nursing home was when she and Debra had gone to visit Debra's grandfather, called Pops. Genie didn't remember much except the smell of disinfectant and urine and the sad moans of a patient on Pops' floor.

They got off the main road and drove down a narrow lane that sloped sharply on either side. Genie had never gotten used to those drainage ditches, a common feature of rural Sonoma County. They passed a sign that said "Heart's Rest—1000 feet."

"That's it," Charlie said. He pulled into a small parking area next to what looked like a large, single-story stucco house. Turning to Genie, he put his hand on her arm. "Don't be nervous. He's gonna love you."

They dashed through the rain to the front door, Genie holding tight to the pumpkin loaf. Inside, a woman seated near a large fireplace looked up from the table she shared with two much older women. They were threading popcorn and cranberries. The younger woman said, "Hello, there. Who are you here to see on this lovely day?"

"Hello to you, too, Melanie" Charlie said.

The woman pulled a pair of glasses out of the pocket of her apron. She got up and said, "Oh, Charlie! I'm blind as a bat without my glasses unless I'm doing close work." She walked over and gave Charlie a hug. "You're here to see Jerry. Let me take you to him." She looked over at Genie. "Is that something sweet? Jerry will love it!" She put out her hand, "Melanie Kantor. Are you Charlie's friend?"

Genie shook Melanie's hand. "Yes. Actually, I'm Charlie's fiancée. My name's Genie Halloran."

"Fiancée?" Melanie leaned over and kissed Charlie on the cheek. "Congratulations! I have some sparkling cider in the kitchen. Let me bring it over to you two and Jerry. He'll want to celebrate, too." She put her hands out and said, "If you give me that, I can put it on a plate for you."

Genie handed her the pumpkin loaf. Melanie smiled and said, "Jerry's sitting in the solarium, just waiting for the sun to come out. Ever the optimist. If you two want to join him, I'll bring you the goodies in a minute."

Genie and Charlie walked down a wide hallway decorated with fall leaves. The air was cinnamon-scented, and classical guitar music played softly. "This place is beautiful," Genie said. "The last nursing home I visited was nothing like this."

Charlie nodded. "It's a shame that more places aren't like this. The emphasis is on encouraging the residents to feel at home and part of a community. There are no more than eighteen people here at any time, and they get top-notch care. Little enough for a rich society like ours to do for its citizens, right? The fact is, though, this place is funded mostly by an anonymous bequest. It could never operate like this otherwise."

At the end of the hallway, they emerged into a large room with floor-to-ceiling windows on three sides. The rain streaked down the glass on the far side, but despite the weather, the room was cheerful. One woman sat quietly reading a book, while a table of four men played cards. Just beyond them a small man sat looking out the window. Charlie said, "That's Jerry over there. He'll probably call me 'chief' or 'pal'—I doubt he'll really know who I am. It doesn't matter. He'll be happy to see us both."

They walked around to face Jerry, who looked up at Genie with rheumy eyes. The skin on his face was remarkably smooth but darkened from years of exposure. When he smiled, only three teeth were visible on top, one on the bottom.

Charlie got down on one knee and put his hand on the old man's shoulder. "Hey, Jerry, my friend. It's Charlie. I've come to say Happy Thanksgiving to you."

Jerry slowly took his eyes off Genie and looked toward Charlie. His smile faded for a moment, as if he was trying to take in this new information. Then he beamed and sat forward, saying, "Hey, there, pal! Where ya been so long?"

Charlie shook his hand and said, "Oh, you know me, Jerry. Just trying to stay out of trouble."

Jerry threw his head back and laughed. "That's a good one, pal. You always were a card, even when we were boys."

Charlie stood and said, "I'm going to bring some chairs over here, Jerry. Then I want to introduce you to someone."

Genie stood a few feet away, not sure what to say to Jerry, who looked at her again, smiling.

Charlie returned with two wooden folding chairs that he placed squarely in front of Jerry. He took the old man's hand again and said, "How've you been, Jerry?"

Jerry smiled tentatively and shook his head slowly, clearly confused.

Charlie put his arm around Genie and said, "I want you to meet someone. She baked you some pumpkin bread. Her name is Genie."

Jerry took Genie's outstretched hand in his. He held on gently and looked at her, then leaned forward and brushed a curl that had spilled out of her short ponytail. "Lillian," he whispered. "You always had such pretty hair."

"Oh," Genie said, looking at Charlie. She looked back at Jerry and said, "My name's—"

Charlie squeezed her shoulder lightly. "Jerry, who is Lillian?" he said, putting his hand on Jerry's knee.

Jerry continued to hold Genie's hand, smiling uncertainly. Then he looked at Charlie, his face showing just a hint of impatience. "Hey, chief. You know Lillian. She's my big sister. She practically raised me when Ma had to go out and work." He looked back at Genie. "Lillian, you look great. I missed you, you know."

Genie hesitated, then said, "I missed you, too."

"Is Ma home yet? I promised her I'd get that shed out back painted before she got home. She'll be plenty mad at me if I don't."

"I, uh," Genie looked at Charlie, who nodded. "No, Jerry. Ma's not home yet."

204

Melanie appeared holding a tray with three flutes of sparkling cider and a plate of pumpkin bread slices. "Jerry," she said, pulling up a small table. "Look at this! We're celebrating some good news. Your friend Charlie is engaged to be married. Isn't that wonderful?"

Jerry let go of Genie's hand and fixed his eyes on the tray. "Is that cake?" he said.

"It's pumpkin bread, Jerry. Just what we need at Thanksgiving time, right?" Melanie put a piece on a plate and handed it to Jerry.

Jerry took the plate and took a big bite of the bread. "Mmm!" He chewed slowly and smiled.

Melanie handed Genie and Charlie a glass each, then said, "Jerry, do you want to drink a toast to Charlie and Genie? They're going to be married!"

Jerry nodded and accepted the glass from Melanie. He extended it with great formality to Genie, then to Charlie, then took a big gulp. Melanie walked around behind Jerry and said, "That was great, Jerry. Do you want to head back to your room, now? It's after two, and you usually like to take a nap around now." She smiled at Genie and Charlie. "Thanks so much for coming," she said. She helped Jerry to his feet. "Do you want to say so long to your friends?" she said as she put her arm around Jerry's shoulder.

Jerry stopped and looked back at Genie and Charlie. "So long, pals," he said, with a little salute.

Melanie looked back over her shoulder and said, "Thanks again. Happy Thanksgiving."

Genie and Charlie watched as Melanie helped Jerry out of the room. When they'd left, Charlie touched his glass to hers. "You were wonderful with him," she said.

Charlie's eyes were sad, but he smiled. "He's spoken to me about his big sister, though I never heard her name until today. Apparently she died when he was in high school. It wasn't long after her death that he started getting into trouble. Who knows how his life would have gone if she had lived?"

For a moment, the only sounds in the room were the cards being shuffled and the rain.

Genie put her glass on the table. "How do you do it, Charlie?"

Charlie took a sip, then placed his glass next to Genie's. "Do what?" He got to his feet and put his jacket on, then helped Genie into hers.

They walked hand-in-hand, waving to the card players as they left the solarium.

"You can relate to anyone you meet. I've never once seen you aloof or judgmental."

Charlie didn't say anything, but held the front door for her and followed her outside. The rain had stopped, but more dark clouds scudded in from the west. When they were in the car, Charlie started to turn the ignition key, but Genie put her hand on his.

"Really, Charlie," she said. "You're so giving to everyone else. Were you always this way?"

Charlie shrugged and looked out the window, then he turned to her and said, "I dunno, Genie. It just seems so obvious that people carry around a lot of heartache with them. Even the people we think have it made. Scratch the surface and you'll find that the richest guy, the woman who seems to have the world on a string, every one of us holds some sort of hurt. I guess I know how to keep clear of the people who get their kicks by being shitty and cruel, and I home in on everyone else. If I can help someone, I'll do it. It's just that simple, I guess." He started the car and pulled out of the parking lot. Looking at Genie, he said, "I'm not noble, Genie. I'm just living the life I want to live, the way I want to live it. I'm a lucky guy."

He turned the radio on and the sound of Mozart's Adagio in E filled the car. Genie watched his face relax as he listened and kept time with the fingers of his right hand, tapping the steering wheel lightly. She smiled and thought, I'm the lucky one.

CHAPTER THIRTY-SIX

Genie and Charlie had agreed to go back to Massachusetts for their wedding. A trip to California was out of the question for Genie's father, and though Charlie's parents were dead, there was his "Nanny" Pat to consider. Though she was too ornery to admit it, age was slowing her down. Attending the wedding at Genie's parents' house in Waltham would save energy for her usual stream of acid comments and critiques.

Genie was careful as she pinned the carnation on her father's lapel. She hadn't seen him in nearly a year and he'd grown frail, but he was all smiles today. His lovely Genie was home and about to marry a good man. He put his hands on Genie's and said, "Dear, your mother and I are so happy for you. Charlie is a great guy."

"That he is, Dad. He's a lot like you. That must be why I love him." She kissed her father's cheek. He wasn't as tall as he'd been ten years before, and he needed help climbing stairs. In fact, Meara, who'd moved back to her parents' house, had set up the front room, formerly a study, as a bedroom for her parents. Today, though, the house was decorated for a Christmastime wedding. The tree had been moved to the corner of the living room, and folding chairs had been borrowed from the neighbors. Only a few people would attend the ceremony besides Nanny Pat and Genie's parents, siblings, and their kids.

Genie felt nervous flutters when she stood with Charlie and repeated the words spoken by Reverend Ingles, a Unitarian minister who'd worked with Charlie when he'd first started Mercy's Family.

Dave Ingles had relocated to Boston, where he'd become involved in a similar program. Neither Genie nor Charlie had wanted to get married in a church, and, as a special favor to Genie's parents and especially Nanny Pat, Dave had worn his collar and stole, and didn't correct anyone who called him "Father." At Charlie's request, Dave had spoken briefly about Charlie's parents, and about Genie's family. In all, the ceremony was exactly what Genie had wanted. It was all about love.

Later, after she and Charlie had said their vows and the Champagne toasts had been made, Genie sat on the couch between Meara and Debra. Charlie was huddled in a corner with Ragsie and Genie's father, talking about the prospects for the Red Sox come next spring. Though Charlie had lived far from Boston for most of his life, he'd always been a fan of the perpetually unlucky team.

"When is your train?" Meara said.

Genie checked her watch. "Not till six. Ragsie said he'd give us a ride to South Station."

Genie and Charlie would have a short honeymoon in New York before flying back to San Francisco. Ragsie had offered to put them up in the Ritz Carlton in Boston, but Genie had told him that Charlie had wanted to spend time in Manhattan. That wasn't strictly true. Although she and Charlie looked forward to seeing New York decked out for Christmas, she wanted to avoid spending time in Boston. In a city of more than half a million, it was unlikely she'd bump into Victor. She wasn't sure if he even lived there anymore. Still, just knowing he might be near made her jittery. If things had been different, if her parents had been up to it, she would gladly have married Charlie somewhere in Sonoma County—at a winery, among the redwoods, or even at the picnic area at Hood Mountain. California had become her refuge, a place that held only happy memories. Still, she honored her obligations to her family, though every trip to Boston would be tainted by the fear of seeing Victor again.

Debra put her arm around Genie and hugged her tight. "I can't believe we're all back here. Do you know it's been fifteen years for me? Since my parents moved to Arizona, I haven't had a reason to come back. Everything looks so beautiful." She jumped up and stood at the window that looked onto the street. "Look at that snow. Isn't it great? I wish it would snow all night."

A few puffy flakes were falling, but they melted as soon as they hit the street. The early snow would soon taper off, but another storm was forecast for the following week.

"You're staying in a hotel and flying back to California in two days, that's why you like the snow," Meara said. "It's another thing entirely if you have to drive in it."

Debra turned from the window and stuck her tongue out at Meara. Just then Nanny Pat entered the room, shouting, "I want a ride home now. Who'll give me a ride?"

Ragsie stood up, towering over the tiny old woman. Sean followed her into the room and said, "I'll take you. I have to get the kids home anyway."

"You won't put me in the back seat!" Pat said. "I'll be carsick and then you'll be sorry. Besides, they're hardly civilized, those children of yours. Did you hear them giggling when the priest was talking? Shameful!"

Charlie put his arm around the old lady and said, "They're young yet, Pat. They're allowed to be silly."

Pat looked up at Charlie, her adoration plain. "You were never silly at that age, Charlie. You were always so well-behaved. An angel, really."

Charlie looked over at Genie and winked. "That's what I always tell my wife," he said. "I'm an angel, really."

Pat put her hand on Charlie's arm and gave it a squeeze. "And so you are. She's a lucky woman."

Charlie said, "We're both lucky."

Sean's wife Donna came into the room, carrying Pat's coat in one hand, holding her younger son in the other arm.

When they'd gone, Charlie and Genie joined her parents and Meara in the kitchen. It looked the same as it had when Genie was a girl, with a spotless tile countertop and a linoleum floor. The refrigerator was festooned with Christmas-themed drawings and yarn-and-popsicle-stick ornaments done over the years by Ragsie's and Sean's kids. A black-and-white Kit Cat clock kept time over the kitchen sink, its eyes and tail clicking back and forth.

"It was a lovely wedding," Genie's mother said. She sat close to Genie's father, their hands entwined. "I wish you both a long and happy marriage, just like ours has been."

"We'd be blessed to be as happy as you've been, Mrs. Halloran," Charlie said.

"I've told you, you must call me Shona."

Charlie put his and over hers and said, "It's been a long time since my own mother died, and I know she'd love you. May I call you 'Mom' instead?"

"Of course you may." Shona got up and wound her thin arms around Charlie's neck, kissing him on the cheek. She giggled and said, "Oh, that beard tickles. Genie, how do you manage it?"

Genie smiled. "I manage just fine, Ma."

Ragsie came into the room and said, "Hey, Genie, Charlie. We'd better get going if you're gonna make your train."

After many hugs and kisses, Genie and Charlie stood at the door. "We'll come back in June, Ma," she said, giving her mother one more hug. "Maybe we can all go up to Maine."

Genie's father's eyes brimmed. "Just come and see us, Genie. We don't have to go anywhere as long as you're here. You and your new husband."

"We'll be back, Dad," Genie whispered. "I love you." She kissed him on the cheek and took Charlie's hand. She had a lump in her throat as she and Charlie walked out with Ragsie. As it turned out, they were back in April, but not for a happy reason. She was able to spend two days with her father before he died. Charlie looked after Sean's and Ragsie's children while the brothers stood vigil along with their sisters and mother. It was a sad time, but the family was together. And before they left, she and Charlie had extracted a promise from Meara to bring Shona out for a visit.

CHAPTER THIRTY-SEVEN

They'd moved into their new house in Windsor, a small town north of Santa Rosa, more than a week before, but Charlie still had a few boxes to deal with. Some of them were twenty years old and had followed him from one Berkeley apartment to another, and then up to Santa Rosa. They were pretty grungy, even Charlie had to admit that. He'd dragged the boxes outside and sat on an overturned bucket, his coffee mug on the ground beside him. Charlie had promised Genie to look through them and throw away whatever he didn't want. She'd gone shopping with Debra earlier, and had said she'd make him a special lunch as a reward for finishing up the boxes. He suspected he wouldn't go hungry if he didn't finish.

Charlie wasn't really a pack rat, but for him, as for most people, the saying 'out of sight, out of mind' rang true. The boxes had sat unopened for a long time, and he was mildly curious to see what they held. He took a deep breath, then got to work. The first two boxes contained notes and papers from his days at Berkeley, first as a student, then as an instructor. There was nothing of value, nothing he was particularly interested in anymore, so he dumped the contents into a big recycling bin.

There were three boxes left. The contents of the third and fourth were a mishmash of odd household items: plastic measuring cups, a few mugs and bowls, some silverware. Charlie shook his head, remembering the day he'd packed those things. He'd lived with Michelle for six years until the day she told him about the man she'd been seeing. Charlie had been surprised, but not stunned. Michelle had told Charlie when they'd met that she wanted to live, if not in Pacific Heights, then in a large house in the Berkeley hills by the time she was thirty. It was clear that on his adjunct professor's salary Charlie was never going to be able to afford more than a modest home, so Michelle had gone to work for an investments firm in San Francisco. It was there that she'd met Brandon, a venture capitalist who drove a BMW. Before she left him, Michelle reassured Charlie that he'd meet some woman whose values were more in line with his.

He'd heard that Michelle had divorced Brandon when she'd found him cheating. According to a mutual friend, she'd done very well for herself in the settlement and had managed to walk away with a gorgeous Victorian in San Francisco. Charlie chuckled. At least he'd kept the matching Tupperware bowls. He set the household items aside; he'd drop them off at the St. Vincent de Paul Society on his way to work one day.

After a sip of cold coffee, Charlie cut through the tape on the last box. It was dusty and discolored on top; clearly, he'd had it a long time. He dug through the packing paper, now yellow with age, then felt something soft. "Well, I'll be damned," he said under his breath. There was the leather jacket he'd bought for himself when he was a senior in high school. He'd taken it with him to Cal and had worn it nearly every day, even in the summer, when the foggy mornings were often chilly. As he reached for the jacket he could feel something hard inside it. He stuck both arms into the box and scooped out the jacket and whatever it was wrapped around. Walking back into the house, Charlie sat on the couch and set the jacket on the coffee table.

When he unfolded the jacket he caught his breath. He hadn't remembered packing the cedar box away, and it had sat forgotten inside that grimy cardboard for years. Charlie cleared his throat, tight with emotion. Billy had given him this box after he had passed the GED. When Charlie had volunteered at a homeless shelter while he taught at Cal, he'd worked with Billy for months on math and English. He could still see Billy, a hulking twenty-one-year old, working his way through a short practice essay, cursing Charlie good-naturedly as he wrote.

Charlie sat back with the box on his lap. He undid the brass clasp and opened it, knowing what he'd find. As he picked up the small envelope, Genie called from the front of the house.

"Charlie? Are you here?"

"In the living room," Charlie called back. He set the envelope on the couch beside him.

"Sorry I'm so late. Debs and I..." Genie stood in the doorway. "Charlie, what's wrong? You look like you've seen a ghost."

Charlie shrugged. "Maybe I have," he said.

Genie walked over and sat beside him. "You found something that surprised you? Want to talk about it?"

"Sure," he said, running his hand over the smooth lid of the box. He said nothing for a moment, then picked up the envelope and handed it to Genie. "Go ahead and open it. There's a card inside."

Genie did as he asked and pulled out a small card. On the front was a photo of a dog wearing a mortarboard. She opened it and read, 'Thanks for everything, Charlie. You've been a good teacher and a good friend. I won't disappoint you—Billy'

"Who's Billy?" Genie asked, slipping the card back into the envelope.

Charlie ran the back of his knuckles over his beard. "Billy was someone I tried to help, a long time ago."

"From what he wrote in this card, it looks like you did help him, Charlie." Genie's voice was soft.

Charlie put the box back on the table. "He was something else, that kid. His mother abandoned him when he was fifteen, and he lived on the streets for a couple of years until he tried to rob a donut shop. Stupid." He shook his head. "He was seventeen and a half, but the judge decided to sentence him to prison anyway. He did eighteen months, and by some miracle, came out with his soul more or less intact. He even learned woodworking." He knocked on the top of the box. "Pretty nice workmanship, don't you think?" He smiled at Genie, but his tears glistened.

"What happened to him?"

"Well, he got his GED. His plan was to work for the city of Berkeley for a while, then maybe try to get into Vista Community College. He definitely had the brains for it, and the job he'd lined up was a good one: maintenance at the Berkeley Marina. There was a lot of physical work involved and he'd be outside most of the time." Turning to face Genie, he said in a strange voice, "You've been to the Marina; it's a great place, right? Plenty of stuff going on, people having a good time..." He stood and looked out the window at the vineyards. "One day, it was late November, Billy was finishing up, putting his tools in a city truck. A witness saw a scuffle going on and ran for the police. When the police got there, Billy was dead. He'd been stabbed. The police caught the guy who did it, strung out on meth, barely knew his own name. Turns out he'd known Billy in prison and had sold him pot a few times. Of course, he went back to prison and Billy never made it to community college, never made it past twenty-three. Two lives wasted."

Genie got up and put her arm around his shoulder. "How soon after that did you leave Berkeley?"

"I gave notice the day after I heard about Billy. Of course, I finished out the year, but I knew I couldn't keep teaching, publishing, and doing the whole academia thing. My father died not long after, and I had a little money, so I came up here and started Mercy's Family."

Genie gave his shoulder a squeeze. "I think we should keep that box in a place of honor, don't you?"

Charlie ran his fingers over the smooth top of the box. "Good idea." He placed the little box on top of the bookcase, beside the photo of Charlie's parents. He looked at it a little longer, then said, "I haven't quite finished out there with the boxes."

Genie kissed his cheeks. "Close enough," she said. "Let's have lunch."

CHAPTER THIRTY-EIGHT

On a glorious July day, Genie drove to meet her mother and Meara at the little Sonoma County airport. She'd spent the days before the visit cleaning the house. The second bedroom was small, just big enough for two twin beds with a little table between them. On a tight budget after buying the house, Genie had found two sky-blue matelassé coverlets at a thrift shop. What the room lacked in size, it more than made up for with its view. Outside, vineyards stretched in every direction, right up to the tan and sage foothills.

Genie hadn't seen her mother since her father's funeral. She wanted to celebrate getting her out to California, but she was troubled. She and Charlie had found out earlier in the week that she would never be able to conceive. She hadn't grieved at the news, but still felt a pang. Having a child with Charlie would have been wonderful, but she would be glad just to be with him for the rest of her life. And with a new crop of students every year, she could help shape the intellects and guide the lives of scores of children.

After finding a parking spot nearby, Genie went into the outdoor waiting area of the small terminal. Clutching a bouquet of red and purple anemones, she scanned the sky. Then, there it was, a small commuter jet. After the plane landed, a short line of passengers made their way down the stairs and across the tarmac. The last people out were Meara and Genie's mother, who had linked her arm through Meara's. They walked across the tarmac slowly, both of them looking for Genie. When they came through the old-fashioned turnstile gate, Genie ran to them and put her arm around her mother's shoulder, handing Meara the flowers.

All three women huddled together, weeping and laughing. Genie's mother blinked in the bright sunshine. "It's so lovely here, Genie," she said, letting Genie guide her into the terminal to get the bags.

"Warm, but no humidity," Meara said. "It was like a steam bath for the last week back home." She pulled her hair out of a ponytail and gave it a shake.

"Good hair weather," Genie and Meara said at the same time.

As they drove the short distance to her house Genie said, "Charlie won't be home till later tonight, so I thought we might have an early dinner, just the three of us. You're on East Coast time, so to you it's," she checked her wrist, "nearly seven o'clock. I've made some cold salads, and there's bread from a local bakery. Sound good?"

"Will there be wine, too? Something from one of those vineyards we saw when we landed?" Meara said.

"Ed sent me a couple of his Chardonnays, and one's in the fridge. Do you like white wine?"

Meara snorted. "Is the Pope Catholic?"

"How about you, Mom?" Genie looked in her rear-view mirror. Her mother was sleeping, her hands resting on her lap.

"How has she been?" Genie said in a quiet voice.

"Oh, you know. She misses Dad, but she's coping okay. She sees the grandkids a couple of times a week, and that's a real shot in the arm for her."

Genie pursed her lips, willing herself not to cry. If the news had been different, if she and Charlie could have a child...She had thought about what it would have been like to introduce her child to her mother, how wonderful it would be to see her mother hold her baby. She turned her head so Meara wouldn't see her face.

"What is it, Genie?"

"Nothing," Genie said, exiting the freeway. "Everything's fine."

"Don't shit a shitter," Meara said. "Tell me now while Ma's asleep. Are you and Charlie okay?"

Genie wiped a tear, angry at herself. "Charlie and I are wonderful, Meara. It's just that we just found out that we—I mean, I—can't have a baby." She waved her hand in front of her face. "I'm just being stupid about this now. I guess seeing you and Ma has got me emotional."

Meara put her hand on Genie's arm. "You're not being stu-pid," Meara said. "Having a baby is a really big deal, Genie." She looked out the window and said, "Would you think about adopting?"

"I don't know," Genie said. She turned on the directional and swung onto her street. "We just found out. I guess we'll talk about it. In the meantime, let me get you home. You and Ma have had a long day."

• • •

Genie and Charlie took Meara and Shona all over Sonoma and Marin counties—from the wineries in the Russian River valley to the funky shops in Sebastopol, and down the coast from Fort

Ross to Point Reyes National Seashore. They even spent a day hitting the tourist spots in San Francisco. On the last day of their trip, Genie packed a picnic lunch for their visit to Armstrong Redwoods State Natural Reserve. Charlie offered Shona his arm as they walked the soft paths among the towering old trees. As they stood in front of the "Colonel Armstrong" tree, at over fourteen hundred years old the most ancient in the grove, Shona said, "Oh, my. If only Enok were here. He always said he wanted to see the redwoods." She dug a tissue out of her purse and dabbed her eyes.

Genie put her arm around her mother, feeling how thin she'd become in the last year. "Mom, you know Dad's with you here in this beautiful place."

The four of them stood silent a moment, the only sound a far-off owl hoo-hooing. Although it was a warm day, the wide, lofty branches filtered the sunlight and cooled the air. The stillness and shadows gave the forest a church-like quality. Genie offered up a silent prayer of thanks that she was able to bring her mother here.

Later, after they'd had their lunch and driven home, Genie sat outside with her mother and sister as Charlie made some calls for work.

"It's wonderful to see you so happy, Genie," Shona said. She took a sip of Chardonnay, something she'd rarely do at home. She closed her eyes and eased back against the Adirondack chair, lazily scratching the top of Tramp's head.

"You look like you belong out here, Mom," Meara said. "You and Genie: a couple of California girls."

Shona smiled. "Not me. It's beautiful out here, but I could never leave my home."

"Yeah, you'd really miss the blizzards and the cold. Who wouldn't?" Meara popped a fig into her mouth.

"You're both welcome here any time," Genie said. She took her mother's hand. "Any time, Mom."

Shona opened one eye and smiled. "Be careful what you say, Genie. I might just take you up on it."

"I hope you will." Genie got up and kissed the top of Shona's head, then went inside to get Charlie. He'd worked enough for one day.

CHAPTER THIRTY-NINE

Genie hummed to herself as she put the rolls on the baking sheet. It was a Saturday and she'd received a phone call that would make a huge change in their lives. She couldn't wait to tell Charlie about the three-book contract her agent had secured. After the success of her first teen romance novel, publishers had taken notice. Now she could write full-time if she wanted to, but she'd keep teaching. She didn't mind being busy doing the two things she loved. As usual, Charlie had gone to his office to do paperwork. He was so busy with meetings, phone calls, and emails all week that Saturdays were almost always set aside for him to do the necessary bookkeeping and grant-writing that kept Mercy's Family going. His small staff was as dedicated as he was, and Genie had asked him to bring the three of them home for dinner. She'd made lasagna and a big salad. Paired with sourdough rolls and a great California red, it would be a feast. When Charlie came home, though, he was alone.

"Where are the others?" Genie said, looking behind Charlie.

"At the last minute Laetitia got a call to babysit her grandkids, and Maria said she was coming down with something and didn't want us to catch it. I think Max felt a little awkward about coming here by himself, so we agreed we'd do it another time. Man, that lasagna smells good," Charlie uncorked a bottle of J pinot noir and grabbed three glasses.

"I thought you said that the others weren't coming. Who's the extra glass for?"

"Marty was at the office today checking with Laetitia on the budget. There's a board meeting next week." He poured the wine and took a sip. "He said he'd follow me."

Marty Edmund was chairman of board of Mercy's Family. A successful lawyer and venture capitalist, he'd moved with his wife Estelle in Sonoma County a few years before. Marty had wanted to spend more time with his wife, who'd been ill for years. After her death Marty had given up his law practice to devote himself to working with local charities.

"I hear a car," Charlie said. "That must be him. Hey, you don't mind that I invited him, do you?"

Genie pulled the giant pan of lasagna out of the oven. "Of course not. I made enough for an army. And anyway, I'm glad Marty agreed to come. It's been hard to get him to do social things since Estelle died."

The doorbell rang. "It's open, Marty!" Charlie called. "Come into the kitchen and have some wine."

"Something smells wonderful," Marty said as he entered the kitchen. He was a tall, trim man with a full head of grey hair. In his late fifties, he still had the physique of the cross-country runner he'd been in college. Marty handed a small bouquet of cornflowers and daisies to Genie. "For the chef," he said, leaning down to kiss her on the cheek.

"Oh, Marty, you didn't have to! But I'm glad you did. Wherever did you get cornflowers?" She opened a cabinet and found a handmade jug, just perfect for the little bouquet.

"I have my sources," Marty said, accepting a glass of wine from Charlie.

"Shall we eat here in the kitchen?" Genie said. "Marty, why don't you sit down with Charlie while I get the plates and silverware?"

"Can I help?" Charlie said.

"No, go sit with Marty. It was bad enough you had to work on a Saturday. Just relax."

Marty looked around the cozy kitchen from the small table in the corner. He laughed. "Estelle always loved that clock," pointing to the Kit Cat clock on the wall.

"It used to be in my parents' kitchen," Genie said, bringing the lasagna to the table. "I remember loving it when I was a little girl. To tell you the truth, the ticking kind of gets on my nerves now, but you can't hear it in the rest of the house. Still, it makes me smile whenever I look at it."

Charlie cut a portion of lasagna and put it on Marty's plate. "Our cat thinks we got it to honor him."

Genie passed Marty a basket of warm sourdough rolls. "Eat," she said. "You're looking too thin."

Marty rolled his eyes. "Yes, Mom," he said, taking two rolls. "It's all the running I've been doing. I found this trainer who takes me out to Shell Beach and we run up and down the coastal trails. It's tough, I'll tell you, but man, the beauty of the place! It almost makes you forget how much you hurt." He took a bite of lasagna and washed it down with some wine. "Mmm! Genie, this is great. Glad I ran into you today, Charlie," he said, nudging Charlie with his elbow.

"You're welcome anytime, Marty," Genie said. She caught Marty's eye and saw he was tearing up.

"Sorry." Marty used his napkin to wipe his eyes. "I've been trying to get out more. Estelle nagged me so much about that before she passed. She made me promise that I'd see you guys and that I'd get out into the world. Those last two months before she died, I never once left the ranch. Frieda did all the shopping and cooking...she really bailed me out." He breathed deeply and took another sip of wine.

"She and Eduardo are still at the ranch?"

Marty nodded. "For a while. They plan to leave in a few months, though. Their kids are all down in Santa Maria now, and there's a grandchild on the way. Who could resist that, right?" He had a sad smile on his face. Years before, Marty and his son had argued, and Alec had taken off. Estelle had stayed in touch with their son, who had moved to Australia. When Estelle had died, Alec and his wife and son had come to the funeral, but they'd left the next day. Marty never talked about it, but Genie knew how much the estrangement hurt him.

He shook his head and sat straighter. "Anyway, I decided I'm going to sell the place. It's way too much work to take care of, and now with Estelle gone..."

"Are you going to move back to Palo Alto?" Genie asked. She'd hate to see him go; he'd been such a help to Charlie at Mercy's Family. She'd become fond of him and would miss his friendship, too.

Marty laughed. "No way. I'm not getting near Silicon Valley ever again. As a matter of fact, I'm surprised your friend Ed hasn't mentioned it. He pretty much set this up for me. I'm buying Elysian Farms. What a cliché, right? Rich guy buys a boutique winery."

Charlie put his arm around Marty. "That's fantastic, Marty! Are you going to live in that gorgeous house on the property? We'll practically be neighbors."

Elysian Farms was a small winery situated northwest of Windsor. It had a reputation for producing some of the best red wines in the county, maybe in the state. The winemaker, an eccentric Frenchman who went by the single name Claude, was known to be exacting and a little crazy. Still, his wine was highly rated by the critics year after year.

"You're not planning to become the new Claude, are you?" Charlie said, pouring Genie a little more wine.

Marty shook his head. "No, Claude comes with the deal. As a matter of fact, the sale could only go through with Claude's approval. I had to have an interview with the great man himself."

"Well, I think that's great, Marty," Genie said, resting her hand on his arm. "I hope you'll have us over a lot. And you should make a point of hanging out with us here, too."

Marty put his hand around Genie's. "I will, I promise." He pushed his chair back from the table and looked around the little kitchen again. "You know, when I'm here with you two I feel closer to Estelle. Not in a sad way, though. I just remember how good it felt to spend time with her doing little things: eating dinner, walking around the ranch, sitting inside and listening to the rain. I was busy with my go-go career for so long that I missed out on those things. Thank God we moved here before it was too late. And of course, we met you guys."

"Well, the road goes both ways, Marty. If you hadn't come along and joined the board when you did, I don't know if Mercy's

Family would have made it." Charlie got up and cleared the plates off the table.

"I didn't do that much, Charlie. Just a few adjustments to your fundraising campaigns and a little tweaking of the budget."

"Face it," Charlie said, taking the silverware to the sink, "I'm not great with numbers. Never was."

Marty shook his head. "I've known a lot of guys who had great heads for numbers but had exactly zero heart. Stay the way you are, Charlie." He winked at Genie. "Don't ever let him change."

Genie stood up and smiled. "Not much chance of that." She opened the refrigerator and pulled out a lemon meringue pie. "Who wants dessert?" she said.

Later, after Marty had left, Genie and Charlie sat close together on the couch. The gas fire was on and Tramp lay on the rug in front of it, stretched out, belly exposed to the heat. Genie put her head on Charlie's lap and closed her eyes as he stroked her hair.

"I'm glad you brought Marty home with you," Genie said. "It's been a while since we've seen him. Now that he's moving closer, I hope we'll see more of him."

"I think we will," Charlie said. "Selling the ranch is a good move for him. That place is beautiful, but way too isolated."

"And we'll have him here a lot," Genie said. "He needs his friends."

"Yeah," Charlie said, leaning back against the sofa. "I could get used to this." He stretched his feet out toward the fire.

Genie smiled. "Me too. Hey, I have something to tell you. I didn't want to say anything when Marty was here, though. I got a call from Philip today."

"How is that agent of yours?"

"He was the bearer of glad tidings. I've been offered a three-book contract."

Charlie pumped his fist. "That's fantastic! You've been working so hard; you deserve this, Genie." He leaned down and kissed the tip of her nose.

Genie smiled. "I'll start writing again on Monday. I declare tomorrow a day off for both of us." She sat up and faced Charlie. "What shall we do?"

Charlie put his hand on the back of her head and guided her toward him. "I can think of a few things," he said, and kissed her. "We can spend all day in bed, then eat lasagna all night."

"Let's plan on some exercise, too. I want to keep you healthy," she said, kissing Charlie's cheek. She tried to shake the image of Marty's sad face. "I intend to grow old with you. Will you love me when I'm wrinkled and grey?"

"I'll love you forever," Charlie said.

CHAPTER FORTY

Debra and Ed sat at a picnic table in the shade, slightly apart from the crowd that milled through the Windsor Farmers Market. Ed had just bought cappuccinos from the local café; Debra sipped hers as she read last week's Press Democrat. "I can't believe this interview with Genie," she said. "And the photo of her and Charlie is priceless."

She passed the paper to Ed, who laughed. "Figures the cat's in the center of the picture."

Debra crooked an eyebrow. "You know that cat rules their lives." She looked over at the crowd, and waved. "There they are now."

"Sorry we're late," Genie said, a little breathless. "It's getting harder every week to find a parking space around here."

Charlie put his arm around Genie's waist. "Windsor's a victim of its own success. Of course, now it can boast a famous author." He looked down at the paper on the table. "I see you're finally getting around to reading about your best friend."

Debra picked up the paper and swatted Charlie gently with it. "It's been sitting under a pile of magazines. The boys were home this week and everything is a mess. But that article, Genie...it's so complimentary."

"Embarrassingly so," Genie said. "Apparently it got picked up by the Globe. Meara said she saw it a few days ago.

"So you're famous in Boston, too?"

Charlie took the paper and smiled. "That's a great photo of Tramp, isn't it?"

"We were just talking about your cat-worshipping tendencies," Ed said. He got up and stretched. "Well, shall we see what looks good here? I have to be at the winery by one, unfortunately."

They wandered through the crowd, stopping to try slices of peaches and tomatoes set out by the vendors. While Ed and Debra picked out food for lunch, Genie walked up to a small booth selling macramé plant holders.

"Didn't you get this macramé stuff out of your system in the seventies?" Charlie said as he joined her.

"It's these things, these little plants. They don't need water. I'm thinking you should get some for your office since you've killed every other plant I've given you." Genie pulled a small pot suspended in a macramé holder closer and inspected the tiny plant with spindly leaves. "They're called air plants. They don't need soil or water. Kind of cool, don't you think?" She looked over at Charlie, then froze. Just twenty feet away, a tall, blond man stood watching her. He wore sunglasses and a fedora, but the way he held himself looked so much like Victor. She stared at him for a few seconds then turned away. She let go of the plant and grabbed Charlie's hand.

"Hey, are you all right, Genie? You just went really pale."

Genie said nothing and took a tentative glance back to where she'd seen the man. There was no one there but a young mother and her toddler son.

"Genie?" Charlie put his arm around her. "Are you okay? Your hand's like ice."

Genie looked around, down one end of the market and up the other. She couldn't see that tall man anywhere. She shook her head and smiled at Charlie. "I'm fine. I think I'm just hungry."

Charlie kissed her cheek. "Well, we'll fix that right away. Here come Debra and Ed with some goodies. We'll be out at the winery in twenty minutes. Do you want me to get you a peach or something to tide you over?"

Genie looked around once more, then said, "No, I can wait till lunch." She turned to Debra, not wanting to make eye contact with Charlie. "What did you guys get? Looks like you bought out the market!"

"Genie's starving," Charlie said. "Me too. Shall we head out?"

"Let's take our car," Debra said. "Ed has to stay at the winery until later tonight; he can catch a ride home."

Debra and Genie got into the backseat of Ed's Outback. Fortunately for Genie, Charlie started talking baseball on the way to the winery. He and Debra were rabid Red Sox fans, and Ed was a Giants fan. Genie had heard it all before: the superiority of the American League over the National League, the validity of using a designated hitter, Fenway Park versus the newer stadiums. While the three of them chattered away, Genie looked out the window and tried to convince herself that the man she'd seen couldn't have been Victor. After all, what would he be doing in a poky little place like Windsor? If he ever came to the Bay area he'd stick close to San Francisco or maybe Marin County, right? He'd never drive an hour up to the North Bay. On the other hand, they were in wine country, and the rolling hills and vineyards had been catnip to photographers going back decades. If he really did show up at the Farmers Market, had he seen her? Would he...a sharp poke in her arm pulled Genie out of her reverie.

"Jesus, Genie, what planet were you on?" Debra's face was only inches away. "I asked you three times about those air plants you looked at."

"Air plants?" Genie tried to hide her confusion by pretending to yawn. "Sorry, I'm a little out of it I guess."

Charlie turned around, a grin on his face. "I told you, Debs. She's been in the clouds since we started walking around the market." He winked at Genie and said, "We're almost there, Genie. Once you've eaten you'll be fine."

Genie sat back, hoping Debra hadn't noticed anything unusual, but she could feel her friend's eyes on her the rest of the way.

When they got to the winery, Ed went straight into the tank room to talk to Luis, the assistant winemaker. Debra and Charlie set out the food on a patio shaded by olive trees, while Genie played with Frodo, Luis' dog.

"Come and get it!" Debra shouted.

Genie threw the dilapidated football once more for Frodo, then walked over to join Debra and Charlie. "Aren't we going to wait for Ed?"

"He'll be back in a few minutes. Besides, you need to eat," Debra said, motioning for Genie to sit down. "Maybe you'll be less of a space cadet if you have some food."

They had started in on the olive-and-gruyere bread along with the tomatoes and cucumbers Charlie had sliced when Ed came out, holding an open bottle of red wine and four wine glasses.

"Sorry about that," Ed said. "Crisis averted, thanks to Luis. Looks like I can go home after lunch."

Charlie picked up the wine and pulled his reading glasses out of his pocket. "What's this?" He inspected the label, then handed the bottle back to Ed.

Ed shrugged as he poured the wine. "It's from a new place on the coast. The winemaker was here the other day and brought a few bottles. It's not bad for a first bottling, I guess."

Genie took a sip of her wine, then another. Again, she let the other three chat while she pondered whether she'd really seen Victor after all. The more she thought of it, the sillier it seemed. Still, even the thought of being near him again left her feeling shaken. When lunch was over, she picked up the plates and utensils and followed Debra into the kitchen behind the tasting room. Debra ran hot water and placed the wine glasses in the sink while Genie put the other things in the dishwasher.

As she rinsed a glass, Debra said, "What's up with you today? Are you feeling okay?"

Genie didn't say anything at first. She shut the dishwasher door, pushed the 'on' button, and turned to face her friend. "You're going to think I'm crazy," she said, folding her arms. "I think I might be crazy, actually."

"Why? What's bugging you?"

"Today at the farmers'...I thought I saw...um...I thought I saw Victor."

Debra bobbled the glass she was drying, managing to put it on the counter without dropping it. "Victor? What would he be doing in Windsor? What did you see, exactly?"

"I knew you'd think I was nuts," Genie said. "It was just, well, this guy was tall and blond, like Victor."

"His face? Did you see his face?"

"Not really. The guy was wearing sunglasses and a fedora."

Debra rolled her eyes. "Perfect hat for that douche." She looked serious again and put her hand on Genie's arm. "I'm sure it wasn't him, Genie. After all these years, how likely is it that he'd show up here?"

"You're right," Genie said. "It was more the way he stood there and looked at me. It was only a few seconds, though. He disappeared right after that. I'm sure you're right; it couldn't have been him."

Debra squeezed her arm. "No, but I can see why you'd be shook up. If I ever saw that creep again, I'd be pretty skeeved out, too."

"You won't say anything to Charlie, will you?" Genie looked outside. Charlie and Ed were playing with Frodo. "I feel dumb enough as it is. I don't want him to think he has a loon for a wife."

"He'd never think that, Genie. Charlie worships you." Debra put the glasses away, then grabbed Genie's hand. "Let's go! Now that Ed can come home, I have some work for him in the backyard. He'll be so pleased."

Genie laughed. "Lucky guy! Come to think of it, Charlie promised to fix the window in the bedroom."

The two of them went out to join their unsuspecting husbands.

CHAPTER FORTY-ONE

It was late, but Genie couldn't sleep. She and Charlie would be leaving from SFO in the morning for their Christmas trip to Boston, and they had to make an early start. She knew she'd just lie awake if she stayed in bed, so she slipped into the study to check her email. Tramp didn't stir from his place on the window sill, but she crept quietly anyway, not wanting to wake Charlie.

Genie scrolled through the list, happy as always to see email from her readers. One message popped out from the others, and while she was reading, she heard Charlie get up.

"What's going on?" Charlie said with a yawn.

"Go back to bed. I just want to read one thing. It's that interview from that online magazine I told you about. You know, the one for young adult readers."

Charlie pulled up a chair beside her. "You mean "Young Hot Sex" magazine?

She gave him a side eye. "No, it's called "Young Love," and you know it." The page appeared and Genie leaned forward. "Want to read it?"

"Sure," Charlie said. "Why sleep when you can read?"

Young Love Blog—December 2011

Interview with Genie Halloran

We're thrilled to end the year with our interview with Genie Halloran, author of best-selling young adult romance novels such as "Again and Again" and "Whisper Kisses". Genie lives in Windsor, California, and teaches high school English. She's been writing for nearly twenty years and says her students inspire her with their fresh ideas and openness. She's been living a real-life romance of her own with Charlie Maguire, her husband of fifteen years. Here's our Q & A with Genie:

YL: Your books tend to run against the latest trends in Young Adult romance, in that they're unabashedly, well, so darned romantic. They've been called throwbacks to an earlier time. What do you think?

GH: I know that YA novels have headed into all sorts of directions, from gritty stories torn from the headlines to sci-fi and fantasy novels that feature young heroes fighting scary villains. Those books are great, and I envy the inventiveness of the authors. I guess I'm just more down-to-earth. I've been a high school teacher for a long time, and I've tried to be a careful observer. I see my students— girls and boys—as they discover love for the first time, go through crushes, and have their hearts broken. I haven't met one yet who doesn't yearn for a happy ending, whatever that might mean to a fifteen-year-old.

YL: Tell us about your own romance, Genie. How did you meet your husband Charlie?

GH: Charlie is incredibly committed to social justice, so it's not surprising that we met for the first time at an event to support farm workers' rights.

YL: What's one thing that's unique about you and Charlie?

GH: Well, I wear a wedding band, but Charlie wears a gold Celtic knot on a chain around his neck. He would have worn a wedding ring, but he'd crushed the fingers on his left hand when he was a teenager. He was helping a friend move a piano, and well, things turned out badly. Rather than have him wear a ring on his right hand, I thought the lover's knot would be more special. He's never taken it off since our wedding day.

YL: And it's been happily ever after for you two. But there must have been others before Charlie...

GH: There were, but no one as special, as wonderful as Charlie. I think part of the reason I write stories that focus on traditional romance is that I had pined away (do people really pine away these days?) for so many years, hoping to meet a really good, solid man. I finally did, and in time for my late father to meet him. I'll always be grateful for that.

YL: I take it your Dad approved.

GH: He did, indeed.

YL: Still, what about those other guys? Any bad boys? Did anyone ever break your heart?

GH: There was one guy, someone who hurt me pretty badly.

YL: Are you ever tempted to base a character on him?

GH: No, I wouldn't want to spend time with someone like that again, even if I had made him up. Over the years I've come to realize that something important in that man's soul was badly broken. I don't think he can ever be happy, and I'm afraid he'd never make anyone else happy. In fact, I think he goes out of his way to make others feel bad. It's pretty sad, really. A real waste of a life.

238

YL: You sound like you've forgiven him.

GH: Well, I pity him. I don't know if that's the same thing.

YL: Well, there's nothing pitiable about your sales, Genie. Everything you write has been a best-seller. What's up next?

GH: I'm in the middle of a first draft, so I can't say much. I will say it involves an American kid who befriends an Italian exchange student.

YL: Sounds dreamy. Thanks for taking time with the "Young Love" blog, Genie. Best of luck to you and Happy New Year!

Genie closed the browser window and turned to Charlie. "Ready to go back to bed?"

Charlie put his arm around her. "I'm always ready to go to bed with you. Even if it's only to sleep."

She turned off the computer and they left the room. Tramp stood up, stretched his spine, flexed his toes, then turned around and settled back to his long nap.

CHAPTER FORTY-TWO

Genie stood at the baggage carousel, wondering how many hours of her life she'd frittered away at Logan Airport. Their plane had landed over half an hour before, but there she stood with all the other San Francisco passengers, wearing winter coats and eyeing the dismal weather beyond the doors. She and Charlie had long ago agreed that they'd make their Christmas visit to Boston every other year, but this year was different. Genie's mother had passed away in May, and Genie wanted to be there for Meara and her brothers. She was especially concerned about her niece Beatrice, who'd been close to her grandmother.

The alarm announced the arrival of the bags, which clumped together at crazy angles on the sluggish belt. Genie looked around for Charlie. He'd gone to find Beatrice, who'd called Genie's cell phone to say she'd driven to the wrong terminal. When their bags appeared, dead last, Genie did a clean and jerk to get them off the belt. The checked bags were filled with gifts. They'd gone overboard this year, but they could afford it. Genie's books were selling well.

"Auntie Gee!"

Genie looked past knots of bedraggled passengers to see Beatrice running through the dingy baggage area, her black hair flying. Her beautiful niece was a freshman at Boston University, where she balanced a heavy academic load with rowing on the Terriers women's crew team. She held out her arms and Beatrice hugged her tight, her glossy black head reaching only to Genie's shoulders.

"Merry Christmas! How's my little Bee?" Genie said, cupping Beatrice's face in her hands. She looked around. "What have you done with your uncle?"

Beatrice giggled. "He's parking my car in a legal spot." She looked around. "He said we should meet him outside. Oh! There he is!"

Charlie had a big smile on his face as he walked over. He brushed snow from his hair and said, "I see you managed the luggage again."

Genie playfully waved a fist under his nose then turned to Beatrice and said, "Your uncle has a habit of disappearing just before our bags show up. That leaves me to heft them off the belt myself."

Charlie shook his head, a smile still playing on his lips. "You just read an article saying how important it is for women your age to do weight training. I'm only trying to help."

"Women my age, huh? May I remind you that you're three years older than I am? It won't be long before you can buy senior-discounted tickets at the movies."

"Ah, but I wear my maturity so well," Charlie said, winking at Beatrice.

Beatrice took hold of one bag and looped her arm through Genie's. "You two crack me up. I love it when you visit."

The snow had stopped when they got to Meara's house. Beatrice tucked her Mini-Cooper in behind Meara's car and said, "Look, there's Uncle Ragsie's car. I think Noel and Jeff were supposed to be here, too."

Charlie jumped out of the car and helped Genie out of the tiny back seat. "Ooof," Genie said. "That's a tight squeeze."

"I've got the luggage," Beatrice called as she hauled the two big suitcases up the steps.

Charlie smiled. "That's what happens when you're eighteen and on the crew team, I guess."

Once inside, Genie and Charlie were drawn into the boisterous world of the Hallorans. Meara came running out of the kitchen and put her arms around them. Ragsie's sons Noel and Jeff were talking football, while Noel's very pregnant wife napped in a recliner in the corner. There was a knock at the door, announcing Sean with his wife and sons. Soon the family was gathered around the dinner table. As Meara carved the turkey, Charlie opened one of his suitcases and pulled out two bottles of Ridge Zinfandel. Sean handed him a corkscrew, and soon Charlie was pouring the ruby-colored wine for everyone old enough to drink.

"We'll make a special case for you," Meara said to Beatrice.

Beatrice giggled. "You used to be able to drink legally when you were my age," she said, holding her glass out for Charlie.

"She started earlier than eighteen," Genie said, laughing.

"Then we should be able to have some, too," said Braden, one of Sean's sons.

Charlie patted his head. "Nice try, small fry," he said, making a show of passing over his glass. "What are you, fourteen now?"

Braden rolled his eyes. "Almost fifteen."

"Whatever," Charlie said. "Come talk to me in a few years."

Ragsie cleared his throat. "Let's make a toast."

Candlelight sparkled in the raised glasses, some filled with wine, others with cider or water. The fire crackled in the sudden quiet as each person thought of the ones who weren't there.

"To our dear mother and grandmother, who loved each of us, whom we loved so deeply," Ragsie's voice shook, but he kept smiling. "We miss her, but we know she's with Dad now. Merry Christmas, Mom and Dad."

Beatrice put her glass down and turned into her mother's embrace, crying softly. The others mumbled a response to Ragsie's toast.

"Nice toast, Ragsie," Charlie said. "Your mother was a wonderful woman. It was an honor to know her."

"She loved all of us," Meara sighed. "And she would have loved seeing this table, so full of family."

Noel patted his wife's stomach, saying, "Very full!"

Everyone laughed, and conversations started up again. It was strange for Genie not to see her mother, encouraging second helpings and fussing over her grandchildren. Meara had nursed their mother through her brief final illness, just as she'd cared for their father. Genie and her brothers had agreed that Meara should have their parent's house rather than sell it. Ragsie and Sean didn't need the money, and neither did Genie and Charlie. Genie's book sales, on top of her salary and Charlie's, kept them more than comfortable.

When dinner was over, the family went into the living room. A small tree stood in the corner, nearly overwhelmed by the ornaments the family had accumulated over the years. Frank, a neighbor and, Genie suspected, Meara's boyfriend, came by for dessert. He, too, had come home to take care of his mother and lived just down the street. Once his mother went to bed (eight o'clock every night, right after "Wheel of Fortune" and "Jeopardy") he'd spend a few hours with Meara, always at Meara's house. His mother didn't approve of the Hallorans or indeed any of the neighbors on the street, though she'd lived there more than fifty years.

Genie and Charlie watched with amusement as their nieces and nephews opened the gifts they'd brought.

"Nice one, Auntie Gee!" Noel held up a book titled *Now You've Done It!—What's Next for Dads-to-be.*

"A guy I work with swears by that book," Charlie said. "His wife just had twins."

Sean laughed. "They do run in the family, Noel."

"No twins for us," Noel said. "Not this time, anyway."

Meara stood and said, "Does anyone want coffee? Tea?"

"Sit, Meara," Genie said. "I'll get it. You've been working for days on this dinner."

"But you just got here. Besides, you've been traveling all day."

Ragsie got up and said, "Genie's right, Meara. In fact, I'll help Genie myself."

Genie looked at Ragsie in disbelief. She'd never known him to willingly do any work in the kitchen. When they'd been younger,

Genie had grumbled about Ragsie and Sean never having to set or clear the table, let alone do the dishes. "But they always do the shoveling," Genie's mother used to say, never acknowledging that snow storms hit a few times a winter, but dinner was served every night.

Genie followed Ragsie into the kitchen. She reached into the cupboard for the coffee while Ragsie filled the carafe with water. While the coffee brewed, they took down their mother's china coffee cups and saucers, setting them carefully on a tray along with the Belleek sugar and creamer set.

"Will anyone want tea, do you think?" Genie said.

Ragsie shook his head. He leaned against the dishwasher, an old Kenmore that still worked perfectly. "Hey, Genie. I just wanted to tell you that I think it's great you agreed Meara should get this house. She hasn't had it easy these last few years. Ma was healthy enough until the end, but her mind was...Well, let's just say Meara hardly had a moment's peace."

Genie nodded. "Meara and I talked nearly every day. She's been incredible and she deserves this place. With her share of Mom's money she should be okay for a while till she finds a job, if that's what she wants to do."

Ragsie smiled. "Actually, she's gonna run her own dance studio. I helped her buy a place downtown. Least I could do, right?" He shrugged and poured the coffee into their grandmother's silver pot.

Genie put her arm around Ragsie's waist. "You're a good big brother, you know that?"

Ragsie turned and kissed Genie's cheek. "And you're a good sister. You and Charlie have been great to Meara, and you've been a wonderful aunt to my kids. Plus you've been great role models, both of you. Charlie works hard for what he believes in. And you're a famous author!"

Genie rolled her eyes. "Please," she said. "I'm hardly famous."

"That's not what I tell everyone!" Ragsie laughed and picked up the tray. "I'm proud of you. That's what I'm trying to say." Before they headed back to the living room he said, "Hey, Genie, is that offer to visit you and Charlie still good? Susie and I are thinking about going out to California this summer."

Genie felt a shot of pure happiness. She'd been worried that after her mother died her family might not be as close as they'd been. She'd seen that happen in other families. Of course, she and Meara would always be there for one another. But Ragsie and Sean had always seemed more interested in their wives and children than in their sisters. Ragsie's sons were grown now. Maybe that's what he'd been waiting for.

"Of course," Genie said, following Ragsie into the living room. "Just let us know when you can come." For the rest of the evening and through their Christmas visit, Genie planned Ragsie's visit. She'd be so proud for Ragsie to see the life she and Charlie had built for themselves. She couldn't wait for summer to come.

<u>2012</u>

CHAPTER FORTY-THREE

Genie set Charlie's coffee on his desk as he scribbled down notes and grunted "uh-huh," the phone cradled against his left ear. When his conversation was over he tilted back against the wall where Shepard Fairey's Obama "Hope" poster had hung for years. In addition to his work with Mercy's Family, Charlie was active in the 2012 campaign to reelect Barack Obama. Not that Obama needed much help in the Bay area. Nevertheless, Charlie was determined to do all he could to ensure a big win for the president he idolized.

Genie was about to leave his study when Charlie put the phone down. "Hey, Genie," he said, "You and Debra are planning to go kick-boxing today, right?"

"Like every Sunday morning for the last two years, you mean?" Genie gave him a wicked smile. She rolled his chair back from the desk and sat on his lap.

Charlie kissed her cheek and said, "I'll take that as a yes."

"Then we're going to the Farmers Market and maybe up to Healdsburg for lunch. Why, did you want to come?"

"The lunch part sounds tempting; the kick-boxing, not so much."

Genie stood up and walked a few paces away, then twirled around, doing a sweep-squat-kick. "Hey, you're the one who encouraged me to do this!"

Charlie put his hands up. "Man, I wouldn't want to get you mad at me. You could kick the shit out someone with that move."

"That's the point," Genie said, sitting on the old easy chair in the corner of the study. "Is there some reason you're asking about today?"

Charlie picked up his mobile phone and frowned. "Well, I got a text a little while ago from a group in the City. Never heard of them before...apparently one of them had a friend who'd been helped by Mercy's Family. They're meeting at Glide Memorial at noon today, and they wanted me to come down. Something about planning a benefit concert for the campaign."

Genie looked at her watch. "It's almost ten and they want you there by noon? That's cutting it kind of close, isn't it?"

Charlie smiled and grabbed his backpack. "Yeah, you know how those lefties operate. Couldn't organize a two-car parade."

"That's why they need you." Genie put her arms around Charlie's waist and drew him near. "Will you be long?"

Charlie kissed Genie on the forehead, then on the lips. "I should be home by five, six at the latest if the traffic's bad. What's for dinner?"

"Depends on what I see at the farmer's market," Genie said.

There was a knock on the door, followed by Debra's voice. "Hel-looo! Anyone home?"

"We're coming, Debs," Charlie said. He pulled Genie close and said, "Go easy on your sensei, Genie. He called me the other day and said your feet should be registered as lethal weapons."

"You're nuts," Genie said.

"And that's why you love me."

They walked hand-in-hand down the stairs and met Debra in the living room.

Debra rolled her eyes. "Come on, Genie, you're supposed to be psyching yourself up for class, not acting all lovey-dovey."

Charlie hugged Debra and said, "She can't help it, Debra. I mean, who could resist my charms? I know you can't."

Debra patted Charlie's back. "You're right. In fact, I'm planning to leave Ed and come live with you. Do you think your wife will mind?"

"I don't know if I can handle two warrior women. This one's a terror. You should have seen the move she tried on me just now." Charlie kissed Genie and took his fleece jacket off the coat hook. "I'll see you later this afternoon. You two have fun."

"We will," Genie said. "I love you!"

"Love you too," Charlie said, heading out the door.

CHAPTER FORTY-FOUR

It was nearly three when Debra and Genie left Healdsburg and drove back to Genie's house. As they turned onto Genie's street, Debra said, "Is that a sheriff's car in front of your house?"

Genie leaned forward and said, "Yes, I think so. And it looks like someone's at my door." Her first thought was Charlie. She bolted out of the car the minute Debra pulled into her driveway.

As she ran toward the door, the sheriff's deputy turned and said in a gentle voice, "Are you Mrs. Maguire?" He walked down the steps toward her, his face unreadable. His partner got out of the car and followed.

"I'm Mrs. Maguire, yes," Genie said. She grabbed onto Debra's arm. "What's wrong?"

The deputy took off his hat and said, "Our office just got a call from the SFPD. It's your husband, ma'am. I'm sorry to tell you... he's been killed."

The world went blurry and a strange pressure cut off her hearing as Genie struggled to keep herself upright. She could barely hear Debra, who seemed to be calling her from far away. The next thing she knew she was sitting on her front steps, Debra's arm around her. She was looking into the eyes of a woman she didn't know.

"Who are you?" Genie whispered.

The woman, who was kneeling on the bottom step, leaned closer. "I'm Deputy Shaw, Mrs. Maguire. My partner is Deputy Velez." She handed Genie a bottle of water. "Please have a sip of this, ma'am."

With shaking hands, Genie reached for the bottle. She held it toward her mouth and tried to drink, but ended up spilling the water on her chin and shirt. Debra held her closer and wiped her chin with a tissue.

"She's shaking something awful," Debra said to the deputy. "I think she's in shock."

Deputy Shaw stood, then bent to look in Genie's eyes. "Mrs. Maguire, do you need us to take you to the emergency room?"

Genie looked into the gentle eyes of the officer. She didn't answer at first, as a strange thought floated through her mind. How did the woman manage to keep her hair so neat-looking under that hat? She shook her head, trying to focus. Finally she said, "No, I don't want to go to the hospital." She took another drink of water, then tried to stand.

"Don't move yet," Debra said. "Just stay here." She slipped her fingers through Genie's.

The other deputy came forward and crouched down to Genie's eye level. "Your friend's right, Mrs. Maguire."

Genie took a deep breath. "How did it happen? Was he in an accident?"

"No," the man said, not breaking his gaze. "Your husband was shot, ma'am."

It took her a moment to process those words, then her heart felt like it would burst through her chest. She bolted free of Debra's grasp and ran off the stairs.

"Genie!" Debra shouted, running after her.

Genie had to get away. She couldn't listen to what they were telling her, couldn't listen to those lies about Charlie. He'd be home any minute now, teasing her about her kickboxing and helping her make dinner. She got to the end of her street then stopped, breathing hard. Tears ran down her cheeks as she sank to her knees. She wasn't going to faint now, though oblivion would have been a mercy. She wept as she never had before, harsh, wrenching sobs that came from the deepest part of her.

Debra and Deputy Shaw had followed and knelt on either side of her. "Genie," Debra said. "Let's get you into the house. The deputies need to talk to you."

Genie let herself be lifted to her feet, then stumbled along down the street between Debra and Deputy Shaw. Debra used the key Genie had given her years ago to let them all into the house and helped Deputy Shaw set Genie down on the couch.

"I'll make us some tea," Debra said.

Genie grabbed her hand. "No! Stay with me."

Deputy Velez said, "I'd be happy to make tea, if you like."

Debra nodded her thanks. "It's in the cupboard to the right of the sink. The mugs are over the stove."

When he'd gone, Deputy Shaw went into the dining room, then came back with a chair, which she placed about a foot away from Genie.

"Mrs. Maguire," she said. She leaned forward, her hands on her knees. "I know this is awful for you, but I need to ask you a few questions."

"Can't this wait?" Debora whispered. She handed Genie a box of tissues and put her arm around Genie's shoulders.

Genie blew her nose, and wiped away a single tear with her thumb. "That's okay, Debs. I want to be helpful, if I can. But, Deputy..." She peered at the woman's name tag. "Sorry. Deputy Shaw, you said Charlie was shot? He was going to Glide Memorial. How could anyone shoot him there?"

The deputy pulled a small notebook from her back pocket. "That's not where it happened, ma'am. He was shot on Leavenworth Street. Did your husband drive into the City?"

"Yes," Genie said. "He might have parked in that garage on Leavenworth." She nodded her thanks to the other deputy, who handed her a cup of tea.

"The SFPD will look for his car." Deputy Shaw scribbled something in her notebook.

"Do they know who did this? Was Charlie robbed? How could someone just shoot him on the street?"

"I'm not sure what they know right now, Mrs. Maguire. There are a lot of surveillance cameras in the Tenderloin, so they can get more information on the crime that way."

"Oh." Genie tried to take a sip of tea, but her throat was too tight. She set the cup down on the floor and put her head in her hands. Not looking up, she said, "How do they know it was Charlie?"

Deputy Shaw cleared her throat. "They found his driver's license in his back pocket. His wallet was missing, though."

Genie looked up. "Charlie hardly ever carried a wallet. He'd stuff his license in one pocket and a little money in the other. He used his phone to pay for things when he could."

"I see. We'll let the SFPD know. With no wallet, they always suspect robbery as the motive." Deputy Shaw shifted in her chair. "Uh, Mrs. Maguire, the police in San Francisco requested that you come down to identify your husband's body. Deputy Velez and I will drive you. Of course, your friend can come with you."

Debra frowned. "But they already know it's Charlie from the license, don't they?"

"In situations like this, the police need a positive identification. If there's someone else you'd like to accompany you, Mrs. Maguire..."

Genie stood up. "Debra's my best friend. I want her with me." She looked down at Debra. "Will you come with me?"

Debra took her hand. "Of course," she whispered. "I'll call Ed, then we can go."

"I'll be ready in a minute," Genie said. She went upstairs to the bathroom and closed the door after her. When she caught sight of herself in the mirror she gasped. I'm a widow now, she thought. Charlie's dead, and he's never coming home. She ran the cold water and splashed some on her face. She wouldn't look at herself again. Hurrying into her bedroom, she put a sweater on over her t-shirt. It would be cold in San Francisco.

CHAPTER FORTY-FIVE

In the sheriff's car she sat back and closed her eyes as they rolled down Route 101. Genie had been up and down this freeway with Charlie hundreds of times, and now he was gone. When she looked out the window they were already past Rohnert Park. The hills, some dotted with grazing cows, others lined with neat rows of grapevines, were in their spring-green glory. A lone hawk soared over a gnarled oak, on the hunt for a late lunch. Soon they drove over the Golden Gate Bridge, packed with bicyclists on one side and pedestrians on the other. She looked out the window again at the happy people. Then she closed her eyes, suddenly exhausted.

"Mrs. Maguire?"

Genie opened her eyes to see Deputy Shaw peering back at her. She'd lost track of time.

"We're here, Mrs. Maguire," the young policewoman said. Her dark brown eyes were kind as she laid a hand on Genie's arm. "Are you ready to get out of the car?"

"Are you okay?" Debra whispered.

Genie nodded and unbuckled her seat belt. Deputy Velez opened the door and took Genie's hand as she exited. He put his hand lightly on Genie's back as they walked toward the hospital. Such exquisite courtesy, she thought, almost undone by the simple gesture. Inside, two SFPD officers waited.

"Mrs. Maguire?" said the taller officer.

"Yes," Genie said.

"I'm Officer Hanson, and this is Officer Nguyen. We'll take you downstairs, then we'd like to talk to you for a little while, if that's all right. Is this lady with you?"

"This is my friend Debra," Genie said. She looked over at the Sonoma County deputies and said, "Thank you for your help."

"Our condolences, Mrs. Maguire," said Deputy Velez.

The two San Francisco officers guided Genie and Debra to an elevator and got in behind them. The car was filled with a family: three little boys and a mother sitting in a wheelchair holding a newborn with a pink knit cap. The father held a dozen balloons and some flower arrangements.

"Give the ladies some room, Trent," the mother said to the youngest boy, a freckled kid of about five.

"My sister just got bored!" Trent piped, tugging on Genie's sleeve. "Her name is Tabitha!"

She looked down at the boy whose smile revealed a missing front tooth. The balloons bobbed dopily against the wall and suddenly it seemed very hot in the small space. When the elevator door opened the family exited. "Congratulations," she whispered to the father as he maneuvered around her with the balloons.

"Wish me luck," he muttered as the doors closed again.

The elevator started up again and came to a stop at "B1"—the basement. The morgue. A buzzing started in Genie's head and her legs felt too weak to hold her up.

"Just take your time, Genie," said Debra, putting her strong arm around Genie's waist.

Genie nodded and took a step out of the elevator. Her legs wobbled, but she kept going. It was important for her to be with Charlie now so he wouldn't be so all alone. She looked down as they walked along the highly polished floor, her eyes dead-center on the tiles.

They had walked only a short way when Officer Hanson said, "We're here, Mrs. Maguire. I'll go in with you, if you don't mind."

Genie wouldn't look up to see the sign on the door. It was impossible that her Charlie lay in a place called a morgue. The door opened, and they walked through a little hallway, then another door opened automatically. They stepped into a room with bright lights, white walls, and stainless steel surfaces. It was so cold.

A young man wearing blue scrubs approached them. "I'm Kenneth," he said in a soft voice.

"Kenneth," Officer Hanson said, pulling Genie closer to her. "This is Mrs. Maguire. She's here to identify Charles Maguire."

He didn't like being called Charles, Genie thought.

"Yes, of course," Kenneth said. "Right over here." He pulled on a handle in the wall and out slid a shelf with a light-blue plastic bag on it. He unzipped the bag and turned around, motioning for Genie to come closer.

Though he blocked her view of the body, the top of Charlie's head was just visible. Genie nearly swooned at the sight of those salt-and-pepper curls. Debra tightened her grip around Genie's waist and helped her friend walk toward the cold steel where Charlie lay. Kenneth moved away so that Genie could get closer.

"Oh, Charlie," Genie whispered. She ran her fingers through his hair, then caressed his beard. His eyes were closed and his expression was mild. "I love you, my Charlie." She leaned over and kissed him. His lips—always so warm and soft—were cold now.

"Mrs. Maguire, is that your husband? Is that Charles Maguire?" Officer Hanson stood behind her, speaking gently.

Genie took a step back and gave Charlie's cheek a final caress. "He went by Charlie; no one ever called him Charles," she said. With a final look back at Charlie's body, she turned and straightened her shoulders. "Have you found the person who did this to my husband?"

Hanson shook his head. "Not yet, ma'am. My partner is acquiring videos from the cameras around where the shooting took place. In the meantime, we need to ask you a few questions. Do you feel up to it now?"

Genie nodded.

"Are you sure?" Debra said.

"I'm sure." They followed Hanson out of the morgue and down the hall toward the elevator bank. When the elevator opened, Ed Tignanelli emerged. Marty stood behind Ed, his eyes red-rimmed.

"Ed!" Debra said, hurrying toward her husband.

Ed put his arms around Debra and looked over his head at Genie, tears welling. "Genie, I'm so sorry," he said, his voice breaking.

Marty walked toward Genie slowly, then took her right hand in his. "Genie," he said, kissing her on the cheek. "I have no words."

Genie introduced Ed and Marty to Officer Hanson, then said to Debra, "Would you call Meara to let her know? She can get in touch with Ragsie and Sean." She turned to Marty. "Could you let Laetitia and the others know at Mercy's Family?"

Marty took a shaky breath and said, "Of course, Genie."

Genie turned to Hanson and said, "What about my husband's body? Should I get in touch with a mortuary in Sonoma County?"

Hanson cleared his throat. "Your husband's body can't be released until after an autopsy. That's standard procedure when foul play is suspected."

Genie put her hand to her mouth. "Oh. Of course. When will that happen?"

"I'm not sure," Hanson said. "Detective Haddad is running the investigation."

"Don't worry," Ed said. "We'll take care of everything for you, Genie. We'll be waiting to take you home when you're done."

They all got into the elevator. When the door opened on the second floor, Officer Hanson said to Debra, Ed, and Marty, "I'm taking Mrs. Maguire to the family meeting room just beyond the lobby. Why don't you go get a cup of coffee and come back in half an hour? The guard at the lobby desk can tell you where to find us."

Debra took hold of Genie's hands and said, "We'll be back for you. Will you be all right?"

The pain in Debra's face was clear. Genie said a silent prayer of thanks to have such a friend.

"I'll be okay." Genie said.

She followed Hanson through the large lobby and down a hallway. When they came to the end, Hanson turned to her and said, "In here, Mrs. Maguire."

Genie walked through the door and entered a small, windowless room. A petite woman wearing a charcoal grey jacket and pants stood up from the table and said, "Mrs. Maguire, I'm Alima Haddad." She offered Genie her hand, then said, "Please, sit."

Genie sat across from the detective, and Officer Hanson took the remaining chair.

"I want to tell you how sorry I am about your husband, Mrs. Maguire. He was a fine man."

Genie was surprised. "Did you know Charlie?"

Detective Haddad smiled sadly, her large black eyes locked onto Genie's.

"We never met," she said. "But he and his work are well known down here, especially in the Tenderloin. Your husband helped a lot of men stay out of prison once they'd been released. More than a few have had a better life because of what he and his staff have done."

A wave of bitterness rolled over Genie. Her Charlie had helped men who'd committed horrible crimes find another life, only to be gunned down on the street. She gripped the edge of the table, her grief giving way to anger. "Charlie didn't deserve this, detective. Will you find the person who killed him?"

Detective Haddad handed Genie a Styrofoam cup. "Please drink some water; it's important to stay hydrated when you've had a shock like this. I have a few questions for you, then your friends can take you home."

For the next half hour, Genie answered the detective as best she could. Yes, it was odd for Charlie to have received a text with a last-minute request to come to San Francisco. No, Charlie didn't go to the City much for his work on the Obama reelection; he was kept busy in Sonoma County. Yes, she knew the password to Charlie's phone, and yes, the detective had permission to check the recent activity. No, she'd never heard Charlie talk about enemies. No, no one had ever threatened him or his staff at Mercy's Family, as far as she knew. Yes, the detective could call her with follow-up questions. Yes, Genie would go to the Tenderloin police station on Eddy St. if that was necessary.

"That's all I need for now, Mrs. Maguire," the detective said. "Do you have any questions for me before you leave?"

Genie stood. In the last few minutes she'd developed a terrible headache. All she wanted to do was go home and lie down. "I can't think of anything except to ask again—do you think you'll catch whoever did this?"

The detective stood, and, after she shook Genie's hand, kept hold of it a moment longer. "I'm confident we will, Mrs. Maguire. I'll do my best for you, I promise."

There was a knock on the door. Officer Hanson opened it, letting in Debra and Ed. It was obvious they'd both been crying. "Marty's brought the car out front. Are you ready to go, Genie?" Debra said in a soft voice.

"Yes, please take me home."

CHAPTER FORTY-SIX

Her friends made sure Genie wasn't alone. They brought her home, then Ed and Marty stayed with Genie while Debra went to her house and packed a bag. She and Ed would stay in the spare bedroom for a few days, despite Genie's protests. Marty had left with a promise to return the next day after visiting the Mercy's Family office.

"I have to be by myself sometime," Genie said, standing in the doorway of her bedroom. "You and Ed don't have to stay." It was nearly two a.m. Ed had gone to bed earlier but Genie and Debra had sat up talking by the fire.

"Don't worry, Genie," Debra said, reaching over to tuck a curl behind Genie's ear. "We want to be here."

Genie yawned, putting her hand up to her mouth. Her neighbor Meg Taylor, an internist, had come over a few minutes after Genie had come home. She'd prescribed Valium over Genie's objections, but Ed had dutifully had the prescription filled. By one a.m. Genie realized she'd never sleep without a pill, so she'd taken a Valium with some chamomile tea.

Genie yawned again. "Thanks, Debs. I think I'll sleep for a while." She kissed Debra on the cheek and staggered toward her bed. She was asleep seconds after her head hit the pillow.

At five a.m., as always, Genie's neighbor started his turbocharged truck. Usually she'd wake up and go right back to sleep, but when she reached over for Charlie he wasn't there. Then she remembered everything. "Charlie!" she screamed. Grief ripped through her. "Charlie!" She sat up, then leaned forward, tucking her legs underneath her. She rocked back and forth, barely able to breathe through her agony.

Debra raced into the room and sat next to her, gathering Genie in her arms.

"He's dead!" Genie keened. "Someone shot my Charlie. Why would anyone hurt him? He was so good. I loved him, Debra! Now he's never coming back!" She balled her hands up and dug her fingernails into her palms, drawing blood.

Ed crept into the room with the bottle of Valium and a glass of water. Debra mouthed a "Thank you," and nodded toward the night table. She held Genie tight and smoothed her hair. Ed stood in the doorway and roughly wiped his cheek. After a while Genie took a deep breath and sat up straight, looking Debra in the eye. "Thank you for being here," she said. With her throat raw from crying, it hurt to talk. She spied the Valium and said, "How'd that get in here? I purposely kept it downstairs."

Debra reached over and took out a pill, then handed it to Genie with the water. "That was smart. It's never a good idea to keep sedatives in the bedroom. It's too easy to overdose when you're half asleep."

Genie looked at the pill in her hand. "If I'd been shot instead of Charlie, he'd never take a pill like this. He was so much stronger."

"No one knows how he'll act when terrible things happen. Charlie loved you, Genie, and he'd want you to get through this. You can do it but it will take time. For now, just rest and lean on your friends."

Genie popped the Valium into her mouth and took a long drink of water. "It'll be light soon," she said. "Maybe I should get up."

"It's only six, and you need more sleep," Debra said. She stood up and stretched. "As a matter of fact, I'm going back to bed myself. Ed's called in to take the day off, too. We'll be here when you wake up."

Genie lay down, turning away from Charlie's side of the bed. "Thanks, Debra," she murmured, putting her arm over her eyes. She was exhausted, and sleep, with its balm of forgetting, beckoned.

CHAPTER FORTY-SEVEN

For the first two days after Charlie's death, Genie stayed in bed, getting up only to eat an occasional bowl of cereal and to shower. On Wednesday morning she came downstairs in a skirt and sweater, ready to go back to school.

Ed had gone to work and Debra was sitting in her robe at the kitchen table with the newspaper turned to the crossword, a mug of coffee in hand. She looked up when Genie came in. "You look spiffy this morning. Where are you headed?"

Genie poured herself a coffee and put a piece of bread in the toaster. She joined Debra at the table and took a sip. "To work, of course."

Debra put her pen down and said, "Genie, don't you remember? I talked to Dr. Wetherington at your school. He's put you on leave through the end of this school year."

"I remember." Genie got up and put some butter on her toast. "But I think it would be better for me if I went back. I can't just stay in bed all day."

Debra turned to face Genie. "There's a big difference between staying in bed and having to be bright and cheery for your students. Why don't you—"

The phone rang. Genie froze and gripped her mug harder.

"I'll get it." Debra walked across the kitchen and answered. She listened for a few minutes, then mouthed to Genie "It's Detective

Haddad." She listened a little longer then put her hand over the receiver. "She wants to know if you'll meet her at the Mercy's Family office at eleven today."

Genie's face went pale. "Will you go with me?"

"Of course." Debra told the detective that they'd meet her later, then hung up. When she sat down she took Genie's hand in hers. "She said they got some photos of the guy they think shot Charlie. They know who he is, and they want to show you the pictures. She seems to think there was some connection between Mercy's Family and this guy."

"I can't believe that," Genie said. She took a bite of her toast, then pushed the plate away. "I guess I won't be going to school today after all."

Debra put her hand over Genie's. "Your school will still be there in the fall, Genie. Give yourself some time."

Genie folded her arms across her chest, hugging herself against a sudden chill. "I could live till I'm ninety-nine and it wouldn't be enough time for me to ever feel normal again." She smiled sadly and said, "You'd better go shower and dress if we're going to be there by eleven."

They drove to Fourth Street in Santa Rosa without talking. KQED, the local NPR affiliate station, played quietly.

"Stay tuned to hear about San Francisco's efforts to deal with violent crime—"

Debra reached over and snapped the radio off.

"You didn't have to do that on my account, Debra. I know the world isn't going to stop just because my life blew up."

Debra turned into the small parking lot behind the industrial building where Mercy's Family had its office.

"I'm glad there aren't any police cars parked here," Genie said. "That would freak out the clients." She led Debra through the back door and into the office.

Detective Haddad sat at the large, dinged-up table at the front of the office. She turned as Genie and Debra entered and said, "Thank you for coming, Mrs. Maguire."

"Please call me Genie," she said, embracing Big Max. Max Lopez, a former boxer whom Charlie had hired ten years ago, wept openly as he hugged Genie. Max had gone to prison when he was young, and when he'd been paroled he'd come to Mercy's Family for help. He'd thrived at a manufacturing plant in Santa Rosa and had taken a job with Charlie when that business closed. Since then he'd been a tireless worker, helping clients about to be released from prison and smoothing the way ahead of them.

Genie patted Max's back. "Max, you were one of Charlie's best friends. He loved you, you know."

The big man's voice cracked. "I loved him, too. We all did."

Genie slid out of Max's embrace and hugged the women behind him. "Laetitia, Maria, how are you holding up?"

Laetitia Adams had helped Charlie start Mercy's Family years before. Her younger brother Cory had spent most of his life in prison, always getting in trouble after being released and always being sentenced to longer stretches, until he was found dead in his cell at age thirty-five. Maria Kim, a newly-minted lawyer, had been with Mercy's Family for two years. The two women and Max were as close to Charlie as any employees could be, and Genie had come to think of them as family.

Maria and Laetitia held onto Genie's hands. "Genie, I've been praying for you," Laetitia said softly. "My whole family has been, too."

Genie managed a quiet thank you. She turned to Detective Haddad and said, "Should we get started?"

"Yes, Mrs. Ma—Genie," the detective said. Turning to a serious-looking older man who'd remained seating she said, "This is my partner, Jim Wilson."

Wilson stood and shook Genie's hand, then sat down. Everyone but Debra sat at the table. She said, "Genie, I'll be at Voodoo Brew until you need me."

"Is that the coffee shop across the street?" Detective Haddad said. "I'll walk Genie over there when we're through."

After Debra left, Detective Wilson put a manila envelope on the table and said, "We got some pretty good images from the cameras on Leavenworth, including a few of a guy heading away from the scene." He pulled photos out of the envelope and put them on the table. One showed a skeletally thin young man bending over something on the ground. It was easy to see the tattoos on the back of his neck and on top of his shaved head. Another showed the same man headed down the street. A camera had managed to get a good shot of his face and upper body. He appeared to have no eyebrows, and he seemed to have a rope around his neck. That rope turned out to be another tattoo.

"Do you think he shot Charlie?" Genie said, not able to look at the photos longer than a second or two.

Wilson pulled another photo from the envelope. "We're not sure if he's the perpetrator, Mrs. Maguire. But we know he was at the scene and we know who he is." He put a mug shot on the center of the table. "That rope tattoo and the no-eyebrows were the tipoff for us. He's Clarence Forester, though he goes by the name of Eichmann on the street. He hangs around with some real creeps, skinheads and Nazi types. We've arrested him four times in the last two years for pretty minor stuff; he did six months about a year ago."

Genie looked at the photo. Could this strange-looking person have killed Charlie? Was this death's head the last thing Charlie had seen? She couldn't look at those eyes. She flipped the photo over and slid it across the table to Detective Wilson.

"Have you ever seen that man, Mrs. Maguire?"

Genie put her face in her hands. "No, never," she whispered.

Wilson flipped the photo back and handed it to Maria. "Have you ever seen him? Has he ever been to this office?"

Maria shook her head, but Laetitia said, "Max, isn't this the guy we saw in the parking lot? He had those messed up eyebrows, remember?"

Detective Haddad leaned forward. "You saw this man? When was that?"

Max looked hard at the photo. "I think that's the dude. He was hanging around Charlie's car one night. It wasn't too late, maybe six-thirty or so, but dark. Anyway, we were just finishing up a quick meeting—Maria, you'd already left. Laetitia, Charlie and me were headed out. I was locking up when I heard this guy... what's his name—Clarence? I heard him talking to Charlie and

Laetitia. He was asking about the program. Said he'd been out for like six months and was having trouble finding a job."

"That's right," Laetitia said. "Charlie introduced himself and told him to come back the next day."

Wilson stared at Max and said, "Did you talk to him?"

Max shook his head. "When I went up to where Laetitia and Charlie were, the dude took one look at me and headed out."

Genie had to smile. Max had become the gentlest of men, but with this heavy brow and huge shoulders and hands, he cut an intimidating figure.

"Did he say who he was?"

Laetitia picked up the photo again and slowly shook her head. "Mm-mm. Never said his name. Never came back, either."

"Do you remember the date?" Wilson said. He'd been scribbling notes since Laetitia had started talking.

Laetitia screwed up her eyes. "Not sure...maybe late February?"

Max leaned forward and picked up the photo. "Wait—I remember. I was going to my nephew's birthday party that night. He's my godson, too. He was born on February 26."

"And he hasn't been back since then?" Detective Haddad took the photos and replaced them in the envelope. "Neither of you has seen him?"

They both shook their heads. "I'd remember seeing him again. He was weird." Laetitia shuddered.

Detective Haddad said, "I think we have what we need for now." She stood and reached into her pocket, leaving a few business cards on the table. "If you think of anything else, please get in touch with me. Genie, shall I walk you to the coffee shop?"

"Okay," Genie said, anxious to get out of the office. She'd visited Charlie there so often, sometimes bringing him lunch or a snack, other times just swinging by after school. She liked to sit in one of the worn reading chairs in the corner, grading papers while Charlie worked the phones. Every once in a while, a former client would stop by to say hello, sometimes bringing his family with him. Charlie never stopped smiling during those visits. He took special pleasure in meeting the children, who, because their fathers had straightened out, had a shot at a happy life. When Genie saw him hold a baby or play with a toddler, she felt a bittersweet pang. He would have been a great father.

She kept up with Detective Haddad's brisk pace as they walked a block south, then crossed the street. Just before they entered the coffee shop, Genie turned to the detective and said, "This Forester person—do you really think he shot Charlie? From what you said back there it didn't seem he was particularly violent before."

The detective's face gave nothing away. "No, that hadn't been a pattern. Before now he'd been picked up for a few minor drug offenses and some petty thefts."

"But Charlie hadn't been robbed, had he?"

"It doesn't appear so. By the way, I've brought you his effects. I'll give them to you now, and you can let me know if anything is missing." She passed Genie an innocuous-looking large manila envelope.

Genie took the envelope with icy hands. She wouldn't open it until she was home.

The detective looked inside the café. Spotting Debra, she said, "I'll be going now. We've been searching all of Forester's usual hangouts and haven't found him, but we will. When we get him, we'll find out why he did what he did. That I promise you."

"Thank you," Genie whispered. She ducked into the café, needing to be with her friend. Sitting across from Debra, she said, "They think they know who did it. Now they just need to find him." She couldn't shake the image of that man bending over something in the street. Was he looking down at Charlie as he lay dying?

Debra stood up and said, "Let's get you home, okay?"

Genie held onto the envelope with a tight grip as Debra drove her home. Would Charlie's clothes be inside, stained with his blood? The envelope wasn't really large enough. When they pulled into the driveway Genie hurried out of the car and into the house. At the dining room table she ripped the envelope open, dumping the contents. There wasn't much: a few dollars and some change, Charlie's driver's license and keys, his belt, and three of his business cards, along with a sealed envelope with her name on it. She shook the larger envelope to make sure nothing else was inside, then she opened the sealed envelope. What she was looking for had to be in that. Instead, she found a brief note addressed to her:

Dear Mrs. Maguire,

Mr. Maguire's clothes cannot be returned to you as they are being held as evidence. Please contact Detective Haddad if anything is missing.

That was it? Genie looked inside the small envelope, then ripped it in half. She did the same with the larger one. "Where is it?" she muttered, quiet at first, then in a louder voice she said, "Debra! I can't find his necklace. Where is it? Why didn't they give it back to me?"

Debra came running into the room. "What's wrong, Genie?"

Genie looked up at Debra with wild eyes. "His necklace. The Celtic knot necklace I gave him...it's not in here!" She stood up and rifled through the paltry collection of Charlie's things again, knocking the change onto the floor. "He said he'd never take it off! Now it's gone. Why didn't they give it back to me, Debra?" She was growing more frantic, pulling away when Debra tried to put her arm around her.

"Genie," Debra said, walking around the table and taking a seat opposite her. "If the necklace is missing, the police probably never had it. Maybe it fell off when—"

"No!" Genie glared at Debra. "It couldn't have fallen off. Don't you remember? I took it to a jeweler who put a special safety lock on the chain. There's no way it would have fallen off."

Debra took a deep breath and said in a steady, gentle voice, "Then maybe someone grabbed it...maybe the man who shot Charlie stole the necklace."

Debra's words hit her like a kick to the stomach. Genie sank into her chair, deflated. "He shot him for the necklace? He killed my Charlie for some gold?" Bile rose in her throat as she envisioned the scene in the Tenderloin: a petty criminal had seen a glimmer of gold around Charlie's neck. He followed him down the street, and when he thought no one would see, he'd killed her good man

275

over a piece of jewelry. Charlie had devoted his life to helping people just like the one who'd killed him.

"We don't know that for sure," Debra said. She went into the kitchen and returned with the phone. "You need to let the detective know the necklace is gone, though."

Genie stared at the phone for a second as if she didn't know what it was.

"Do you want me to call her?" Debra said. She sat next to Genie and put her hand on Genie's back.

Genie blinked a few times, then sighed. "No, I'll call her. She might have other questions for me." She took the phone and went upstairs to her bedroom, closed the door, and made her call.

CHAPTER FORTY-EIGHT

A few days later, Genie was upstairs vacuuming. She'd finally convinced Debra and Ed to go home. Debra hadn't left without insisting that Genie promise to call if she needed her. The days since Charlie's death had passed slowly, with Genie craving sleep no matter what the hour. She forced herself to stay awake, and now, finally, she started to feel more like herself despite the aching loss. It was a Monday, just over two weeks since Charlie's death, and she was determined to try to live as normally as she could. She'd spent hours on the phone with Meara, and even Ragsie and Sean had talked to her at length.

Last week she and Debra had visited the mortuary to pick up Charlie's ashes, which she'd put on the little table on his side of the bed. She'd been sleeping on the living room couch, preferring that to the loneliness of the bed she'd shared with Charlie. After vacuuming the bedroom she closed the door and went downstairs to fix herself a cup of tea. While the kettle was coming to a boil she sorted through the mail that had been piling up. When the water was ready she poured some in a cup, dunked in a teabag, and sat down, only to have to get up again when the phone rang.

"Mrs. Maguire...Genie...this is Detective Haddad. How are you today, ma'am?"

Genie smiled at the detective's reflexive formality. "I'm better, Detective, thank you."

There was a pause. "Ma'am, is your friend Debra there with you now?"

What would the detective need with Debra? "No," Genie said, taking a sip of her tea. "Would you like her phone number?"

Another pause. "No ma'am. I just wondered if you had company...Mrs. Maguire, we got some news about the man we think killed your husband."

Genie set the cup down. "Did you find him?" she whispered. "Did he confess?"

"No, ma'am. Some hikers out by Goat Rock Beach alerted the Coast Guard to a body that had washed up. We're pretty sure it was Clarence Forester. They'll check against his dental records, but there was an ID in his pocket, and some of the tattoos checked out, too. We'll have confirmation by tomorrow, but I'm quite certain it's him."

"Oh," Genie said. "If he's dead, how can you be certain he was the one who killed Charlie?"

"We've talked to a witness who saw him on the street right after the shooting. And we found a gun with his prints on it. There's little doubt he did it, Mrs. Maguire."

"How did he die? When did he..." Genie's voice quavered. She couldn't believe she was having this conversation.

Detective Haddad exhaled and said, "He was shot in the head. The coroner thinks he'd been in the water for a couple of days, so most likely whoever killed him dumped the body right afterward. He hung around with a lot of bad actors, Mrs. Maguire. It wasn't too surprising he ended up dead. I know you would have preferred he'd been arrested and punished for what he did to your husband, but unfortunately that won't happen now."

Another wasted life. That's what Charlie would have said. She took another sip of tea but could barely swallow it. She didn't agree with the detective; she didn't want Clarence punished so much as she wanted to ask him why he had done it. Was a human life worth so little to him that he'd shoot a good man to steal a necklace?

"Was there anything else in his pockets?"

"No ma'am. We didn't find your husband's necklace. I'm sorry." Detective Haddad cleared her throat. "Genie, I'm writing this up and, dependent on the coroner giving a positive ID, I'm going to have to close out this case. I wish I could have done more to help you find closure."

Genie clamped her eyes shut. Who could ever find closure when the person they loved most in the world had been murdered? It wasn't the detective's fault for talking this way. No doubt she'd been forced to take sensitivity classes where such trite, meaningless terms were recommended in these situations. "How can you close the case?" Genie said. "You don't really know for sure that he's the one who did it. How certain can you be from a couple of video tapes and photos? Tattoos and shaved heads aren't uncommon these days. And what about the necklace? Maybe he sold it to someone. That would be a lead for you, wouldn't it?"

There was a long pause before the detective responded. "Genie," she said, clearing her throat, "My captain wouldn't permit me to pursue any further leads, even if I pushed for it. Clarence Forester had a record and he hung around with some very bad people. We interviewed members of a gang—they're called the White Devils. They confirmed for us that Forester had been to a few of their gatherings."

"Who are the White Devils?" Genie asked.

There was a pause. "They're a group of white nationalists in the Bay area. Very anti-immigrant, anti-gay—generally hateful people. Apparently Forester sympathized with their views and wanted to join them. But according to the people we talked to, they told him to get lost. They said he was all talk and couldn't be counted on in the clutch."

"Do you think that's why he killed Charlie? To convince them he was tough?"

Detective Haddad cleared her throat. "That could have been his motivation, or maybe not. The fact is that Clarence Forester was a petty criminal on his way down. If even people as bad as the White Devils thought he was a loser, it's not surprising that he got himself killed. I'm sure the coroner will come back with a positive ID for him, and I'd stake my career on him being the shooter. Those videos gave us a good look at him, believe me."

"But where's the necklace?" Genie murmured. She wasn't ready to give up so easily. Charlie's death had to matter more.

"Genie, I'm sorry to say that you'll probably never see the necklace again. I wish I could do more for you, but I can't. If there's anything I've learned in this job it's that life is unfair. In fact, it can downright suck. You have my condolences, you really do. Now, if you'll excuse me, I have to take another call. Goodbye."

There was a click, then the dial tone. Genie held the phone to her ear a little longer, then set it down. She picked it up and called Max at Mercy's Family. "May I come over?" she said. "I need your help."

CHAPTER FORTY-NINE

A week later Genie sat hunched on a bench in Washington Square. Max had been reluctant to set up the meeting, but relented when she'd agreed to let him keep an eye on her. She could see him in the doorway of St. Peter & Paul Church, his hands thrust into the pockets of his fleece jacket. It was a typical morning in San Francisco: chilly and damp, with a fog that might or might not dissipate later in the day. The park, which was almost empty on a Saturday morning, would fill with picnickers and Frisbee throwers if the sun came out later. But for now, Genie wrapped her fingers around the latte she'd bought from the Italian café down the street and tried to keep from shivering.

"Are you Genie?"

She startled, then looked up at a man standing just behind her. He was heavy set and wore a ripped denim jacket and black jeans. His dark hair was shaved nearly to his skull on the sides; on top it was longer and straight, parted on the left. He looked down at her with a slight smile on his face, as if he'd heard a joke that somehow involved her. She nodded and started to stand, but he waved her down, then joined her. He sat closer than she would have liked and put his arm up on top of the bench, touching her shoulders ever so lightly. Sitting so close, she could see faint acne scars on his pale skin. His grey eyes looked her up and down, a smile still playing on his lips.

"Well," he said. "What did you want to know? My brother begged me to meet you...said you were married to that guy who ran

Mercy's Family, the one who got capped in the Tenderloin. I heard that clown Forester wasted him." His laugh was harsh. "Not that it did him any good."

Genie winced. "The police closed the case, but I don't think they should have. Why would my husband be killed like that?"

The man shrugged. "Happens all the time. Anyway, it's none of my business."

Genie forced herself to continue. "I want to know if he did it to get into your gang." His eyebrows shot up and he laughed again. Genie could smell alcohol on his breath and leaned away. She wasn't going to be deterred. She had to find out why Charlie had died. "I...I heard he was trying to join your...your group."

The man stopped laughing, but his smile was even wider. "My group? You mean the White Devils? That group? What, do you think we assign people little tasks before they can come into the group? Like the Boy Scouts earning merit badges? Lady, I'll say this. It took balls for you to set up this little meeting of ours. I only came cause your husband took good care of my brother when he got out." He stretched his arms, then folded them across his chest. Looking at her with a serious expression, he said, "We already told the cops this. Forester tried sniffing around us a few times, said he wanted to follow Hitler. He was a goddamn loser, and we told him to fuck off. He was stupid enough to get himself killed right after he offed your man, which kind of proved our point."

He stood up and looked around him. "What are you doing here, anyway? Playing Nancy Drew can get dangerous; didn't anyone ever tell you that?"

He reached over and roughed up her hair. Genie pulled away, but he put his hand on her cheek. "Go on home, little Miss. You don't belong here. My brother told me your husband was a good guy, so I'm sorry he had to die. But it happens to us all, doesn't it? I had nothing to do with it, neither did anyone else I know. It was that asshole Forester, and he got his. Leave it alone, now, before you get hurt." With a little tap on her cheek, he turned and walked quickly toward Stockton Street. Genie was relieved to see Max hurrying toward her. She was quiet on the ride home, but she wasn't deterred. There had to be a way to find out why Charlie had been killed.

• • •

"Genie, it's crazy to go putting up flyers in the Tenderloin. Do you know what kind of creeps you'll dig up?" Debra stood in the middle of Genie's living room, with her arms crossed. Genie smiled. If Debra had known about the meeting she'd had the other day in San Francisco, she'd be even more upset.

"Didn't you already put notices in SF Weekly and Craigslist?" Debra said.

Genie put a staple gun and tape in a canvas bag. She wouldn't meet Debra's eyes.

"Genie?" Debra's voice was soft. "Did someone call about the necklace?"

Genie shrugged. "I got a couple of strange calls. Somebody called from the Craigslist lost-and-found the other day. When I asked him to identify the Celtic knot—you know, tell me what's engraved on the back—he said something really awful and hung up." She stuffed the flyers into the canvas bag and faced Debra. "I just don't understand why anyone would call if they didn't really have the necklace. It's so cruel."

"It might have something to do with the thousand dollar reward you're offering. I'm surprised you haven't had more calls. Really, Genie, why are you doing this to yourself? The police told you the necklace is probably gone for good."

"I'm doing this because someone might have the necklace. Maybe they can tell me how they got it, and that might give the police something more to go on. I know there's more to the story, Debra. Maybe I can get the police to reopen the case."

Debra put her arm around Genie's shoulders. "That's a lot of mights and maybes, Genie." She gave Genie a kiss on the cheek. "Okay, if you're determined to do this, I'll drive you. You can look for utility poles to staple. But you have to be careful. There's lots of places where posting handouts is a no-no."

"I'll take my chances. At least I left off the amount of the reward on the flyers." Hefting the canvas bag over her shoulder, Genie said, "Ready?"

"Ready as I'll ever be," Debra said, and followed her friend outside.

On the ride to San Francisco, they listened to *Pride and Prejudice*. Genie was glad to have her thoughts transported to Jane Austen's world, even for only an hour. Debra was probably right that putting up the flyers would be pointless, but she had to try. She couldn't give up on Charlie the way the police had. Once they crossed the Golden Gate Bridge, Debra turned off the recording. She gave Genie a quick look and said, "You still want to do this, right?"

Genie nodded. "I have to try, Debs."

Debra drove toward the Tenderloin, intentionally staying away from Leavenworth Street. She parked in a garage on Jones Street, then she and Genie headed out. Genie dashed toward the first telephone pole she saw, already punctured by hundreds of staples and plastered with handouts touting everything from Chinese food to crystal energy readings. Genie pushed hard against the stapler and managed to get the first flyer up. She looked around and spotted another likely pole across the street. When she stepped off the sidewalk she nearly collided with a bicyclist, who gave her the finger and kept going.

Debra caught up to her and took her by the elbow. "Hey, tiger. No jay-walking, okay? Let's go down to the corner and cross like nice, law-abiding citizens."

When they reached the next pole, Genie took out her stapler.

"Miss?" A small woman stood behind her. She wore oversized clothing and held the handle of a shopping cart overloaded with black plastic garbage bags.

Genie turned around and said, "Did you say something to me?"

The woman, who could have been anywhere between thirty and fifty-five, smiled at Genie. Her teeth were surprisingly sound-looking. "I did. I wanted to tell you that the police will ticket you if they catch you using a stapler on these poles."

"Oh." Genie looked around. "But all the poles have staples in them."

"That's right," the woman said, nodding as if Genie had made a good point. "But those have been there, most of them, for years.

286

There's laws against using staples now. You can use tape, though."
She looked at the pile of flyers in Genie's hand. "May I ask what
you're advertising?"

Genie handed her a flyer. "I'm looking for a necklace like this. It
belonged to my husband."

The woman looked closely at the photo and description. "It's very
beautiful," she said. "I imagine he'd like to get it back as soon as
possible." She looked into Genie's eyes and put her hand on Genie's arm. "Do you mind if I hold onto this? I might come across
someone who can help you. I meet quite a few people on the
street every day. Some of them are extraordinarily well-informed.
In fact, some regularly communicate with extraterrestrial friends.
Those creatures can be very helpful, too, I've heard." She spoke
matter-of-factly; her clear, brown eyes holding Genie's gaze.

Genie was thunderstruck. What had she been doing? The woman
in front of her was like countless others who roamed the streets,
confused and without help, without a home, prey to loneliness
and danger. It was almost as if Charlie was telling her not to keep
trying to find the necklace, to stop trying to find out why he'd
been shot. If Charlie had been there he would have been far more
concerned with the homeless person in front of him than with a
necklace.

"My name is Genie," Genie said softly. "What's yours?"

The woman smiled. "Beth. My mother named me for her sister."

"Beth, do you have a place to sleep tonight?"

Beth smiled broadly. "Oh, yes. I go to the Ladies' Place on Devery
most nights. They're lovely. Have you ever been there, Genie?"

Genie smiled. "No, I haven't. But I'm glad that you like it."

Beth folded the flyer carefully and slipped it into her pocket. "Well, I should be going now. I'm glad we had a chance to meet, and I hope you find your husband's necklace. I'll ask around for you."

Genie had left her wallet at home. She fished into her jacket pocket and pulled out a twenty. "Beth, may I give you this for your help?"

Beth's eyes flashed and she smiled. "Aren't you kind," she said, taking the bill and putting it away. "Well, goodbye now." She pushed her cart up the street and disappeared around the corner.

Debra, who'd been standing off to the side, said, "You okay, Genie?"

Genie gave her a shaky smile and said, "Yeah. Shall we go home?"

"Don't you want to put the rest of those up?"

Genie shook her head. "I just decided to do two things, Debs."

Debra cocked her head. "What two things?"

Genie slipped her arm through Debra's. "One, I'm going to stop this dumb search. The necklace is probably floating in the Pacific Ocean, and I'm never going to see it again. Two, when I get home, I'm going to write a big check and mail it to the Ladies' Place. It's a drop in the bucket, but as Charlie would say, every drop counts."

Debra squeezed her arm. "You're going to be okay, Genie."

Genie sighed. "Maybe someday I will. For now I just want to try to live the way Charlie would want me to. I have to accept the fact that finding the necklace won't bring him back."

CHAPTER FIFTY

On a Saturday morning in October Genie woke early to beat the heat, common in early fall. When Charlie was alive they'd hiked everywhere, but now that she was alone she enjoyed the challenge of running again. She'd push herself to go just a little faster or half a mile farther, rewarding herself with an extra-long shower. If she were more susceptible to the new-age vibe of Sonoma County she might tell herself she was releasing toxins when she pushed herself to breathlessness. It didn't matter, though. She felt better when she ran, and that's why she kept at it.

When she got home she turned on the kettle and put two heaping spoons of coffee in her French press, then went upstairs to pick out clothes for her day. She had an appointment in San Francisco with Philip, her long-time agent. He'd been so kind to her in the days after Charlie's death, not pressing her on her progress with her latest book, and sending her thoughtful notes and miniature wildflower bouquets from a notoriously pricey San Francisco florist. In a burst of energy a few days earlier Genie had called him to see if they could have lunch. She wanted to get back to writing, and she was interested in starting a blog as well. Philip had mentioned blogging the previous year and she'd just rolled her eyes. But all she wanted now was to immerse herself in work.

After showering and blowing her hair dry, Genie dressed in a simple black and white linen dress and Pikolinos sandals. She looked into the back of her closet and found a blazer she'd bought from J.Crew years before. She didn't put it on—at eleven a.m. it was already eighty degrees—but she brought it with her. San Francisco could be chilly most of the time, even when Sonoma County was broiling. She put out fresh food and water for Tramp, found her purse, keys, and sunglasses, and headed out for the city.

Fort Mason was hopping, as usual. Genie did a few spins around the parking area before she found an empty space, finally spotting one facing the bay. She sat in her car, staring out at the water. Alcatraz, that gloomy rock, brooded not far away. Once a grim artifact of a cruel penal system, it had become a popular tourist attraction. Visitors from all over the world, perhaps before riding on a cable car or after snapping photos of the sea lions lolling and bellowing at Pier 39, took ferries out for tours of the prison, all part of a trip to San Francisco.

Genie and Charlie had never wanted to go to Alcatraz, but when Meara and Genie's mother had come to visit, they'd relented. They rented the audio tour, which guided them through the cell blocks and common areas of the prison. The tape ended with a former prisoner describing how it felt to be released after serving a long sentence. At Alcatraz, he'd never been visited by anyone, and when he left he'd been dropped on a busy street corner in San Francisco with no one to meet him. He felt envious of all the people walking purposefully along the city streets. He, himself, had nowhere to go, no one to see. He said he was scared to death. Genie felt a lump in her throat at hearing the man's sad story, but she kept going, trailing her sister and mother. When they went to the gift shop, she found Charlie sitting on a bench outside, mourning all the men he could never have helped.

She shook herself back to the present. With a quick look in the vanity mirror to check her lipstick, she got out of the car and headed for Greens, a favorite restaurant. As usual, the high-end vegetarian place was packed, with customers sitting around the sculptural redwood burl at the front, or standing near the door, waiting for their tables. Genie spotted Philip waving to her from a table by the window. She threaded her way past the young servers and tightly spaced tables, leaning away when a man suddenly jumped from his seat to welcome a friend.

"Did you play running back at USC?" Philip said, rising from his chair to kiss Genie on the cheek. As always, her wore a suit and tie, making him stand out from the crowd in San Francisco, where business casual—medium blue shirt, blazer, and jeans—was the norm. That was, unless you were a super-rich techno-titan. Then you wore ripped jeans, a t-shirt, and a hoodie.

Genie rolled her eyes. "My Dad never let me forget I went to the same school as Frank Gifford. There was that other running back there, though. He didn't end well."

"Best not to mention him," Philip said, motioning for Genie to sit. "I already ordered appetizers. And, oh, here are the drinks!"

A slim young man set down two flutes half-filled with sparkling wine. "Two Brut-de-Blancs," he said. "Your grilled polenta and spring rolls will be out shortly."

Genie eyed him skeptically. "We're starting with Champagne? What's going on, Philip?"

"Who needs an excuse to drink Champagne? Besides, they're only half-glasses. I knew you wouldn't go for a bottle."

"It's one p.m., and I have to drive back up 101 after this. I can't get sloshed during the day on Champagne like your average literary agent."

Philip raised a blond eyebrow. For as long as Genie knew him, Philip wore his white-blond hair in pompadour. It should have looked ridiculous, but on him, it worked. "You wouldn't be making cracks about literary agents if you knew what I was about to tell you." He took a lazy sip and set his glass down, looking out the window at the boats docked nearby, ostentatiously drawing out the pause in the conversation.

"If you think I'm going to beg you to tell me, you're sorely mistaken," Genie said with a laugh.

A server appeared at the table with their appetizers. She wore a serious expression, and after she'd set the food down, said, "Would you like to order your main courses now?"

Philip gave her a smile Genie had seen a hundred times. It never failed to charm. "Thank you, but we'll wait a bit before we do that, if that's okay."

The young woman's face was transformed. With her big smile, she looked about fourteen years old. "Take all the time you need," she said, then headed back to kitchen, running the gantlet through other busy servers and happy diners.

Genie spooned a little polenta onto her plate, then skewered a spring roll with her fork. She was well aware that Philip was leaning toward her, willing her to ask him what he had on his mind. She handed the plate of polenta to Philip and said, "So, are you going to tell me, or are you going to burst?"

Philip rolled his eyes. "I guess I'll tell you." He heaped most of the polenta onto his plate and said, "Guess what literary agent just negotiated a seven-figure deal for the movie rights to *Truth to Tell?*

It took Genie a minute to understand what Philip said. *Truth to Tell* was the title of the book she'd published late last year. She knew it had been selling well, but she hadn't been paying too much attention to such things, not since Charlie had died. She'd seen some financial success from her books in the last few years—that was when Philip had become her agent—but she'd never dreamed of such a windfall. "Seven figures? Like in a million dollars?"

"Try one point seven million," Philip said, picking up his glass of champagne. He giggled and tossed back the rest of the wine. "Can you believe it, Genie? I told you that book would make you rich." He put out his hand and stopped a server going by. "Could you please bring us a bottle of this?" Looking back at Genie, he said, "Don't say it! I'll arrange for a car service to take you home."

Genie felt numb. She'd loved writing *Truth to Tell,* but never thought it was better than any of her other books. "Why this book?" she said in a soft voice. She accepted a full glass of Champagne and took a drink.

Philip laughed. "You're a great writer, but no marketing phenom, Genie. When I read that book I knew Keely would be a hit."

The novel began in the mid-eighties, and that had given Genie the chance to reference Madonna, the release of the Apple Macintosh, the Challenger tragedy, and other events and cultural touchstones that probably seemed like ancient history to most of her readers. She'd had fun with the clothing and hairstyles of the time, too. However, like all her books, it had a serious side. Keely was the protagonist, a young girl who'd grown up the baby of the family, only to become orphaned and without siblings at age twelve after a devastating fire in her Boston home. Sent across country to live with her grape-farming grandparents in Alexander

Valley, California, she's a fish out of water until she meets Elena and Carlos, fraternal twins. The three grow up together, and eventually Keely falls in love with Carlos, setting off conflicts within his family and her own. As in every one of Genie's books, though, love conquers all, and Keely and Carlos eventually marry and inherit the vineyards from her grandparents and Elena becomes an award-winning winemaker. She'd modeled Keely on her sister Meara, making her petite, beautiful, and full of spirit.

Genie held up her glass, "To you, Philip. You're the marketing genius."

They clinked glasses. Philip finished the last of the polenta. "Can't sell unless I have the product, Genie. Oh, and by the way, Pennypacker Press and the studio want you to start blogging on your website. That's part of the deal. This social media marketing is taking over, I'm telling you. Gone are the days when you could stick an ad in a couple of newspapers and set up a press tour to market a book. Now it's blogging, Facebook, Tweeter..."

Genie smiled. "Twitter, not Tweeter. Get with it, Philip. You're younger than I am."

"Whatever," Philip said, looking around for a server. "Your publisher wants you to blog, so you'll blog, okay? It doesn't have to be much—just a couple hundred words twice a week. I'll send you links to other blogs like they have in mind. You could do it in your sleep." He peered at Genie over his menu and winked. "Let's order. I'm starved."

CHAPTER FIFTY-ONE

Genie concentrated on teaching and forced herself to keep her evenings and weekends packed with activities and writing, even if grief stopped her cold many times a day. One of her top priorities was ensuring that Charlie's life's work would continue. In late November she'd called Marty Edmund to discuss the search for a new director for Mercy's Family. Although Maria Kim had agreed to step in on a temporary basis she had made it clear she wanted to continue in her regular role, so someone else would have to be found as a permanent replacement for Charlie. Marty invited Genie to come out to his winery for Sunday lunch, which she'd agreed to readily. She'd never been there before and, unlike at her own house, which Marty had visited often, the memories of time spent with Charlie wouldn't hang over the discussion.

It was an abnormally warm day for so late in the year, the sky a cloudless blue. Genie drove up a narrow road that wound up a hillside covered with grape vines. The grapes had all been harvested, of course, but a large flock of starlings dipped in and out of the tidy rows, perhaps looking for fruit that had been left behind. The road continued to climb, offering a spectacular view of the valley below. When Genie reached the open wrought iron gates of the winery she looked back and saw the birds come together in a murmuration, hundreds of them forming a hypnotic pattern, gliding up and down together over the vineyard.

She drove through the open gates and onto an elegant crushed rock driveway, the burgundy red stone hinting at the wine produced on the site. Poplars grew on either side of the drive that curved slightly as it ascended further. She rounded another curve and there it was, the famous stone and glass structure built sixty years earlier. Elysian Farms was distinguished not only for its wine but also for the unusual architecture of the winery building. The front was deceptively small and served as the reception area and tasting room (by reservation only). Through the back door of that room the building expanded and housed the laboratories, towering vats, bottling room, and wine barrels found in any winery. Behind the winery was a large house, also made from stone and glass. It sat on the edge of the hillside and looked out over Alexander Valley, home of dozens of wineries. Genie had read about Elysian Farms many times over the years; lifestyle magazines in the Bay area always covered it in any issue devoted to wine country. The photos didn't do it justice. Genie parked her car in a space near the front door and stood in the warm sunshine, happy just to be there.

"Genie, you made it!" Marty said as he opened the big front door. He walked over and hugged her, saying, "It's a little tricky finding the turnoff for this place."

Genie smiled and said, "Your directions were impeccable." She looked around again. "God, Marty, this place is even more beautiful than I expected. I guess I don't have to ask you if you like it here."

Marty raised one eyebrow. "What kind of ingrate doesn't like living in paradise?" He laughed and said, "You're right, though. I love it. It was definitely the right move for me. All that, and I'm learning how to make wine."

"Has Claude taken you on as a cellar rat?"

Marty put his arm around Genie's shoulder and guided her to the door. "I stay out of the great man's way when he's working. But every once in a while I have him to dinner. He's a fascinating guy. Too bad it's Sunday; he's never here on Sundays no matter what's going on. Fortunately his assistant is top-notch, and so is the rest of the crew."

"What does Claude do on Sundays?" Genie said as she walked into the reception area. It was at least ten degrees cooler than outdoors.

"Who knows?" Marty said. "He doesn't say, and I don't ask. Hey, would you like a little tour? I know you've probably been to a hundred wineries, so just tell me if you'd rather take a pass."

"I'm more curious to see the house, honestly," Genie said. "By the way, this tasting room is gorgeous. What kind of wood is the bar made of?"

Marty cleared his throat. "It's rosewood, if you can believe it. It's banned now, but when this place was built the owner wanted nothing but the best, which in his mind meant the most expensive. Whenever we do tastings I make sure the manager puts a cloth down on the top of the bar. It seems almost sacrilegious to use it at all, but that's what's here, so..."

Genie ran her hand lightly over the wood. "It's amazing."

"Well, if you want to see the house, let's go back outside. It's a nice little walk around the building."

They went out and turned right, down a pergola-covered lane. "Wow, look at the size of this garden!" Genie said. She put her hands on her hips and looked at the neat beds, most of which had gone into their dormant winter stage. Spinach and kale plants were still thriving, though, as well as purple-tipped broccoli.

"You have to see it in the summer," Marty said. "The tomatoes and cucumbers were unbelievable. And the blackberries! I had blackberry ice cream almost every day through August. Sam is the master-gardener. He and his husband Matt are quite a pair. Sam grows the stuff and Matt cooks. I had to up my running once they came to work here. In fact, Matt's made us lunch. Come meet him before he takes off for the afternoon."

"I'd love to," Genie said. A hawk soared overhead as she ran her fingers over the rosemary bushes lining the walkway. "What a place," she murmured.

Past the main winery building stood the house, a rambling structure made mostly of glass and redwood with a tiled roof. Marty opened a glass door trimmed with Art Nouveau-inspired copper scrollwork and Genie followed him into a large open space. Before she could look around, a young man came through a doorway near the patio.

"Would you like me to set out your lunch now, Marty?" he said. He was about thirty, slim, with short dark hair and a scruffy beard. He smiled and said, "You must be Genie. I'm Matt." He wiped his hands on his black apron and said, "Sorry, I was just in the kitchen." He came closer and held out his right hand.

"Nice to meet you, Matt," Genie said, shaking hands.

"Matt comes from Massachusetts, too, Genie," Marty said.

Matt nodded. "I'm from the western part of the state. Ever hear of Tyringham?"

Genie thought a moment. "No, sorry. I haven't been out to the western part of the state much."

Matt laughed. "No worries. Most people haven't heard of my town; it's a tiny place not too far from Stockbridge."

"Stockbridge I've heard of."

"Mmm," Matt said. "Everyone's heard of 'Stockbridge to Boston' thanks to James Taylor." He turned to Marty and said, "I don't want to rush you, but Sam just called and said his mother's plane's getting in half an hour early. Would it be all right if I served your lunch now?"

"Of course," Marty said. "It's nice enough to eat outside, right?"

Matt smiled. "I was thinking the same thing. The table's already set for you on the patio. I'll bring out the food right away."

"Shall we, Genie?" Marty said.

They walked out onto a large patio. Beyond lay Alexander Valley, its tidy rows of grapevines nestled among stands of oak. Two rattan chaise lounges were well-positioned to take in the view, and a terra cotta mosaic table ringed with four chairs sat nearby. On the table set for two sat a pitcher of iced tea and a small glass holding a single red dahlia.

"Sit here, Genie, so you can enjoy the view," Marty said. He took the chair opposite and poured tea for the two of them. Matt came out with a tray and set it on the table. "Thanks, Matt. We can serve ourselves. You need to get going," Marty said with a smile.

"You're sure?" Matt said, setting a bowls of polenta in front of Genie and Marty. "I mean, everything's here on the tray, but if you need coffee or anything after lunch..."

Marty waved his hands. "Matt, thank you for this beautiful lunch. I'm sure if Genie and I need anything else we can manage. Now get going!"

Matt put his hand on Genie's shoulder. "It was nice meeting you, Genie. I hope to see you again soon."

"Thanks, Matt," Genie said. When he'd gone she looked down at the bowl of polenta topped with an aromatic stew. "This smells incredible," she said.

"It's my favorite. Wild boar ragu," Marty said, setting a small dish of salad by Genie's plate. "And before you ask, no, I didn't bag a boar. One of Claude's helpers did. His father has a ranch up north and they sometimes have problems with those wild pigs. Anyway, dig in. No need to think too much about where this came from. If Matt prepared it, it's going to be good."

They ate in silence for a while, content to enjoy the warm afternoon and delicious food. When they'd finished, Marty said, "So, there are two things I want to talk to you about today, if you don't mind. First is finding someone to take over as director of Mercy's Family. I might actually have a lead on that, by the way."

Genie took a sip of tea. "What's the other thing?"

Marty shook his head. "Let's talk about the director position first, okay?"

"That's fine," Genie said. She set her glass down and leaned back, turning her face to the sun. "You said you had a lead?"

"I do," Marty said. He picked up a folder that sat on one of the empty chairs and pulled out some papers. "His name is Burt

Macauley. I got in touch with your friend Dave Ingalls in Boston and he recommended Burt. Here, take a look at his resume."

Genie took the pages from Marty and started reading. "Wow, he's done a lot of work in prisoners' rights. Five years in Chicago, three before that in Miami. But he must be pretty young. He graduated from college less than twelve years ago."

"He's young, that's true. But you should see some of the recommendations. I think we'd be lucky to get him. He and Maria talked by phone the other day and she was impressed."

"He's been in Chicago a while and went to Northwestern, too. Why would he want to move out here?"

"He's from Northern California originally. His family is in Chico, mostly. He wants to come back here to raise his kids nearer their grandparents. Plus, Mercy's Family has a great reputation. Oh, by the way, he'd like to talk to you when he's out here for some final interviews. Is that okay?"

"Me?" Genie sat straighter. "If you and Maria think he's okay, why would he want to talk to me?"

"He wants to talk to you about Charlie," Marty said, reaching his hand out to Genie's. Giving her hand a squeeze, he said, "He wants to make sure you approve of him, I think."

Genie took a deep breath and rubbed her hand over her eyes. She was quiet for a while, then looked up at Marty. "Does it ever get easier, Marty? Sometimes I'm doing fine, hitting on all cylinders, then—bam!—something will remind me of Charlie and I can barely function." A tear rolled down her cheek, but she wasn't embarrassed. If anyone could understand what she was going through, it was Marty.

Marty poured himself a little more tea and shrugged. "I don't know that it gets easier, but moments like that, those moments of absolute gut-punching sorrow, those don't happen so often over time." He smiled and said, "Walk with me? I want to tell you something kind of great."

Genie nodded and followed Marty down the path through the patio and out to a grassy area behind the house. Close-packed eucalyptus trees stood guard nearby, suffusing the air with their medicinal fragrance. Marty stretched his arms over his head and said, "Days like this are a gift, aren't they? Hey, there's a bench down there. Feeling like catching a few more rays?"

They walked to the small wooden bench, then sat. "So, Marty, tell me something great," Genie said.

Marty looked down at his hands. "You know, it's been a couple of years since Alec was here for Estelle's funeral. He came with his wife and son and stayed exactly two days. I didn't get a chance to get to know my grandson Chris; he'd lived in Australia since he was born and when he was here I barely got to talk to him. Those days after Estelle's death were just a blur."

Genie nodded. She remembered how grueling Estelle's last few weeks had been.

"That time was—I can't even find the words to express how bad it was, Genie." He wiped his hand over his face, then sat up straight. "But now something wonderful has happened. Alec, Beth, and Chris are coming for a visit next week. They're planning to stay here for a couple of weeks."

"That's great, Marty," Genie said. "Congratulations."

"That's not even the best part," Marty said, getting to his feet. "Alec told me they might move back here permanently. Beth's parents moved back to the States last year; they're up in Oregon. She wants to be closer to them, and well…" He took a deep breath. "I keep telling myself not to get my hopes up. But Genie, I gotta say, this is the best thing that's happened to me in a long time."

"Oh, Marty! I'm so happy for you. How did this happen? I mean, I know you tried reaching out to him years ago, but he never responded. Why did he get in touch with you after all this time?"

Marty smiled and said, "Actually, it was Charlie who reached out to him. Apparently he and Alec had a chat after Estelle's funeral, and about a year ago Charlie started emailing Alec, letting him know about me and asking him how his life was going. It seems they communicated pretty regularly. I guess you didn't know about that, right?"

Genie shook her head. "No, Charlie never said anything about it."

Marty shifted and turned to face Genie. "Alec emailed him a few times after, well, after Charlie died. He was concerned when Charlie didn't write back and did some Googling…"

"And he found out that Charlie had been killed," Genie said. She got up and took a few steps, then turned back to Marty. "When was that?"

"Two weeks ago. Right after Alec found out what had happened to Charlie, he gave me a call. He said that Charlie had wanted him to get back in touch with me. Charlie hadn't put it so directly, but it was more the way Charlie let him know about my life, what I was doing, how I was coping after Estelle's death…you know, kind of keeping Alec in the loop without lecturing him.

Alec said he'd come to look forward to hearing about me and realized how much he missed me." Marty's voice quavered, but he was smiling. "When he called me, Genie, when I heard his voice …I can't tell you how much that meant to me. I have Charlie to thank for bringing my son back to me. He's not here anymore, so I'll thank you instead."

Genie nodded. In a quiet voice she said, "I'm so glad this is happening. I hope I get to meet Alec when he's here."

"Of course you will. He wants us all to get together for dinner."

"After our lunch today, I'm going to have to insist that dinner be here, Marty. Matt's an amazing cook."

"Wherever we eat, we'll make a toast to Charlie, the man who got my family back to me."

CHAPTER FIFTY-TWO

Genie was surprised by how much she liked to blog. She wasn't ready to start writing another novel, but she wanted to write every day, a habit she'd developed years before. Posting to her blog a few times a week not only kept her writing, it also put her in touch with her fans, mostly girls aged ten and up. Their comments and questions to her often went far beyond the content of her novels, and she soon found herself offering advice and comfort to girls navigating the challenges of puberty and being a preteen. It also gave her a chance to talk about herself, something she couldn't do with her novels.

As Christmas grew near, Genie sat down to write her final blog post of the year. She was determined not to fall into the trap of writing a clichéd "year in review." After all, what could she say about 2012? It had been the worst year of her life and the pain she felt at losing Charlie would never go away. She wouldn't burden her young readers with her own torment, though. So she wrote something else:

The holidays can be a hard time for people, both young and old. If you've lived a long life, you might find the holidays sad because they remind you of all the people you've lost. If you're the parent of young children, money might be hard to come by and you feel you can't give your kids the holidays they deserve. Or say you're a young person—maybe twelve or thirteen—and you think you should feel happy around this time of year, but you don't. Maybe it's pressure at school, or maybe your parents have split and you can't celebrate the way you used to. For all of us, the worst part of the holidays may be that we feel that there's something wrong with us if we don't feel happy.

I'm old enough to have lost some people very close to me, and I'll always miss them. I'll be sad about that, not just this holiday season, but forever. But I'm looking forward to the holidays anyway. I'll be back in Boston area through the new year to see my family—my sister, my brothers, their spouses, and my niece and nephews—even a grandnephew. I'll surround myself with people I love, and people who love me. I'll stay in the house I grew up in and, if the weather is right, maybe challenge my brothers to a snowball fight. (My sister has a killer arm, so I'm always on her side.)

I hope the holidays hold a wonderful surprise for each of you, something that delights you and warms your heart. When I come back I'll start blogging again. I can't stop myself, you know. It's a joy to keep in touch with all of you, my dear blog-friends. Happy Holidays and all good wishes for a wonderful New Year.

CHAPTER FIFTY-THREE

Genie pulled her suitcase from the overhead bin and looked out the window. At five p.m. it was already dark, and snow swirled in the lights of the ground crew's vehicles. She shuffled off the plane behind the other passengers, grateful to have mailed her presents to Massachusetts ahead of time. As she wheeled her Travelpro through the crowded terminal she tried not to listen to the nonstop Christmas music. There was no escaping it from November through the first week of January, no matter where you were. Swinging into the ladies room, she splashed cold water on her face and dabbed on some lipstick. Meara and Frank would be picking her up, and she didn't want them to see she'd been crying. They'd try to comfort her, of course, which would only set her off again. This Christmas would be excruciating, but she was determined to gut it out. She was luckier than many people in her situation: she had a loving family and friends, work that she adored, and she was financially set. None of that made up for Charlie being gone and nothing ever would. But she'd enjoy the good things that remained.

She spotted Meara standing near the baggage claim and ran toward her.

Meara saw her and yelled, "Genie!" and threw her arms around her. She looked behind Genie and asked, "Is that all you brought?"

"Yep," Genie said. "I've learned to pack light, finally. Besides, if I need to wash something, you'll let me use your machine, right?"

Meara rolled her eyes. "Darn! I knew I should have installed those coin slots on the washer!" She pulled Genie's scarf tighter around her neck. "Bundle up. It's freezing out there, and the wind just picked up something awful."

Genie looked around. "Where's Frank?"

Meara grabbed Genie's hand. "Come on! He's parked right outside. I swear he's gonna get a ticket. We've been here nearly half an hour."

Genie had known Frank nearly all her life. If anyone could get away with live-parking in front of a terminal patrolled by Massachusetts State Troopers, it was him. As they rushed through the automatic doors, Genie staggered from a blast of arctic cold. Not for the first time she asked herself how she could have lived so long in this climate.

Meara ran toward Frank's black Tacoma with a "Semper Fi" Marine Corps sticker on the back bumper. Through the open window, Frank was chatting with a State Trooper, who roared with laughter, his breath visible in white puffs. As Genie caught up with Meara, she heard Frank say, "I told that son of a bitch he could go straight back to New York. Never heard from him again."

Genie clambered into the back seat, pushing her suitcase ahead onto the seat beside her, as Meara got into the front passenger seat.

Frank said to the trooper, "Well, looks like my friend's arrived. It was wonderful to talk to you, Izzie."

The trooper patted Frank's arm and said, "Same to you! You have a Merry Christmas, now. And drive safe."

As they moved away from the curb, Meara shook her head in amazement. "How the hell do you do that, Frank? If that was me, your pal Izzie would have towed my car and taken me to the Suffolk County Jail."

Frank smiled broadly and said, "I told you a million times, Meara, I got the magic touch. No Trooper is gonna hassle a Marine, hence the sticker. Once I get them talking, I just charm the bejesus out of them."

He turned quickly and winked at Genie. "How was your flight, kiddo?"

Genie laughed. "The flight was fine, but this welcome is even better. I didn't think Staties were capable of being charmed."

Frank pulled out of the airport and headed toward the Ted Williams tunnel. "Everyone's capable of being charmed. You just gotta know how to do the charming. You warm enough back there, Genie?"

"Fine." Genie pulled off her coat and set it on top of her suitcase. The snow was coming down fast, and the traffic going into the tunnel was crawling. "Looks like it's going to be a long drive home," Genie said. "Last time I tried this during rush-hour it took me two hours to get to Waltham," she said.

"You forget, I put myself through college driving a limo," Frank said, making an abrupt left turn. "I know every shortcut there is, and we're gonna use one of my favorites."

Meara laughed. "Hang onto your hat, Genie. Prince Charming here is about to show off!"

Forty minutes later, they pulled into Meara's driveway. "I'll help Genie with her suitcase, then bring the snow blower over," Frank said.

"I can get it," Genie said. "Thanks for the ride, Frank. It was extremely stimulating."

Meara gave Frank a quick kiss on the cheek. "When you finish with the snow blower, come inside. We're having beef stew."

Meara looped her arm through Genie's as they walked up the steps to the house. "Don't worry, Genie. You'll get through this Christmas."

Walking into the warm house, Genie's throat tightened. "Absent friends," she whispered to Meara.

Meara hugged Genie tight. "They'll be with us in spirit."

CHAPTER FIFTY-FOUR

A few days after Christmas, Genie sat in the kitchen of Meara's house. The late-afternoon sun streamed through the flowering stems of a hanging Christmas cactus, and Genie helped herself to another butter cookie. She and Meara had shared a pot of tea, catching up. The house was finally quiet, and Genie enjoyed the mellow feeling of being warm and cozy inside while the weak December light made long shadows on the snow. It had been hard for Genie to be alone with her family this Christmas. Last year Charlie had been with her, and, though she'd made a point to mention him often, she could tell that most of her family tiptoed around the subject of his absence. She couldn't blame them. They loved her and didn't want to make her sad, though nothing they said or didn't say would have made a bit of difference. She was grieving and would always miss Charlie, whether it was Christmas, Independence Day, or any other day of the year.

When she heard Meara clomping down the stairs in her favorite clogs, Genie got up and cleared away the cups and spoons, putting them into the dishwasher while she put the Belleek teapot in the sink to hand wash. She'd promised to fix dinner for Meara and Frank and needed to get the chicken in the oven soon. As she was about to turn the oven on, the doorbell rang.

"I'll get it!" Meara shouted.

The front door opened and closed, and Meara walked into the kitchen. "Will you look at this!" she said. "These flowers just came for you. I think there must have been a mistake—they're not in good shape." Meara set the large bouquet on the table and stood back, folding her arms. "I didn't see a delivery truck. You should open the card, Genie, then call the florist. These flowers are half-dead."

It was a pitiful-looking arrangement, with withered red and white carnations and blackened sprigs of holly. A few broken pinecones were interspersed with the flowers. Genie plucked out the large envelope, ready to give the florist a call. Opening it with a frown, she said, "I can't think of anyone who'd send me flowers here."

"Maybe your agent?"

"No," Genie said, opening the card she'd taken out of the envelope. "This isn't his style. He's more into glam—"

There was nothing written on the outside of the card except Genie's name, but a glossy 3 x 5 photo slipped out and onto the floor. Genie picked it up. The photo showed a gold chain and pendant resting on a black background. It was the necklace she'd given Charlie. In the corner of the photo was a small VP. "Oh my God!" she whispered, swaying a little.

"What is it, Genie?"

She handed the photo to Meara, who looked at it, then frowned. "I don't understand. Is this a picture of Charlie's necklace? Did the police find it? But why would they send you a photo like this, with the flowers? Why not call you?"

Genie held onto the edge of the table, forcing herself not to black out. "It wasn't the police who sent it," she whispered. "It was Victor."

"Victor?" Meara's voice shook. "Victor Pulnik? Have you been in touch with him?"

Genie shook her head slowly as she tried to make sense of what she was seeing. An awful certainty seized her. Victor was taunting her. He had something to do with Charlie's death. How else could he have the necklace? She grabbed Meara's arm. "I need your car, Meara. Where are the keys?"

"Why? You can't seriously be thinking of seeing him."

Genie was moving too fast to respond. Driving was a bad idea, actually. She didn't trust herself behind the wheel given the way she was feeling, and she doubted she could remember how to get there, anyway. She ran into the front hall and grabbed her coat and purse, making sure her iPhone was in her coat pocket.

Meara caught up to her and held her arm. "Genie, be reasonable. If Victor knows something about Charlie's death, you need to call the police. You can't go confront him on your own. He's a dangerous man; you should know that!"

Genie gently pulled Meara's hand away. "The police haven't been much help to me. This is something I have to do, Meara. Don't worry about me." She kissed Meara's cheek and hurried out the door.

Meara ran after her, calling, "Where are you going? You don't have the car keys! Genie, come back!"

Genie jogged up the street, oblivious to the puddles that were icing over in the late-day cold. She pulled her phone out and tapped Victor's name into Google. His studio was still on Jenton Street. She brought up her Uber app and typed in Victor's address, then kept going. She'd meet the Uber in ten minutes at the end of Lake Street. When she got there, the car, a Nissan, was waiting for her at the corner. She jumped in without a word to the driver, who picked up on her urgency and pulled away from the curb in a hurry.

As they drove, Genie looked again at the photo. What kind of game was Victor playing? Perhaps he knew about Charlie's murder and found a necklace like Charlie's, then took a photo of it to taunt her. But the police had never said anything publically about the missing necklace, so how would he know it had been stolen? She thought briefly about calling Detective Haddad in San Francisco, then decided to wait. She had to get the truth out of Victor herself. She drummed her fingers on the armrest while the car crawled down Storrow Drive, choked with traffic as usual. It was dark by the time they pulled onto Beacon Street. There were only a few blocks to go. Genie's mind was racing, but she tried to force herself to think clearly. If Victor knew something about Charlie's murder, she couldn't go flying into his studio making accusations. She had to stay calm and get the truth out of him. When the car pulled up at his address Genie thanked the driver and hurried out. She looked up at the third floor, where she remembered the studio was. Light shone through the windows. He was waiting for her.

She punched the buzzer and the door opened automatically. The interior of the building had been renovated, with gleaming white walls and a trendy poured concrete floor. The freight elevator was gone, too, replaced with a shiny stainless steel door that slipped open noiselessly when she pushed the button. Her heart pounded as she rode up the three floors. She breathed deeply and told herself to stay calm. For so many years she'd dreaded bumping into Victor again, and now she was rushing toward him. She couldn't let him get the upper hand; she had to stay focused.

The door opened. Across the room an elderly man in a wheelchair sat at a small table. Did she have the right floor? "Excuse me," she said, taking a few steps forward. "Is Victor Pulnik here?"

The old man turned the wheelchair around slowly. "Don't you know me, Aideen?" he said in a raspy voice.

"Victor!" Genie didn't take another step.

He was barely recognizable. His blond hair had thinned and gone white, and his face, a sallow, sagging mask, was recognizable only by those icy green eyes. He sat slumped, wearing a too-large black tracksuit that exposed a bony clavicle. Victor placed his hand on the joystick and maneuvered the chair toward Genie. "You're looking fit. Older, of course, but fine for your age." He got closer, and Genie took a step back. "What's the matter, Genie? You've seen people in my condition before. What about your father? He was in pretty bad shape by the time he died, right? Or did you bother to come back from California before he kicked the bucket?"

"What's wrong with you?" Genie whispered.

"That's quite a question," Victor said. He'd stopped a foot away from Genie and looked up at her, his grey face twisted into a grin. "I don't think I have time to go into all the ways there's something wrong with me. When I was in prison—" He stopped and took a breath. "When I was incarcerated many years ago, before you and I had our little reunion, I was told I had sociopathic tendencies. But you'd probably figured that out for yourself. If you're asking why I look the way I do, there's a simple answer. I'm dying. My smoking and whoring around finally caught up with me. You didn't come here to ask about my health, did you?" He reached into his pocket and tossed something at Genie's feet.

316

A gold chain and pendant skittered onto the floor. Genie picked the necklace up and turned the pendant over. On the back a small heart was etched into the gold Celtic knot. There was no doubt: this had been Charlie's. Her fingers closed over the chain, rage coursing through her. "How did you get this?"

Victor maneuvered his chair back to the table, then picked up a length of clear tubing and pulled it over his head, fixing a nasal cannula into his nostrils. "Sorry," he said, his voice hoarse. "I don't usually talk so much these days." He smiled again as he sat with his head back. "Would you mind coming closer? My last round of chemo did a number on my hearing."

Genie took a few steps toward him.

"Sit down, Genie," Victor said, pointing to a chair on the other side of the table.

"No." Genie was shaking, but not from fear. "Just tell me how you got this. And how did you know I'd be at Meara's house?"

Victor shrugged. "I'll answer the easy question first. I'm an avid reader of your blog. You said you'd be going home for Christmas, so that's where I sent your festive bouquet. As for the tougher question, well... a man named Al got the necklace for me. Well, I should say, the guy Al hired to shoot Charlie got it for me. Then he...what was his name, Al?"

A burly, dark-haired man slipped out from behind a stack of photographic equipment. He held a gun.

"Clarence Forester," he said in a mocking tone. "Dude called himself Eichmann, thought he was some kinda Nazi or something. He was an idiot."

"Anyway, Clarence killed your husband and took the necklace, which he gave to Al. Then Al killed Clarence. And now, you have the necklace back."

Genie's legs nearly gave way. She reached out for the back of a chair by the table and sat down. Victor sat with his eyes closed, a smile on his face.

Genie bit the inside of her lip, forcing herself not to scream. She leaned toward Victor and said, choking out the words, "But why? Why did you do this?"

Victor opened his eyes and took one of Genie's hands in his. She could feel the bones in his hand as she tried to pull away, but his grip was strong. "Aideen...," he said, pulling her toward him. "Don't you remember I told you that you belonged to me? Did you think I'd let you and your dear husband live happily till your golden anniversary?"

"You're crazy, Victor."

He took a labored breath and said, "That may be. But I made a promise to myself when you left me that day..."

"Left you? When?" Genie managed finally to pull her hand away. "After you humiliated me in Paris or after you tried to kill me at your apartment?"

Victor shrugged. "I'm not convinced I would have killed you. Either way, I tried talking to you, I wanted to beg you to forgive me. But you had your little sister send me away. When you turned your back on me, you might as well have killed me. You pushed me away and my life turned to shit. You were to blame for that. So I've been keeping tabs on you, making sure I know what's going on in your life. After our little Paris fling it was difficult, but when the Internet came along things were so much easier."

"What are you talking about?"

"You disappeared for a while, then when Google came along I found you again. In fact, I went out to California after one of your books was published. I'd read all about your happy life with your wonderful husband, and I had to see for myself. I tried to stay hidden, but I think you might have seen me once."

"The Farmer's Market," Genie said in a flat voice.

"Right. You and your roly-poly little husband were looking at a hideous crafts booth. What were they selling? Some kind of macramé? Anyway, once I'd seen him I lost interest. If that's the kind of guy you settled for, then I couldn't really feel too jealous, though I did follow your career. The Google alert I set up for you worked great. I even read a few of your books. I was content to watch from a distance. That is, until you decided to psychoanalyze me in public. Remember the interview you gave to that silly magazine? You were gushing about how happy you were, how wonderful your husband was, and how magnificent your life turned out. I didn't care about any of that. But then you started talking about me. You said I had no heart and had probably never been happy. You said you pitied me. I read that the day I'd seen my doctor. I asked him to be straight with me, and he told me there was no hope, and that I'd die a painful death very soon. I didn't think was fair for me to suffer like that and for you to be happy, so I paid my friend here to take care of your precious Charlie. It was only fair after you said those things about me. Said you pitied me. I would have left you alone if you hadn't attacked me that way."

She couldn't look at Victor anymore. Al had been sitting silently with a little smile on his face, seemingly proud of himself. But when she looked at him he averted his eyes.

"I have to get out of here," Genie said, jumping up.

"You're not leaving, Genie," Victor said, nodding at Al. "I didn't lure you here to confess my sins. And you're crazy if you think I'll let you go to the police with this. I'm not going to die in jail."

Al pointed the gun at Genie.

"Please sit down, Genie," Victor said. "I'll tell you why you're here."

Genie sat and put Charlie's necklace in her pocket. "Go ahead," she said. "If you just want to torture me about Charlie, though, I can't understand why. How could you have done this? What you did in Paris was bad enough, but to have my husband killed? Because I said I pitied you? You've been holding a grudge against me since we were seventeen—we were just kids playing at love."

"Not me," Victor said, raising his voice. "I wasn't playing." He sucked in his breath and writhed, gritting his teeth, then exhaled. "I loved you, Genie, and you betrayed me. I've never forgiven you for that. When the doctor told me I was going to die, I didn't mind. I'd been in pain for a long time and was sick of it. In fact, I thought about killing myself that day, but then I saw your interview. I knew I had something to live for, at least for a little while." He turned to Al and said, "Tell Genie how her Charlie died, Al."

Genie turned to Al. "You were there?"

Al nodded and said, "I watched from a second-floor window across the street. I wanted to make sure it was done right."

"What do you mean, 'done right'?"

"I wanted Charlie to feel the same pain I do," Victor said, his voice hoarse. "Every day, every night, my guts are in agony. Do you know what that's like, Genie?"

She shook her head. She didn't want to hear any more.

"Well, Charlie found out. Al's buddy shot him three times in the belly. It was as close as you could come to disemboweling him. I hear Charlie screamed for a while before he died."

She put her hand over her mouth and moaned. Her Charlie had died in agony, alone on the street. And Victor had made it happen.

Victor grimaced. "He must have been in terrible pain, Genie. Just like I am right now. Do you still pity me, or do you hate me?"

Genie couldn't speak.

Victor removed the cannula and leaned over to turn off the flow of oxygen. "I'll bet you'd like to hurt me, wouldn't you? It wouldn't be the first time, of course. But now, things are different. I want to die, and you want to kill me. What would be more fitting? All you have to do is take that gun from Al—don't worry, he'll give it to you—just take the gun and shoot me, right here." He pointed to the center of his forehead.

"I'm not going to do that, Victor," Genie whispered. "Charlie devoted his life to helping people like the man who killed him. He helped anyone he could. He'd probably even try to help you. He wouldn't want me to take revenge."

Victor took a deep breath, then started coughing. He fished a cloth out of his pocket and put it over his mouth until the hacking stopped. "I thought you might say that. It's very important to me that you be the one to kill me, Genie. That's why Al's here to help. I want to make sure your fingerprints are on the gun, and for everyone to see what a vicious little bitch you really are. Killing a man in a condition like this, just to get revenge for a teenage relationship gone wrong."

Genie looked over at Al and, for the first time, noticed he was wearing latex surgical gloves. The man still would not look at her. He fidgeted, nervous and breathing hard. "Hey, Victor. I thought you said that Charlie guy was a prosecutor. You said he was a racist and he went out of his way to get guys put away for life, guys like my brother. He died in prison cause of some bastard prosecutor. She's saying something different."

"My husband worked with released prisoners," Genie said, her eyes welling. "He helped them find jobs and places to live."

"Don't listen to her," Victor said, his voice grating. "Her husband hated people like you and your brother."

Genie pulled her purse onto her lap. She ignored Victor and looked straight at Al. "I can prove what I'm saying. Let me take my iPhone out. I'll show you his obituary. You can read it yourself."

"Let's get this over with. I paid you a lot of money, Al!" Victor's breath came in gasps now. "She's a liar."

Genie kept her eyes on Al. "Okay? Can I get my phone out?"

Al shrugged. "Sure, why not?"

While Genie took out her phone and tapped on the screen, Victor moved his chair back and grabbed the cannula. Fiddling with the oxygen tank, he took a couple of breaths.

Genie handed Al the phone, saying, "This is Charlie's obituary... it's from our local newspaper."

Al took the phone and put the gun in his lap. He frowned as he read, his lips moving as he sounded out the words.

Genie stared at Al and tried to ignore the sounds of Victor gulping for air. Finally, Al looked up and said, "Hey, Vic. Says here that her husband helped a lot of guys after they got out. Got them jobs, places to live. One guy said he owed him his life." He stood, holding the gun loosely by his side. "Vic, why are you hassling her this way? Just cause she broke up with you when you were kids? Is that why you hired me to kill her husband? He was a good guy."

Victor glared at him. "Stay out of this, Al. You got your money. In a few minutes I'll be dead and you can go. You agreed to this."

"I would'na gone along with you if I'da known the truth. You're a sick bastard, Vic. If you want to die, that's your business. Take some pills or jump out a window. Why does this lady have to suffer more?" Al put the gun on the table and started to remove his gloves.

"I paid you a hundred grand, Maricel! I'll tell the police you came in here to kill us both," Victor said, his eyes bulging as he lurched forward, dislocating the cannula and knocking his oxygen tank on its side. "I'll tell them about what you did to Charlie. I'll tell them you killed the man who shot him." His breaths came in little gasps, as if he was drowning. He leaned over, his hands flailing as he tried to find the tank.

They jumped at the sound of sirens. They sounded close and were getting closer. Al got up and looked outside. "The cops are coming down the alley." He ran to the other side of the studio and stepped out onto the fire escape, yelling "Rot in hell, you piece of shit!"

Victor managed to get the oxygen going and replaced the cannula. He looked Genie in the eyes and whispered, "Please, Genie. Before they get here, please do it. I can't take the pain anymore. I don't want to die in prison." His bravado was gone. He sagged in his chair, a tear rolling down one cheek. Then he moved quickly, reaching for the gun.

As he picked it up, Genie jumped out of her chair and kicked his hand hard, knocking the gun away.

Victor smiled horribly, tucking his hand under his other arm. "You still have time to kill me, Genie. Don't you want to?"

Genie trembled, but her voice was strong. "If I had known what you were going to do to Charlie, I would have killed you then. But now, what's the point? It's not my fault that you're sick and in pain. And it certainly wasn't Charlie's. No, I won't do what you want. You're going to have to live out whatever life you have left to you. I won't have anything to do with it."

The elevator doors opened. "Don't move!" shouted a police officer. He was young and had his gun drawn.

"The gun's over there," Genie said with a slight upturn of her chin.

The officer came forward and carefully picked up Al's gun, handing it to another officer right behind him.

"Are you Mrs. Maguire?" the young cop said softly. He'd replaced his gun and put his hand lightly on Genie's arm. "Are you all right, ma'am?"

Genie couldn't answer at first. She was dimly aware of the other officer talking to Victor, then rolling his chair away. Other police came into the room, talking loudly to each other and into walkie-talkies, the static scratching the air. The room seemed to fill with a grey fog, but she held on, willing herself not to faint. She felt someone holding her hand, calling her name, but she couldn't answer at first. A cold, wet cloth placed on the back of her neck stopped her lightheadedness, and she saw Meara's face close to hers. She was surprised to find herself on the floor.

"Genie!" she said. "Are you all right?"

Genie looked up into Meara's heart-shaped face, trying to focus her eyes.

"Help me!" Meara shouted, turning back toward the police.

Suddenly four black-uniformed police were standing over Genie. One of them, the one who'd spoken to her, knelt beside her. "Mrs. Maguire, can we get you up onto this chair?"

Genie nodded. Two other police officers bent to help her to her feet, their strong hands supporting her shoulders.

"Be careful with her!" Meara snapped. "She's not a sack of potatoes, you know."

Genie smiled. Only Meara would talk that way to a room full of police. When she was on the chair, she looked around. "Where's Victor?" she said. "He's very sick."

Meara rolled her eyes. "Why do you give a flying fuck about him?"

A woman Genie hadn't seen before stood next to Meara. "Ms. Halloran," she said to Meara, "Perhaps you'd like to talk to my colleague over by the elevator."

Meara looked her up and down, weighing whether or not to comply. With a shake of her head, Meara stomped away, and the woman pulled up a chair near Genie. She was dressed in a checked jacket and black pants, and wore a police I.D. tag around her neck. Leaning close to Genie, she said in a soft voice, "Are you all right?"

Genie licked her lips. Her mouth felt like it was stuffed with cotton. "Do you think I can have some water?" she whispered.

"Of course," the woman said, nodding to an officer who stood nearby.

Someone handed her an open bottle of water, and Genie took a sip, then another. She set the bottle on the floor and said, "Who are you?"

The woman smiled. Though she looked young, there were light lines at the corners of her mouth. "My name is Detective Santangelo. I'm with the Boston PD. I've been in touch with Detective Haddad in San Francisco. She's the one who worked on your husband's case. Do you remember?"

"Of course I do," Genie said, straightening up.

The fuzziness in her head had disappeared and she was acutely aware of her surroundings. She looked over at Meara, who was ticking off points to a couple of police officers, one of whom scribbled notes furiously. Frank stood just a few feet away, his eyes on Meara. Other police searched a small desk in the corner and rifled through files in a couple of wooden cabinets. Victor had been taken away, but just being in his studio made Genie jumpy.

"Do I have to stay here?" Genie said. She picked up the water bottle and drained it.

"Just a few questions," Detective Santangelo said. "I don't blame you for being anxious to get out of here. Detective Haddad is taking a red eye to Boston tonight. She'll want to talk to you, too. I'll bring her out to your sister's house tomorrow morning."

"What happened to that man—his name was Al, I think?" The big window was still open, letting in the cold December air.

"Alberto Maricel," the detective said, her smile disappearing. "We caught him running down the alley. He said he was sorry he'd ever met Mr. Pulnik, and told us that Mr. Pulnik had hired him to have your husband killed. He's being booked now, as is Mr. Pulnik."

"But Victor's dying," Genie said. "He needs to be in a hospital." She gripped the bottle hard enough to hear the plastic crinkle.

Detective Santangelo pressed her lips together. "We're aware of his condition, Genie. After he's processed, he'll go straight to the hospital. I'm surprised you still care, after all he's done to you. According to Mr. Maricel, he'd been paid to force you to shoot Mr. Pulnik, then to kill you after you'd done it. Mr. Pulnik wanted it to look like a murder/suicide. He's a very bad man." She sat back and blew out a breath. "Sorry, I shouldn't have said that. I don't come across people like you very often. Most people in your situation would be screaming for the death penalty."

Before Genie could answer, Meara left the police standing by the elevator. She stood beside Genie, her hand on her hips. "Can I take my sister home now, Detective? She's been through enough today. You and that woman from San Francisco will be talking to her tomorrow. Save your questions till then."

Frank came up behind Meara and put his hands on her shoulders. "Meems, honey, if the police still need to talk to Genie, I'm sure it's fi—"

Meara whirled around. "It sure as hell is not fine. If Genie doesn't have sense enough to take care of herself and tell the cops to back off, I do." She turned back to the Detective. "Your friends in San Francisco weren't much help to her after Charlie died; they closed the case as fast as they could. When I called the Boston police today I had to go up the line and finally talk to a sergeant who checked on Charlie's murder. Otherwise you and your buddies wouldn't have gotten off your asses to come over here. If it had been up to you, my sister would probably be dead right now."

Detective Santangelo smiled thinly and stood up. "Well, we're here now, Ms. Halloran. As long as we can come talk to Genie tomorrow, our questions can wait." She looked down at Genie, smiling more normally now. "Genie, we'll see you tomorrow. I'm so glad you're safe. And I can see your sister will take good care of you from now on." She put her notebook back in her purse and called over to the other officers. "Are you ready to leave now? Have you found anything besides the gun?"

A petite redhead carried something in a plastic bag. She brought it to the detective and said, "All we found was this little knife. Not really a weapon, I guess."

Genie saw the glint of silver and stood up. "May I take a look?" she said. The officer handed her the plastic bag. Genie recognized it right away. It was the pen knife she'd given Victor for Christmas so long ago, the one that had belonged to her great-grandfather.

"He kept it all these years," she murmured. She handed it back to the police officer and said to Meara, "Let's go home."

CHAPTER FIFTY-FIVE

It was a Saturday afternoon in late January, and Genie was at her desk, working on her new book. The rain had been relentless the last few days, but she thought it might let up soon. She was looking forward to getting outside after putting in hours at her computer. When the phone rang she was tempted to let it ring through to voicemail, but picked it up when she saw the Boston area code.

"Genie, this is Detective Santangelo."

Genie shifted in her chair. She'd tried not to think about what had happened the month before, though she'd spent hours going over things with Detective Haddad in Boston and back in San Francisco. Alberto Maricel had been extradited to California, and his trial was set for April. As far as she knew, though Victor had been charged, he'd not left the hospital.

"Yes, Detective," Genie said. "How are you?"

"Fine, ma'am. I have some news for you. I don't think it will be a shock or anything. Mr. Pulnik passed away today."

"Oh, I see." Genie got up and went to the window seat, sitting on the quilted cushion.

There was a pause. "He never left the hospital. He'd been in a coma the last couple of days. We'd visited him while he was conscious, but he refused to talk to us. The nurses said he never said a word to anyone."

"I guess I'm not surprised," Genie said. "Did he have visitors...I mean, did anyone ever come to see him?"

"We couldn't find any next of kin, if that's what you mean. You already told us his parents had died and he had no siblings. We did find a lawyer who handled some of his business transactions. He'll take care of the burial."

"'Unwept, unhonored, and unsung,'" Genie muttered.

"What was that, Genie?"

"Sorry," Genie said. She went back to her computer. "My students will tell you I have a bad habit of quoting poetry."

"Oh, okay," the detective said. "There's just one more thing. The nurses found a piece of paper on Mr. Pulnik's bedside table. There was something written on it, but it's hard to figure out what it means. Plus the handwriting was pretty shaky. Anyway, I wonder if you might be able to help us. Do you mind?"

Genie closed her eyes. She promised herself this was the last time she'd say anything or think anything about Victor. He'd done all he could to ruin her life, and she wouldn't allow him to do more.

"Genie? Are you still there?"

"I'm here. Go ahead, Detective."

"Well, like I said, the handwriting is pretty bad. But it looks like it says, 'Sorry little fire.' That's pretty strange. Maybe he was confused when he wrote it. Anyway, does that mean anything to you?"

Genie hesitated. "No," she said. "It doesn't mean anything to me. Nothing at all. Goodbye, Detective."

She set the phone down and went back to work.

2015

CHAPTER FIFTY-SIX

It was just after dawn and Genie was dressed and ready for the day. She sat in the study and sipped her coffee as she looked through an advance copy of her latest book, *Man of Mercy*. Her agent Philip had balked at first when she'd told him she wanted to write a novel based on Charlie's life. He'd said that writing it would be too hard on her emotionally, though she suspected he also feared it wouldn't sell. But when he'd shopped it around—Pennypacker Press would never want such a gritty story—he'd found a major publisher in New York who'd been interested. Genie knew the book probably wouldn't make much money, not compared to some of her YA titles. She didn't care. Charlie's story needed to be told. She'd pledged all her revenue from the book to Mercy's Family. Now that the new executive director had come on board the program would expand and live on, a testament to Charlie's life and work.

She put the book down and sighed. She'd promised herself that today was the day she'd deal with the letter that had come the week before. Genie knew who'd sent it, but couldn't bring herself to read it when it had arrived. Taking a deep breath, she opened the desk drawer and pulled out the envelope stamped with the return address: San Quentin, CA. She took the letter and her coffee cup into the kitchen. The day was growing lighter, with pink clouds glowing in the east. Pouring another cup, she headed out to the bench outside. She slid her nail under the flap, then took out the piece of lined paper.

Dear Mrs. Maguire,

I dont want to bother you to much, but I want to thank you for what you did for me. My loyyer told me that you were the one who said that the prossacuter shouldn't try for the deth penalty at my trial even tho he coulda won on account of aggrivating circimstanses. You didn't have to do that. I'll be in prison the rest of my life, but I promiss you I'll do something to make you proud. And your husband would be proud to. Im in a litterasy program now and also learning about computers. Some of the guys here no about Mercys Family and tell me how good they are. Your husband must of been a hell of a guy, and Im so sorry I ever did what I did.

I hope you have a happy life. Dont worry about me. I no I screwed up and I don't mind paying the prize.

Sincerly,

Alberto Maricel

Genie put the paper back into the envelope. She thought about throwing it away, but instead, went into the study and slid it back into the drawer. She'd read it again, but not for a long time. Looking at her watch, she saw that she had an hour to prepare before Marty and his family would arrive. She hurried back into the kitchen to assemble the sandwiches and treats for their hike and the little gathering afterward.

CHAPTER FIFTY-SEVEN

Genie had just finished filling her backpack when a car pulled up outside. She wiped her hands on a dish towel and went out front. Marty, Alec, and his son Chris were already out of the SUV while Alec's wife Beth stayed inside with Emily, the baby. Genie opened the door and said, "I'm all set. Chris, will you help me with this stuff, please?"

Chris, a freshman at Sonoma State University, bounded up the steps and grabbed the insulated food carrier from Genie. "Is this all? What about your backpack?" he said. Though he'd been in the States a couple of years, his Australian accent was still strong.

"That's it. The others will be bringing food, too. I'll hang onto this bag, though." Genie said.

"Grandad's brought some wine," Chris said. "Wish it was beer, but I got outvoted." He winked and used his key fob to open the tailgate.

Genie climbed into the backseat next to Emily, her godchild. She'd been born a year after Alec had moved his family back to California. Genie had helped Beth in the days leading up to the birth and doted on the baby ever since. Beth worked part-time as a nurse and dropped Emily off twice a week at Genie's house after Genie came home from school. Now a sturdy toddler, Emily amused herself by chasing after Lucy, Genie's kitten, and sitting with a book next to Genie as she worked at her computer.

As Genie adjusted her seatbelt Emily handed her a book. "Read now, Genie!" she commanded.

Chris jumped into the third row and grabbed the book from Emily. "Hey, peanut, give Genie a break. I'll read to you."

Emily turned to her brother and narrowed her eyes. "Read it right," she said. "No funnies."

Genie laughed. "I never add any commentary to Emily's books. She knows them by heart and won't allow any riffing."

Chris put his hand over his heart. "I promise, Emily, no funnies."

Mollified, Emily sat back in her car seat and said in the manner of a grande dame, "Read now."

While Chris read to Emily, Alec drove to the foothills, keeping up a quiet conversation with Marty. Father and son had reconciled and, after Alec's visit to California at Christmas in 2012, lived together for a while in Marty's sprawling home. By the time Emily was born, Alec had put his Australian experience to work. As a master woodworker, his reputation for innovative and artistic designs caught on among people who owned expensive second homes in Sonoma and Napa counties, allowing him and his family to buy a house near Genie. Both Alec and his father never forgot the debt they owed Charlie for helping bring them back together, and when Emily was born, Alec and Beth agreed her middle name would be Charlotte.

"How much farther?" Alec asked Genie, meeting her eyes in the rear view mirror.

Genie glanced out the window. "About half a mile. The sign for the parking area will be on the right."

They were headed to a park in Windsor, where Genie and Charlie had hiked dozens of times. Soon after they'd married, they'd vowed to climb the Alta Vista trail in the park on their twentieth anniversary. Genie had moved the date up a few months, since December could be rainy. She knew Charlie would understand.

When they reached the parking lot, Debra and Ed were leaning against their car, chatting with Frank and Meara, who'd flown in for the occasion. The night before, the four of them had joined Genie and Marty for dinner and everything had gone well, just as Genie had hoped.

Genie hopped out of the SUV and walked across the parking lot, saying, "We've got a beautiful day for our hike."

Frank gave her a hug. "It's always beautiful in California, right?" He turned around and held his arms out. "Look at this place! Driving over we saw all those mountains and grapevines everywhere. We should live out here, Meems!"

Frank and Meara had married a few months after Frank's mother died. Genie had been Meara's matron of honor at the small ceremony at Meara's house. Meara and Frank had stood just where Genie had stood with Charlie when they'd been married years before.

"What about my studio?" Meara said, looping her arm through Frank's.

"Open a studio out here," Frank said. "Genie, there's people who dance around here, right? I can work anywhere. Besides, there's never any snow. This back of mine ain't getting any younger, you know."

Genie laughed. "As long as your back can get you up the trail today, we should be fine." She put her hand on Meara's shoulder. "I'd love it if you ever did move out here, Meara."

Meara gave Genie a quick hug. "I'll think about it, I really will. My husband has already made up his mind, and I suspect he'll be working on me when we get home."

Frank laughed. "It's August, Meems. I won't have to do much convincing when we're under a foot of snow this January."

"Hey, everyone, we should probably start before it gets too hot," Genie said. "Ready to go?"

She put her hand on her chest, feeling the gold knot and chain under her T-shirt. "Okay, Charlie," she whispered. "Let's go hiking."

"One sec," Alec said, trying to put a squirming Emily into a child carrier.

"I wanna walk!" Emily said, arching her back. "I'm a big girl now! Mommy says I am."

Beth folded her arms and said under her breath, "Why did I ever tell her that? That's all she says these days." She smiled at Genie and said, "Genie, what do you think? Will Emily be able to climb this tall, tall hill all by herself?"

Emily pushed her father's hands away and walked over to Genie, beaming up at her doting godmother.

Genie squatted down beside Emily and said, "I have an idea. Do you want to hear it? It's a secret, though."

Emily nodded and Genie leaned over and whispered in Emily's ear. The little girl's face lit up then she ran over to Alec and said, "Okay, now," trying to put one chubby leg into the carrier.

"What did you say?" Beth asked as Alec secured Emily in the carrier.

Genie laughed and said softly, "I told her that if she let someone carry her up the hill, I'd walk with her and hold her hand all the way down. I also told her we could hunt for lizards."

"Hmm," Beth said, "It might take you a few hours to get down, then. Emily can be a determined hunter."

Chris picked up the child carrier and set Emily on his back while Alec checked the fastenings. "Ready to go, squirt?" Chris said, not seeming to mind as Emily grabbed his hair to steady herself.

Brother and sister set off up the trail and the group was under way. It wasn't a long climb, a loop of about two and half miles, but there was an elevation gain of four hundred feet, so they moved slowly.

They fell into line two-by-two, with Marty and Alec up ahead, followed by Debra and Ed and the rest of Marty's family. Meara walked along beside Genie, the two of them lagging behind. Genie put her arm around Meara and said, "It's so nice that you and Frank came out here for this. Your being here means so much."

Meara squeezed Genie's hand and said, "We wouldn't have missed it."

They walked along quietly for a while, avoiding the roots and rocks that littered the trail. At one point Emily said something that made everyone up ahead laugh, though Meara and Genie were too far away to hear. The trail got steeper and they slowed their pace, happy just to walk together in companionable silence. Turkey vultures circled high overhead, silently riding the thermals.

Meara took a deep breath. "This place is so great, Genie."

"It is," Genie said, taking a sip of water and offering her bottle to Meara. "It sounds like Frank is ready to move out here. Do you really think you would?"

Meara took a drink and handed the water back to Genie. She stopped walking and looked up the trail at the rest of the group. "We've talked about it a lot. It's possible." She leaned against the twisted trunk of an old oak. "After what happened to Charlie, we wondered at first if you'd move back to Massachusetts. Clearly that's not going to happen."

Genie wiped her forehead with the back of her hand. "No way," she said. "This is home for me. It was hard that first year after Charlie died, but I had a lot of support here with Debra and Ed and all the people at my school."

"And Marty?" Meara said with a gentle smile. She started walking again and Genie fell into place beside her.

"Marty and I..." Genie shrugged.

"You don't have to talk about it if you don't want to," Meara said. "It's clear that he and his whole family mean a lot to you. That's wonderful, Genie."

Genie paused a moment. "Well, you can see for yourself how close I've become to them, right? When Alec and Beth first got here, Chris was in high school. It was tough for him to make the transition from everything he'd grown up with in Australia. Fortunately they enrolled him in Jenner, so I was able to kind of look out for him. I didn't have to for long, though. He got involved in sports and even did some tutoring. By the time he graduated it was as if he'd known the kids in his class since kindergarten. Then Emily came along. She's a little charmer. I fell in love with her the moment I saw her." Genie smiled. Her eyes glistened with tears.

"Hey," Meara said. "Are you okay?"

Genie took Meara's hands in hers. "I'm more than okay, Meara. I mean, I still miss Charlie every day. Sometimes I get a feeling right here," she said, her hand on her chest, "I feel like my heart is just going to break sometimes, you know? Then I spend time with Emily, or Marty and I go see a movie, or I sit in my study and work on a new book, and I think that life is so wonderful, so precious. Charlie will never mean less to me even if I have more people in my life to love. Does that make sense?"

"It makes total sense, Genie."

"As far as Marty goes," Genie said, walking around a hole in the trail. She smiled and wiped the tears from her cheeks. "We're taking things slowly. I mean, we're together, but don't feel like we're ready to take the next step. Not yet."

"You mean marriage?" Meara said.

"Well, we talked about me moving into Marty's place. Maybe I'll do it one of these days, but for now I'm happy with my little house. As far as marriage goes, I don't know, we'll see. We're both still grieving, you know, even though it's been years since Estelle and Charlie left us. We probably always will be."

Now it was Meara's turn to pause. Finally she said, "He's a good man, Genie. Charlie would approve, I'm sure of it. Just because love has come into your life again doesn't mean you'll forget what you had with Charlie."

Genie adjusted the straps on her backpack and said, "You're right. Like I said, we're going slowly, but we are together." She shaded her eyes and said, "Look, the others are almost to the top. We'd better get moving."

It took little time for Genie and Meara to catch up with the others. Soon the group reached the top of the trail. Meara and Debra set their packs down, and Ed and Frank walked a little way to where the view was best. "Amazing," Frank said. Marty joined them and Frank said, "If I lived out here I think I'd hike every chance I get."

Marty smiled. "So move out here. Genie would love it, and I think you and Meara would too."

"We just might do that." Frank said. Meara came up and slid her arm through his. "Marty says we should move here, too," Frank said, kissing the top of Meara's head.

Meara rolled her eyes. "Everyone's saying that. You're all in cahoots with Genie, aren't you?"

Marty laughed. "She can be very persuasive."

Debra sat down on a rock next to Genie. She took off her hat and raked her fingers through her hair. "Man, that breeze feels great. Hey, Genie," she said, turning to where Genie sat cross-legged. "Did you order this perfect day?"

344

Genie turned her face to the sun and smiled. "It's always perfect up here." She took a few deep breaths, then picked up her pack. "Well, I guess it's time. Marty's going to take everyone back down to the picnic tables and get lunch set up. Emily's sleeping now, so she won't be upset if I don't walk her down."

"Are you sure you want to do this by yourself?" Debra said.

"I won't be by myself," Genie said. She reached into her pack and pulled out the small cedar box that Charlie's friend Billy had given him years before. "Charlie's right here with me."

Debra leaned over and kissed her cheek. "Okay, we'll see you in a little while."

Marty helped Genie off the rock and put his arms around her. "Are you okay?"

Genie pressed her cheek against his chest. When Charlie died she'd never dreamed that she'd ever love another man, but Marty had come to mean more and more to her. When his son Alec moved back, he and his family became part of her life. She couldn't love Chris and Emily more if they'd been her actual grandchildren. She'd never stop loving Charlie and she'd miss him till the day she died, but Marty had filled her grieving heart with love. They might marry one day, as she'd told Meara. It didn't really matter to her, though. The love was enough.

She smiled and said, "Don't worry; I'll be fine."

Marty squeezed her hand then started down the trail with the others. She watched him until he was out of sight, then turned away. She walked past the edge of the trail and stood overlooking the valley. She and Charlie had stood in the same spot many times, picking out the far-off mountain peaks, listening to the breezes blow softly through the grasses, and holding each other close. Genie smoothed the top of the box and brought it to her lips. "Charlie, we promised we'd come here on our twentieth, and here we are. I'm going to let you go now, so you can be here forever. I'll come to visit you, and one day I'll join you."

She opened the box and shook the ashes into the air, smiling as the gentle wind spread them out ahead of her into the valley below. She watched for a while until nothing was left, then closed the box, put it into her pack, and headed back down the trail. Genie brushed away a few tears as she descended, then smiled to see Meara standing at the bend of the next switchback.

"I thought you'd gone down with the others," Genie said.

"You know me, always keeping an eye on you," Meara said. Suddenly serious, she said, "That must have been tough. Are you okay, Genie?"

Genie took a deep breath and looked around. "Not really," she said. They started down the path again. Genie took a deep breath and said, "Charlie wanted this; he didn't want to be buried in a cemetery or stuck in a wall somewhere. That's why I brought that empty urn back to Massachusetts years ago. Nanny Pat was satisfied, and that was enough for me. But I wasn't going to leave him there, so far away. This way I can hike up the trail and talk to him anytime." She stopped and shrugged. "You probably think I'm nuts, right?"

Meara put her arm around Genie's waist. "Not at all. You and Charlie had something rare, and this place is part of it. I think what you did was perfect."

"Thanks, Meara," Genie said. She looked at her watch. "Yikes, it's after one. We'd better get down there. Everyone will be starving by now."

When Meara and Genie got to the picnic tables near the small pond, the others were setting out containers of food on the cloths Beth had brought. Ed, Marty, and Emily stood near the edge of the water, where the tall reeds swayed in the breeze.

"What are they up to over there?" Genie asked Debra.

Debra laughed. "Emily woke up just as we got to the bottom of the trail and was none too happy that you hadn't walked her down there. Marty figured he could distract her by hunting for red winged blackbirds."

"I'll go over and see if I can make it up to her," Genie said.

When Emily saw Genie coming she yelled, "Genie! The black-birds have red shoulders! You can hear them talking to each other."

She hurried toward Genie, who scooped her up and said, "You can? Can you show me where they are?"

Just then a blackbird shot out of the reeds, alarmed by the loud voices.

"There's one right there!" Emily said. Her long-lashed eyes were bright with excitement as she pointed toward the pond. "There's a bunch of them in there. Poppa says they live there and hunt for bugs and snails. They eat them." She scrunched her nose. "I don't like bugs and snails."

"You don't?" Genie said, following Ed and Marty back to the tables. "Then I guess it's good I didn't pack any for lunch, then.

I thought about it, but couldn't find any big, fat ones in my garden."

Emily put her arms around Genie's neck and whispered, "You're kidding, right Genie?

"I am," Genie said with a wink. "I'm a kidder, remember?"

Emily closed both eyes, her mouth cocked to the side, in imitation of Genie's wink, then planted a sticky kiss on her cheek. They got to the tables as Ed was setting out plastic wine glasses. He took a bottle out of a wine tote and pulled a small corkscrew from his pocket. As he removed the cork, he said, "Genie, this Chardonnay will be released later this year. We made it at my winery, but most of the grapes came from Marty's vineyard. Come take a look at the label."

Genie handed Emily to Beth and took the bottle. The label, a beautiful gold with Art Nouveau lettering, said Charlie's Chardonnay, 2014. "Oh, Ed, Marty," she said, putting her hand over her mouth.

"Read what's on the back," Ed said.

Genie did as he asked but once she started reading, tears came to her eyes. "I can't," she said. "Marty, you read it. Everyone should hear this."

Marty took the bottle from Genie and put his arm around her. "Sure, Genie," he said. He cleared his throat and read. "Charlie's Chardonnay, named for a Sonoma County man who lived a life of service and loved deeply, is meant to be shared with friends and family. It goes with any food you eat with others, whether a formal meal or an impromptu dinner for two. Raise a glass and toast Charlie, a guy you'd be proud to know."

"That's beautiful," Genie said. "Ed, Marty, thank you for this. Charlie would have loved it."

The group took their places around the two picnic tables that had been moved together. Emily sat across from Genie on Beth's lap. "I'm hungry!" she said.

"That's good," Meara said. "We have enough here to feed an army."

Ed handed Genie a glass of wine saying, "Why don't you taste this, Genie. Make sure it's fit to drink."

Genie took a sip of the golden liquid, so cool and crisp. "It's delicious," she said. She watched as Ed poured glasses for everyone, pretending to pour some in Emily's sippy cup.

When everyone had a glass, Marty raised his and said, "To Charlie."

"To Charlie," they all said, and took a sip.

Genie looked around at the faces of those dearest to her. Meara and Frank, who, she hoped, would soon live nearby. Ed and Debra, her friend for nearly all her life. And Marty and his family, whom she'd grown to cherish. She'd always feel the pain of loss, and she'd never stop missing Charlie, but life had been kind.

She raised her glass. "To love," she said.

ACKNOWLEDGEMENTS

Elaine and MaryAnne, my younger and wiser sisters and the inspiration for Meara; my partners in reading Lori, Diahanna, Shawn, and Larry; Edie, a superb designer and true friend; and John, my husband and best editor, who believes in me more than I ever believed in myself.

ABOUT THE AUTHOR

Joan Broughton gladly traded snowy winters and a career in business to live and write in Northern California. She lives there with her husband and two cats.

For more information, visit www.joanbroughton.com.